UNDER A GILDED SKY

IMOGEN MARTIN

Storm
PUBLISHING

This is a work of fiction. Names, characters, business, events and incidents are the products of the author's imagination. Any resemblance to actual persons, living or dead, or actual events is purely coincidental.

Ebook ISBN: 978-1-80508-171-5
Paperback ISBN: 978-1-80508-173-9

Cover design: Emma Rogers
Cover images: Shutterstock

Published by Storm Publishing.
For further information, visit:
www.stormpublishing.co

For my daughter Rebecca, whose bravery and determination inspired this book.

1991–2018

PART 1

ONE

SNOW FARM, MISSOURI—FEBRUARY 1874

The front door banged open and a blast of air swept down the passage to Ginny at the kitchen table.

"Mary Lou! What're you doing? It's freezing!" Ginny called out, keeping her concentration on pouring oil into the well of a lamp.

"I need help."

Ginny caught the breathless tone in her sister's voice and glanced down the dark hallway. Mary Lou was outlined against the gray sky, struggling under the weight of a disheveled man who looked ready to crumple.

"Good Lord above." Oil splashed as Ginny dropped the canister. Wiping her hands on her pinafore she rushed to her sister. "What on earth—"

"Found him. Bottom of the track."

"Found?"

Ginny hooked herself under the man's left shoulder. She kicked open the parlor door and together the sisters maneuvered the man toward an armchair in front of the fire. He growled as he sank down. Ginny shoved away a footstool to give room for the man to extend his left leg. He winced and let out a low moan.

"The front door." Ginny nodded to Mary Lou, who ran to pull it shut against the wind, dropping the heavy latch and securing the bolt to keep out the February storm.

Ginny stared at the man. Dust and dirt were so crusted on his skin, it was hard to tell what age he was, but she guessed early thirties. A shaggy beard covered much of his face and matted hair escaped from his hat. His eyes were clenched tight shut.

"Where on earth did he come from, Mary Lou?"

"I was at the chicken coop and saw him, right down by the gate. Barely standing. He seemed in pain, so I ran down the track."

Ginny glared at her sister. At fourteen, Mary Lou really should know better. Her trusting nature was going to get them both into trouble someday. And this just might be the day.

"I couldn't leave him there." Mary Lou met her sister's eyes. "No other shelter for miles around. He'd be frozen harder than an iron rail come the morning."

She was right. But what were they going to do now?

Ginny hastily pushed back a golden-brown tress which had worked free from her braid as she went to the cabinet under the window. She pulled open the top drawer, and carefully took out a Smith & Wesson. Her fingers shook as she opened the barrel to make sure it was loaded.

"I'll keep it on him while you go fetch water."

Mary Lou rushed from the room and soon returned with a tin mug of water.

"Put it on the cabinet," Ginny instructed. "Now, take Papa's gun. You remember how to use it?"

Mary Lou nodded and stood by the window opposite the fireplace, both hands on the gun directed at the man. His eyes were still shut.

Ginny pushed the cool mug against her brow and tried to bring her breathing under control.

She knelt and offered the mug. The stranger seemed too dazed by the pain to respond, so she lifted it to his cracked lips. Feeling the water, he steadied the cup and gulped it down.

"More." His voice was a croak.

Ginny mouthed to Mary Lou to check she was prepared to stand guard, then she went to get a second cupful from the kitchen. The man lifted a grubby hand to hold it. After a few swallows, he fell back in the chair, his eyes closed once more.

Ginny got to her feet and stood shoulder to shoulder with her sister, staring at the man.

"He say anything when I was out?" Ginny whispered.

Mary Lou shook her head. "But when I first got him up from the road, he said something 'bout his horse. Thrown from it. Thinks he might have broken his leg."

"Did he say when? He looks in a bad way."

"I didn't ask. But he seemed pretty desperate. Couldn't jus' leave him there to die, could I?"

"No, course not." Ginny bumped shoulders with her sister. They had been brought up to help those in need, and she hoped Mary Lou would never have to grow out of her innocent generosity.

"So I told him to come with me. It took quite a while. He had to hop and hobble all the way."

The man's head fell forward, his hat still in place.

"No wonder he's tired." Ginny bit her lip. "You keep that barrel fixed on him while I get his gun."

Mary Lou's eyes widened, but Ginny shrugged. What else could she do?

With a racing pulse, she crept forward and lifted the man's damp jacket. It was made from a dark worsted fabric but had turned beige from the dirt. Ginny began to unbutton the holster and the man's hand clapped over hers. She froze and glanced up at his rugged face. Their eyes met.

Ginny swallowed hard. "Fella, you want my hospitality, you gonna have to give this up. You can always go back into that storm."

His eyes, gray as the winter sky, held hers. He seemed to size up the situation, then he slowly eased out his Colt and handed it to her. Ginny nodded and stood.

"You stay there. We'll just be out in the hall."

"I ain't going nowhere," he growled.

Ginny urged Mary Lou out of the door with a nod of the head and then she followed, closing the parlor door behind them.

Mary Lou stood by the kitchen door, Papa's pistol in her hand. "Have I gone and done the wrong thing?"

Ginny paced up and down the passage. "No, honey. I just need to think." She looked at the gun in her hand. It was far heavier than Papa's Smith & Wesson, with a long barrel. It looked new. A giggle bubbled up. "Look at us both, like we're going on a raid. Let's hide this thing in the kitchen somewhere."

The kitchen was warm from the fire banked up to cook the evening stew. Ginny tucked the gun behind a jar on a high shelf, while Mary Lou took the lid off the pot and gave the vegetables a stir.

Ginny grabbed a rag to mop up the lamp oil and threw it on the fire. She went to the sink and washed the smell from her hands, looking out of the window. The storm was whipping up the debris in the yard and a barn door needed tying shut again.

"Did he tell you anything more? Where's he come from?" asked Ginny.

Mary Lou shook her head.

"Was he with anyone?"

Another shake.

Ginny cleared the lamps from the table, her task half-finished. "He looks like a farm worker. Or a cowboy. Most like traveling one place to the next, looking for work." She didn't voice the fears that were running through her mind. An outlaw on the run? A robber? Or worse?

She keenly felt the vulnerability of running Snow Farm by themselves. Papa had died two years ago, but she'd been determined to keep the family homestead, the one thing that connected them to memories of their parents.

"Now, Marie-Louise, you must do as I say."

Mary Lou looked up at her, blinking her big brown eyes. Things were serious when Ginny addressed her sister by her full name.

"We mustn't let the stranger know it's just us two here. We need him to think there's a man in the homestead."

Mary Lou cocked her head, a line appearing between her brows.

"Trust me on this. We're gonna pretend Papa is here. But he's upstairs. Sick. We're looking after him in his bed, and any day now, he'll be better."

Mary Lou stared into the pot. "That's easy. I pretend Papa is still around all the time."

Ginny walked over to the fire and laid a hand on her sister's head. Mary Lou had adored their father, too young to see his faults. Their mother had died when she was a girl and Papa had fallen into a stupor with the grief.

Ginny took Mary Lou by the shoulders and gave her a reassuring smile. "Right. Let's see what we can find out about this man."

TWO

They returned to the parlor to find the stranger asleep, breathing heavily. Mary Lou put Papa's gun in the pocket of her pinafore and sat on the ladder-back chair in the corner. Ginny bit her lip and went over to touch the man's arm. He raised his head and his eyes snapped open. There was something wolflike about his look, watchful of each move she made.

Ginny pulled back her hand. "I think I should try and see what's wrong with that leg."

"You a nurse?" His voice was low, rattling from a still-dry throat.

"Well, no—"

"So I don't see how you can help."

Ginny sprang upright and put her hands on her hips. "Maybe you don't want any help at all and we can sling you straight back outside."

The man screwed up his eyes. "I forgot my manners." He removed his hat and dropped it to the wooden floor beside him. Like the jacket, it was hard to tell what color his hair was originally, it was so matted with dirt. "Ma'am, I am indeed grateful for your ministrations."

Ginny didn't care for his tone. "Apology accepted. Now. Where's it hurt?"

"Bottom of the leg. All round the ankle."

She pulled back the footstool and sat directly in front of him, her back warmed by the stove. She pushed up the black serge of his trouser leg and unbuckled his boot. Ignoring the mud caked around the heel, she firmly put her hand below and started to ease off the boot. The man gasped and gripped the arms of the chair.

"I'm afraid I'm gonna have to pull this harder."

The man nodded and Ginny tugged the leather past the heel until the boot slid free. It dropped onto the hearth. Lifting his foot onto her skirt, Ginny rolled back the white jersey long johns and peeled off his sock. She could see swelling around the ankle.

"Well, for the good news, I can't see no bone coming through." She felt her way around the man's foot, glancing up for reactions in his face. As her hands kneaded up to the ankle, he groaned.

"That's not surprising. It's where the swelling is. Can I see what movement you've got? Should tell us if anything's broken." Ginny met the man's eyes, which were fixed intently on her. Her breathing hitched for a moment. The lines around his eyes were traced in dirt.

He made a slight grunt, which suggested he trusted her, and Ginny began to rotate the foot. The man took a sharp intake of breath; she paused and then carried on.

"Now a bit further up the leg." Ginny ran her fingers over the Achilles tendon and then up the shin. "Nothing seems broken up here either." She sat upright on the stool. "So, an injured ankle. Might be a broken bone in there, but I think it's just a ripped tendon."

"Just?"

Ginny glanced at him and thought she could see the faintest sparkle in the stranger's eye.

"How d'you know all this?"

Ginny smiled. "As you say, I'm no nurse. I'm taking this from years of looking after livestock on the farm."

He raised an eyebrow. "I'm being examined by a veterinarian?"

"We're all built the same way. Bone, muscle, tendons. You get to know with animals which ones are gonna heal and which ain't."

"And which d'you think I am?"

"I think you'll heal. What to do to help it, though?" Ginny frowned a moment. "Mary Lou, honey, bring me the remedies from the dining room."

Mary Lou dashed out and returned with a wooden box.

Ginny lifted out a screw-top jar and some bandages. "This is comfrey and elder salve. It will take down the swelling."

The man nodded his approval and Ginny massaged the milky-colored gel into his ankle. The astringent smell filled the room.

"Sir, when d'you last eat?" Mary Lou asked.

He looked up at her, as if remembering there was a second young woman in the room. "Not for a few days."

"I'll get you something." Mary Lou glanced at Ginny for approval to return to the kitchen and Ginny nodded.

She turned back to the man's foot and began to wrap a bandage around it.

"Whoa! Does it have to be so tight?"

Ginny paused, doubting herself. "I think it best to keep the foot and ankle fixed." She continued to wind the fabric.

When she'd finished, she gently lowered the foot to the floor so she could stand up. The man leaned forward, taking his weight on the arms of the chair to rise.

"No, no, no. You're gonna have to rest that foot up for a while. Sit back down and put it on that stool."

"Truly?"

"Yes. I'm sure that trying to move too soon will make it worse."

He sat back in the chair with a heavy sigh.

"No use fightin' it," Ginny said.

Mary Lou returned with a bowl. "Chicken stew. To be honest, it's mostly vegetable stew, but if you dig around a bit, you should find some chicken."

The man took the bowl and spoon and devoured the first few mouthfuls before pausing to savor the taste. "Miss, that's the finest thing I ever tasted." He scraped the bowl clean and handed it to Mary Lou with what Ginny thought was a smile, but it was hard to tell under the beard.

"What now?" Mary Lou whispered to her sister.

Ginny slid her eyes over to the window. The sky was the dappled purple of late afternoon. It would be dark soon and the wind was blowing harder. There was nothing for it; they were stuck with this stranger in their home. A tremor went down her spine.

"Did Papa enjoy his stew?" Ginny asked, louder than necessary.

Mary Lou frowned. "Papa?"

Ginny glared meaningfully at her. "Yes. Papa. Upstairs."

"Oh yes, of course. Papa. He loved it."

"You see, sir"—Ginny turned to the stranger—"our father is a little unwell at the moment. He's upstairs in bed. That's why we didn't want to disturb him. When Marie-Louise first brought you here, I mean." Ginny clamped her mouth shut to stop rattling on. Lying didn't come easy.

The stranger made a slight "uh-huh" of acknowledgment.

"Clearly you'll have to rest here tonight."

"That's very kind." The man's voice was softer than before.

"We could bring down the trundle bed," Mary Lou suggested.

Ginny nodded. "I was thinking that too."

"I don't want to put you ladies to any trouble. I can sleep fine in this chair. Or on the floor if you got a blanket."

"You'll get better quicker for a good night's sleep. We won't be a moment."

The trundle bed under Mary Lou's bedstead hadn't been used for many a year. Ginny rolled it out and brushed away the dust. The sisters maneuvered it down the stairs and through the parlor door. Ginny cleared away a chair and trunk to make space so they could lay it in against the wall. She tightened the ropes with a bed key, while Mary Lou made a few more trips to bring down the mattress, bedding and a chamber pot.

"You finish here, Mary Lou, and I'll make our guest some tea."

Ginny slipped a vial from the medicine box and took it to the kitchen. She put the kettle onto the hearth and stoked the fire, then filled a muslin bag with tea leaves and put it in a china cup, pouring warm water over it. She gave it a stir, squeezed out the flavor, and took the bag out to hang it to dry. Ginny measured three drops of liquid from the dropper in the lid of the bottle and stirred the tea once more; a familiar ritual she remembered only too well from her mama's final illness.

Ginny returned to the parlor and handed the cup to the man. "Drink this. It will help with the pain."

The man sipped at the tea.

"All of it." Ginny stood over him.

He glanced at her and frowned but drank it down.

"Mary Lou, will you fetch an oil lamp from the kitchen."

Her sister did as she was told as Ginny closed the wooden shutters on the windows, feeling the wind creeping between the glass panes.

"I'll bring wood for the stove. And more water. Then we'll

leave you till the morning. I suggest you try and rest. I'll thank you to be quiet. I don't want Papa disturbed during the night."

Ginny took the empty cup from the man and turned toward the door, but the man grasped her free hand. She froze.

"Thank you for your kindness, miss."

Ginny looked down at his hand. The back had dark hairs and the veins stood out; his fingers were strong, roughened by outdoor work. She tried to speak but could not find the words, and when his hand dropped back to the chair, she almost ran into the passage.

Ginny hid her face in her father's coat hanging from a hook, trying to take comfort from the faint smell and longing to have him there. The stranger wasn't going to be able to move any time soon. Even when his leg was better, he had no horse. And who knew how long the storm would last. She was responsible for Mary Lou, for keeping her safe. Being trapped in their home with an unknown man was the last thing they needed.

THREE

His head throbbed as the wind banged a gate somewhere, over and over. It wasn't blowing directly on him, though. That was an improvement after the last few days. He was warm, thank God.

He opened his eyes. A room in shadow. Was it dark because the shutters were bolted or was it evening? He dragged his thoughts from the comfort of sleep. There was a girl, with a round face, heavy eyebrows the same color as her dark hair. She'd brought him here.

And a woman. That was right. Sisters. A woman with equally dark eyes but a finer shape to her face. Beautiful. Even half-dead he was still man enough to notice that. A full mouth that hadn't smiled. But she'd fed him, given him shelter. He was grateful for that. Met plenty on his travels who'd have walked on by.

His body was too long for the trundle bed, but he could feel that the woman had put sacks beneath his feet. He caught the sweet smell of hay, so maybe that was what filled them. Hauling himself up with his arms, he rested his back against the wall. Damn if that didn't set off pains all over his body.

As his eyes accustomed to the gloom, shapes emerged. A hearth to his right with a stone fireplace, solidly made, with smooth plaster that may have been white once. A wood burner. Logs stacked next to it to dry out, and above, a big wooden lintel. Heavy brass candlesticks.

He swallowed, his throat rasping with thirst. Hadn't the woman said she'd leave water for him? He felt round by the bed and knocked the cup over, spilling water onto the threadbare carpet. He cursed under his breath. A pitcher stood on a side table, so he swiveled to get up and gasped in pain as he moved his left leg. Jeez, that was not good.

He tried again and pushed himself to standing, making sure all the weight was taken on his right leg. His foot was cold from stepping in the wet patch, but at least the room was carpeted. Better than rough wood or a stone floor. Or the open field.

Snatching up the cup, he hobbled to the table and poured out the water, downing it in one go, then drinking a second cup, relishing the soothing sensation.

Thirst sated, he hopped to the nearest window and unhooked the lock on the shutters. Pushing back the wood, he thought it must be dawn. Or maybe evening. He couldn't tell how long he had slept.

He crept back to the armchair and slumped heavily into it. Light fell onto the glass doors of a cabinet in the alcove next to the fireplace. A fine piece of furniture with shelves full of books. Maybe that would show him the sorta people he'd landed on.

His eyes shifted around the room to the shadows in the far corner, where there was a shape like a piano.

A piano?

He peered more closely through the crepuscular murk. Yes, it was an upright piano—quite a fancy one to judge from the gleam on the wood. A stool wide enough for two people but one side piled high with what looked like music scores. There was a further pile on top, next to an oil lamp with a tall glass chimney.

He smiled. He'd been traveling for close on two years now. Had experienced all sorts of people, good and bad. And folk kept on surprising him. Why the folks on a small farm in the Midwest would need a fine piano was beyond him.

FOUR

Ginny was clearing ash from the kitchen hearth when she heard the man moving. She took a deep breath, steadying the anxiety of having a stranger in her parlor. She hurried down the passage and opened the door to the darkened room.

"You're up."

"Yep. Felt more comfortable in this chair."

"How are you?"

"Been better," he shrugged.

She bit back a retort and folded the shutters from the other two windows, letting in the half-light before the sun had properly risen. She was troubled by how large he was, filling the armchair in a way her father never had. Pa would never have slumped back like that neither, resting rangy limbs on the hearth.

"The house faces southwest," she said. "You don't get much light in here at this time of day."

"What time of day would that be?"

"Around six."

"Morning or evening?"

Ginny looked at him to see if he was joking, but his face

remained solemn. "Morning. You must have slept at least ten hours."

"Ten hours!"

"It will have been good for you. The rest, I mean."

There was a tap at the door and Mary Lou poked her head around. "Is he awake?"

Ginny frowned at Mary Lou's tone. Her sister might be finding this the most exciting thing to have happened in their homestead for months, but it was excitement they could do without.

"You can come in. How's Papa?"

Mary Lou sat on the same chair as the night before and caught Ginny's eye. "Oh, fine. Great. I mean, not *great*, with him being ill an' all..." She darted a panicked look at Ginny.

Ginny turned to the man. "As I told you last night, our father is a little unwell. Upstairs. Not too unwell, I'm glad to say. Will be up in a day or so. You can meet him then. If you're still here, that is. Hopefully, you'll be gone." She knew she was sounding rude and decided to stop before she said more foolish things.

"You could do with more light in here."

She took a taper from the mantelpiece and crouched to open the stove. The taper caught at the smoldering log. First, she lit the candles on the fireplace, then reached up to the oil lamp hanging in the center of the room from the main wooden beam. The room took on a honey hue.

Ginny slid a small log on top of the embers before raddling the grate to get air flowing through. She felt the man's eyes upon her and wasn't sure if the heat around her face was from the fire or the effect of this stranger sitting so close. She tightened the stove door and sat in the second armchair. She needed to take control of the situation.

"Seeing as you're stuck here for now, I think we should

make some introductions. I'm Ginny. Ginny Snow. And this is my sister, Marie-Louise."

"You can call me Mary Lou," she said. "Everyone does."

"Pleased to make your acquaintance." The man turned and put out his hand to Mary Lou in mock solemnity. She shook it shyly and waited expectantly for him to shake Ginny's hand too. He leaned forward to oblige. The grip was firmer than the night before and Ginny's skin prickled. "And I'm Lex, drifter from outta state."

Ginny saw a slight smile behind the whiskers. For a moment, his eyes met hers. She pulled her hand away as if she had touched a hot stove.

"Ginny." He rolled the name around his mouth. "Short for Virginia?"

Ginny narrowed her eyes. Was he prodding to find out if they had allegiances with the South? "No. Geneviève."

"Geneviève and Marie-Louise Snow. Sounds fancy."

Now he seemed to be making fun of them.

"Not particularly. It happens I was born in Sainte Geneviève."

He nodded. "I've heard of it. On the Mississippi."

"That's right."

"So, can you tell me where I am?" he asked.

Ginny hesitated, so Mary Lou cut in. "Snow Farm. Run by me an' my sister. And our Papa, of course." She glanced at Ginny.

Lex leaned back in the chair. "Is there a town nearby?"

Ginny replied: "The nearest is Brownsville. Only three miles away."

"Good. I've heard of Brownsville."

Ginny raised her eyebrows. She thought Brownsville too small for anyone from outside the county to have heard of it.

"The railroad runs through it. Am I right?"

"Yes, it does."

The railroad had been laid in 1869, just five years earlier. Five years to have gotten used to it, but Ginny still felt it had changed the Missouri town out of all recognition.

A gust of wind rattled the windowpanes.

"Seems the storm's still raging," Lex said.

"But a little less than yesterday. Maybe it'll blow itself out by tomorrow."

There was a pause. Ginny wanted to know who this man was that she had sitting in her father's armchair. It seemed rude to ask outright, but then, this was her house.

"You'll be wondering how I came to be here," Lex said, as if reading her thoughts.

"It does seem a little... strange."

"I was working in the Ozarks, lumbering in the hills for a farm with plenty of forest. It felt like time to move on. I heard about the caves and wanted to take a look."

Ginny opened her mouth to comment but changed her mind.

Lex laughed. "You're looking at me like I'm crazy. Maybe I am."

"You wanted to visit some caves. In this weather?"

"Weather wasn't so bad when I set off. And I was told they were something special."

"And were they?"

"The caves?" He smiled and shook his head. "Can't say. Never found them. I kept on north, down out of the hills. Bivouacked a couple of nights. Then the weather changed." A frown came to his brow as he remembered. "I've been in worse, but I didn't reckon on my horse being spooked by a mountain lion. Came right at us, must have been looking for food in the snow. My horse reared me off and bolted into the distance. I tried to jump clear but must have landed badly on this ankle. I'd always thought of myself as pretty good in the saddle, so I admit, miss, to feeling pretty foolish now."

"It could happen to anyone," Ginny said, but she wasn't quite sure this was true.

"What did you do?" Mary Lou leaned forward.

"Waited for my horse to come back. He's a beautiful Paint, black and white patches, jet black mane and tail. You haven't seen him, by any chance?"

Ginny shook her head.

"That's a darn shame. When I gave up waiting, I found a big branch to make a crutch and started limping my way northwards. I knew the railroad lay this way somewhere and I'd reach it eventually. But I can tell you, limping and hopping is slow progress. Even more so when you're frozen and got no food."

"My!" said Mary Lou, getting up and standing behind Ginny's armchair so she could see him more clearly. "How did you manage?"

"My shotgun was on my horse, along with all the rest of my kit. I shot a rabbit with my handgun and had my knife to skin it. There were plenty of streams to cross. I've found over the last couple of days that food you can do without. Water..." He shook his head. "Now, that's the stuff of life. The important thing was to keep moving."

"And then I saw you on the road near the bottom lake." Mary Lou eagerly moved the story along.

"Have to say, I'm mighty pleased you did. Otherwise I might be lying out there now, waiting for my end."

Mary Lou traced the pattern of the carpet with the tip of her shoe. "Don't be so silly, you were fine."

Lex was still for a moment. Ginny took in the sunken cheeks not quite hidden by the dark, unkempt beard; she had a better grasp than her sister of how precarious Lex's situation had been.

Lex breathed out. "No, truly. I think it likely I owe you my life."

The gravity of his words hung between the three of them.

"Well," said Ginny to break the silence, "you're not saved yet. Hopefully that foot will heal, the storm will pass and you can be on your way."

The log in the stove had caught and Ginny opened the door to let its heat radiate into the room.

"Breakfast?"

"That would be much appreciated."

"Mary Lou, you go make some pancakes. There's only two eggs left, so I'll go see if those chickens have laid more. This man needs feeding up."

She put another log on the stove.

"You look pretty beat-up, sir. May I suggest you sleep after you've eaten? My sister and I have a farm to run and the animals haven't yet been trained to muck out their own stalls."

"Whatever you say, miss." He made a mock salute.

Ginny followed Mary Lou out of the room but paused at the door to glance back. There was something soothing about the man's voice. His accent was old-fashioned somehow, the tone deep. Part of her wanted to stay sitting in the chair and listen to him speak. She shook her head to dislodge such sentiments and reminded herself to be on her guard.

FIVE

Half-light again. No, more than that. Near darkness. The reddish light came from the embers in the stove.

Lex pulled the woolen blanket around him. The storm was making sure no one thought it had passed. The rattle of the shutters, the rat-a-tat-tat of droplets falling on hollow wood, high-pitched and sharp. There must be a water barrel nearby. The gusts: like an old man pushing air out, sometimes short and low, sometimes softer and longer. And in the background, a low continuous rumble. Where was that coming from? The wind through a building somewhere? Maybe a barn. It reminded him of steam trains he'd traveled on: that rumble in the lower register.

Every few minutes, it would all settle and there would be near silence. Then the gentler sound of water threading its way through the building somewhere. The staccato of raindrops falling from eaves. Had the storm passed? Could he return to sleep? But no, the gusts started up again. And then rain, almost like a brush on the roof.

Lex remembered how he had felt much sicker whilst sitting

in the chair earlier in the day, his head throbbing and his skin sticky with sweat. The sisters had helped him back to the trundle bed, one under each arm as he'd struggled his way across the room. He remembered the older one bringing him more bitter tea and standing there to make sure he finished it. The younger one removing the chamber pot without comment.

He fell back to sleep once more. He dreamed of piano scales. Fingers running up and down the notes, then the leapfrogging arpeggios. Finally, they transformed into a tune. Hesitantly played, but a tune nevertheless. A tricky passage repeated several times until it ran smoothly. Yes, this was real.

Lex opened his eyes just enough to see the girl sitting at the piano, straight-backed with long dark hair, lit by the oil lamp.

The woman brought in logs and stacked them by the stove in order of height. The woman with the fancy name. Geneviève. Ginny. That was it. The one with startling brown eyes and hair that wouldn't stay in its braid, tendrils softening her fine features. She returned with a heavy metal scuttle. Placed a few pieces of coal on the fire.

"That should keep in 'til morning." Her voice was soft.

Lex closed his eyes and prayed thanks to whatever gods were looking over him that he had been brought into this warm refuge.

The girl spoke: "Your turn."

"Perhaps not tonight. It might disturb our guest. He's been running a temperature all day."

"He's fast asleep. An' you say we have to practice *every* day. No matter what. That's what Mama taught us. How about the Nocturne? It's so peaceful, might help him get better."

He heard her move across the room. "Just a few minutes then."

She started to play something, sweet and harmonious, her fingers tripping across the keys. There was a gentle rhythm, a slow waltz. Something he had heard before somewhere. He drifted back to sleep, his dreams now ranging through scenes of a different life.

SIX

"You ready for breakfast?" Ginny asked as she entered the room carrying a small table. Her hair was secured under a cotton scarf.

The stranger opened his eyes and squinted. Ginny had folded back the shutters earlier. "Guess so."

"I thought you could eat it here, by the window." Ginny pulled the high-backed chair over as Lex dragged himself up to his feet. He leaned on different pieces of furniture to make his way over. "You sleep OK?"

He nodded.

She noted that he had taken off his jacket and vest, and was in his shirt. "You were unwell all yesterday. Something like a fever."

"Seems to have passed now. Although I feel like my horse turned round and kicked me after he threw me."

Ginny brought the footstool over. "You need to keep that ankle lifted."

Mary Lou came in with a mug of coffee in one hand and a plate in the other. She laid them on the table in front of Lex.

Two fried eggs, the yellows bright against the white. A piece of crusty bread. Two slices of bacon.

"Never seen a tastier feast," he said, wolfing down a rasher.

"Mary Lou, take breakfast up to Papa," Ginny said, with a subtle nod in the direction of the stairs. Her sister seemed to be taking a lot of trouble to provide the best for their unwanted visitor and was enjoying his compliments more than was wise.

Mary Lou glared at her and left the room and soon heavy footsteps could be heard across the wooden boards above.

"It's an early start for us. Plenty of work around the farm. We'll do the chores in here first, if you don't mind. Then you can rest undisturbed. With luck, the weather'll be calm enough tomorrow for us to take you to town. If you're feeling strong enough."

"That would be very kind. I don't want to impose on your hospitality any longer than necessary."

Ginny studied him for a moment as he mopped up the egg yolk with the crust. He was wild-looking, with his hair still tousled and his nails crusted with earth, but she'd known cowboys with worse manners. Maybe this one was just down on his luck.

She crouched by the stove and selected a log to place in: too small and it would burn through in no time, too large and it wouldn't pick up the embers from last night's coal. She slid out the tray of ashes, carrying them through the kitchen to the backyard and tipping them into a metal bin.

Returning to the room with a brush and pan under her arm, Ginny pushed back the ash tray and twisted the stove door shut. Mary Lou's steps could be heard coming downstairs and she came back into the parlor with a broom.

Ginny raised her eyebrows meaningfully to Mary Lou and wiped her own mouth with a finger. Mary Lou rolled her lips inwards, removing the remaining egg from the corner. It wouldn't do for the stranger to notice that Mary Lou had eaten the plate of eggs herself.

Ginny looked around the room. The storm seemed to have blown dirt into every space in the homestead. It was a daily battle for the sisters to keep the natural elements outside of the house and keep civilization in. She handed the brush and dustpan to Mary Lou, who began sweeping from the corners inwards, working her way across the floor, looking at the pan full of dirt with satisfaction at the end. Ginny pulled a duster from her apron pocket and ran it over surfaces, replaced a candle that had burned down, trimmed the wick of the lamps in readiness for the evening. She returned a book to the shelf and tidied the scores back under the seat of the bench.

She picked up the man's overcoat, jacket and vest piled on the floor near the trundle bed. "I can give these a shake outside."

As she folded them over her arm, a photograph slipped from a pocket of the vest. She picked it up and saw a young woman in an elegant dress, standing in front of a painted backdrop, her elbow resting on a pillar and her hand touching her chin. The woman's hair was parted and pulled back into an elegant twist. Her eyes looked wistful.

Ginny placed the photograph on the table. "This fell from—"

Lex frowned as he swiftly scooped it up and tucked it into the pocket on his shirt.

Ginny swallowed, feeling she had intruded on something private.

"Right, we can leave you in peace now." She surveyed the room. "We'll be in the kitchen or outdoors for the day. Papa is upstairs. Try to rest that ankle."

She took the empty plate and left the man alone once more.

. . .

Running a farm with only her younger sister for help needed a daily dose of optimism and a large dash of resilience. Over the past two years, since her father's death, Ginny had discovered the farm was deep in debt. Papa had hidden it from her, and now she was hiding it from Mary Lou. Ginny brought in hired help for the big jobs and ones she was not physically strong enough to tackle. But she found ways to solve most of the day-to-day challenges. Keeping the farm going during a sudden storm was just one of those challenges.

Ginny changed into her outdoor working clothes: a thick cotton blouse over her woolen undershirt and buckskin pants. She pulled on Papa's leather coat and pushed her feet into stout boots that came up to her knees. Ginny would never dream of dressing in this masculine way if she were going to town. She pulled on her wide-brimmed hat over her headscarf, knotting the cords beneath her chin, and tugged on her leather gloves.

Stepping down from the kitchen porch into the yard, she saw that the remains of the February snow were melting and were scattered with small branches and twigs which had been ripped off the trees. She picked up a stick to crack the ice at the top of a water barrel.

Mary Lou followed her out, equally wrapped up against the cold, and trudged to the chickens. This was her personal domain and she was proud of their contribution to the farmstead, keeping the sisters in regular supply of delicious eggs and occasional treats of a roast dinner.

Ginny went into the barn. Her two horses poked their heads out over the wooden partition and she stroked the muzzles before setting to work, mucking out their stable, replacing hay and replenishing water in the bucket.

"You two seem happy enough," she said, patting their necks. "No time for a brush-down today, but I'll be back soon."

Next, she went to the double stall on the opposite side of the barn driveway to her four cows. She speared some hay into the trough to keep them quiet, then took up the stool and pail and milked each one.

Ginny secured the lid on the disappointingly small amount of milk to take to Mary Lou to make into butter. The cows would not produce much until they were released into the field in spring.

Leaving the milk can by the back door, Ginny skirted the back of the house to the kitchen garden on the other side. An area had become muddy because a fallen branch had blocked the creek. She dragged it away—it would make good firewood when seasoned—and pulled at the debris gathered behind it. The stream began to flow better. She prodded the earth, hoping the potato crop had not been damaged.

When she returned to the kitchen, her back aching and fingers cold, she found that Mary Lou had made the morning coffee as usual. Ginny pulled off her gloves and threw her hat and headscarf on the chair, releasing her untamed honey-brown hair.

She dropped onto the bench beside the wooden kitchen table and took her first sip. "That tastes good. Have you taken any to Lex?"

Mary Lou nodded. "I brushed out his coats and vest as well. Got some of the dirt off them. I left them on a chair in the parlor."

Ginny's stomach tightened as she remembered the photograph. That beautiful woman. What must it be like to know that someone, somewhere, was holding your image close to his heart?

"How was he?"

"Seemed asleep in the armchair when I went in. Said thank you for the coffee, though. D'you think he'll get a little—well —bored?"

Ginny blew her coffee as she thought. What wouldn't she give for a couple of days sitting doing nothing, being brought coffee and meals? In truth, she would be bored in no time, her fingers itching for something to do.

"I'll give it some thought. I'm praying we can take him to town tomorrow and that'll be an end of it." She drained her coffee and finished the bread and cheese Mary Lou had fixed. "Good bread, Mary Lou."

Ginny brushed crumbs from her lips as Mary Lou smiled with pleasure. Making the bread early in the day was one of her chores. "I added some herbs to the dough."

"Right. That's it for me. I'm off over the hill to the cattle." Ginny looped her hat on securely and pulled on her gloves once more.

Ginny saddled up the bay mare and took the track up through the wood that covered the ridge behind their house. The trees were bare and the path soft from the thick layer of leaves made damp by the snow. As Ginny came out to the valley east of the ridge, the sun broke through the ash-gray clouds.

The herd of Durhams were nearby, trying to get shelter from the trees. They looked underfed after the long winter. She pushed down the feelings of frustration with her father for gambling so much of their land on cattle. Most farms in the county were mixed, or dedicated to crops. The Snow farm was larger than most, but still did not have the open land to make the most of beef cattle. She prayed for a warm spring. If the grass grew lush, the cattle might put on enough weight to get a few dollars a head more, particularly if she could sell them to a dealer for the railroad and send them east.

As she wheeled her mare around, her eye was caught by a horse beside the stream. It was a fine-looking stallion, a Paint with black and white patches flecked across its body. It was stocky with good hindquarters: perfect for working with cattle. On its back was a leather saddle, full bags and a rifle. The reins fell forward as the horse nosed through the couple of inches of snow to find some grass.

Ginny stood up in her saddle to see where the owner was, though she was pretty sure the owner was sitting in an armchair in her parlor. She called out, in case there was someone she couldn't see. Silence. So she slowly and carefully walked her horse up close. The Paint looked up, watched her for a moment and then decided the grass was more interesting.

"All right, boy," she murmured. "Let's see if I can tempt you to follow me."

She slipped to the ground and took a rope from her saddle. As she approached, making soft clucking sounds, the animal raised his head, took a step nearer and then changed his mind and walked further away.

"Hmmm, is that how it's gonna be?"

Ginny started walking in a wider circle so she would not come straight at the horse. When she got a few feet away, instead of pushing closer, she turned and calmly walked away. Intrigued, the horse began to follow. Ginny didn't stop and look back; she kept on walking slowly. Before long, she felt the Paint nudging her shoulder.

"*Now* you want to make friends, huh?" She stroked his neck and then his muzzle. "Happy with me now?"

She tied her rope to the bridle and walked back to her mare, the Paint content to follow. Ginny knotted the cord around her saddle and mounted.

"We'll take this easy, because I know you're a stranger round these parts. But I've a feeling someone is gonna be very pleased to see you when we get back to my homestead."

SEVEN

They were looking after him, that was for sure. A hearty breakfast and now a strong cup of coffee. After the girl went back into the kitchen, Lex decided to try out his ankle. He couldn't stay here long, even if it was a welcome change from the laboring that had filled the winter months.

Lex sat upright, his right leg on the floor and brought his left leg down to meet it. The swelling had gone down overnight. A good sign? The pain bit into him, but it was nothing like the day before.

He pushed himself up with the chair's arms, all his weight on his right leg. Then tried some pressure on the left leg. No, not ready for use just yet. But Lex needed to test how much he could move. Leaning on the back of the armchair, he shuffled a step, then another. He looked through the window at the front of the house. There was a porch just outside, protected by a roof. The track on the right led down the gentle slope to the valley below. The landscape seemed as gray as the sky.

Two pictures on either side of the window caught his attention. To the left, a daguerreotype of a man in a velvet jacket, a dark cravat knotted below winged collars. The pose struck Lex as unexpected: the man's arms were crossed and his face quizzical. Although the mouth was a line, it looked like he was about to smile. His hair was thick and stood up from his forehead.

On the other side of the window was a fine oil painting of a woman in an oval frame. Lex was struck by the resemblance to Geneviève. The woman was standing sideways, her head turned to look straight out, with dark eyes that forced the viewer to step closer. She wore a turquoise dress with black lace and violet bows, a fan in her left hand. Her hair was the color of a chestnut just broken free of its bur. Sunshine fell on her bare shoulders. The necklace and a rope of pearls twisted into a bracelet told Lex that the woman was wealthy. He scrutinized the label at the bottom of the frame: LUCILLE LEROUX.

Lex was intrigued by the wallpaper behind the painting. The delicate swirls were hand-painted, but, peering closer, it was newspaper pasted on the wall. He saw the masthead and stepped back in surprise: *The Liberator*. Lex knew this abolitionist newspaper and that it had not been published since the War. How would this homestead in Missouri have ended up with copies of this radical newssheet? And did using it as wallpaper indicate that they did not agree with its views?

Turning back to the room, Lex made his way to the piano. He hopped from one support to the next, like a man climbing a cliff face, making sure each hold was strong enough before reaching for the next. The piano had a walnut veneer with rich patterns of honey-and-chocolate-colored swirls. The cover of the score on the stand said *Chopin, Nocturne No. 2*. The upholstered piano stool was long enough for two people to sit side by side. He raised the hinged lid and inside was full of scores: yellowing parchment, the edges of the pages well thumbed.

Was this rude to be snooping? How would he feel if one of the young women came back into the room? Embarrassed, to be sure. But he couldn't sit here all the darn day doing nothing. And everything about the room aroused his curiosity. Maybe the girls' father would be well enough to come down soon. If he were as interesting as his daguerreotype, Lex hoped so.

He turned to the cabinet, tucked into the alcove between the fireplace and the side wall. He took his time to limp closer, step by step. Like the piano, it was out of place in this rough-hewn house. He ran his fingers over the wood, smooth and glowing. Maple, he thought. The top part was glazed and packed with old books, the leather spines faded. He saw three volumes of Alexis de Tocqueville's *Democracy in America*. Lex could not resist opening the glazed doors and lifting them out.

Opening the first volume, he looked at the frontispiece where there was a name and date: ELIJAH SNOW, 1858. Volume two had the same name but was dated 1859. Leafing through, sentences were underlined and there were notes in the margin. The third tome was a copy of the first volume but in the original French. He was surprised to see even more pencil notes, some in French, some English, with paper bookmarks on important pages. Turning to the frontispiece, he saw the name LUCILLE LEROUX, 1859. He shook his head in surprise.

The next shelf up was mostly novels; there was *Little Women* and *The Scarlet Letter*. The presence of *Uncle Tom's Cabin*, after the discovery of *The Liberator* wallpaper, made him pretty sure of the social leanings of the household. He let out a long breath.

He took down a novel with a burgundy cover and gilded lettering. *Madame Bovary*. Lex grinned. He stacked it on top of volume one of the Tocqueville and pushed them onto the table by the fireplace. He returned the other books to their place and then swung himself down into the armchair.

Madame Bovary. He had heard of this book—whispers of something scandalous. What on earth was this European novel doing out here in the Midwest? He opened it and raised his eyebrows: it was in French. The same woman's name was signed on the frontispiece. He was beginning to like the enigmatic woman in the fine oil portrait. He wondered if the girls in the homestead knew about the nature of the smartly bound book.

His pulse quickened as Ginny's candid face came to mind, her intense brown eyes. A farm girl. The last person he'd expect to be reading a disreputable French novel.

EIGHT

Ginny swung down from her horse as the weak sun lengthened the shadow of the barn across the yard. She tied the stallion to the hitching rail in front of the barn and took her mare into its stable, then hauled the saddle off onto the half wall dividing the stall and hooked the bridle over the horse's head. Soon, the mare was brushed, fed and watered. Ginny took a pail of water to the Paint and patted his side. She dropped a pile of hay in front of him and headed back to the house.

Pushing the kitchen door open, Ginny was met by an aroma of herbs and onions.

"Dinner's nearly ready," said Mary Lou, stirring the pot.

Ginny went over to smell the stew and popped a kiss on Mary Lou's head. "How's our visitor been?"

"He's moving. I heard him hobbling round the room."

Ginny raised an eyebrow. "Well, that's good. Maybe we can get him to town tomorrow."

"He was sleeping a moment ago."

"Good. I'm gonna creep upstairs and get changed." Although Ginny was happy to wear her buckskin pants around the farm, she was embarrassed to do so with this stranger here.

She felt uneasy enough having an unknown man in her home, she didn't want to add to the air of impropriety. And there was something about this man that unnerved her.

Ginny came back down a few minutes later in her blue cotton dress buttoned up to the neck, with a short calico jacket which emphasized her narrow waist. She had splashed water on her face and pulled a brush through her hair, which was now coiled and pinned to the back of her head.

She entered the parlor. "Just checking on Papa." She twisted a tendril that had escaped down her neck, feeling awkward as she tried to keep the fiction in place. "Mary Lou says you're moving."

"Indeed I am." He edged his leg to the floor and pushed himself upright from the armchair. "All I need is a crutch an' I'll be... well, not exactly good as new."

"Can you get to that window?" Ginny pointed to the one overlooking the yard.

He raised an eyebrow and maneuvered his way over while Ginny pushed the shutter back.

A grin broke out across his face and he whooped. "Oh my! Isn't that the finest sight?"

The horse had eaten most of the hay and kicked the water pail on its side.

"I'm guessing he's yours," Ginny said, smiling.

"Sure is. That's Arion. Looks like the saddle is there and everything. Goddamn! How did you— Any injuries?"

"Nope. You been lucky. Y'know, I think he's enjoyed living wild."

"We've been through a lot together."

Ginny took a sideways look at Lex. Light from the window showed laughter lines at the edge of his gray eyes. His happiness at seeing his horse had softened his features—at least those she could see between his beard and shaggy hair. His grin made her stomach flip.

Ginny moved away. "I'll stable him after dinner. We thought maybe we should eat together. In the kitchen." She noticed the pile of books on the table and stopped.

"I hope you don't mind," Lex said.

Ginny turned back to him, her heart beating hard. There was so much she hadn't asked of this stranger, thinking he'd be gone in no time. The contents of the bookcase hinted that her family had stood with the North during the war that had torn the country apart. Feelings ran deep and if it turned out he had fought for the South, things could turn nasty.

Lex scratched at his beard. "I know, I should've asked."

Ginny ran her fingers over the book which lay open. "*Democracy in America*. It's old, so I hope you were careful. It was—it is my father's."

She picked up the Flaubert, her cheeks flushing, having read it the previous winter.

Lex stepped closer. "Course, that one's in French. So I couldn't read it. Wonder what it's about?"

Ginny stole a look up at him. Was he teasing her? Trying to embarrass her?

"I wonder too." She briskly put it back in the bookcase. "I could find you a novel in English if you wish."

"I wouldn't want to trouble you, miss. I'm not much of a reader."

Ginny closed the bookcase door and eyed him. She'd never met a cowboy who had wanted to read anything at all. The man said he was not a reader but had staggered his way over and pulled out some books. Maybe that's what boredom did for you.

He followed her down the passage, limping and making the odd grunt of pain.

"We have a dining table through there." Ginny nodded to the room on the opposite side to the parlor. "But it's always covered in things. Sewing and whatnot." She opened the kitchen door and stood to one side to let the man through. A wooden table dominated the kitchen and she watched as he carefully lowered himself onto a bench beside it.

Mary Lou brought a cast-iron pot of stew from the hearth. "Here we are," she said, plonking it on the table.

She served three bowls of the aromatic stew, then slipped onto the bench beside Ginny. Lex picked up his spoon, but Ginny coughed.

"We usually take a moment to give thanks."

Lex placed his spoon back on the wooden table. The women bowed their heads briefly and then picked up their spoons.

"That it?" he asked, with that smile creeping back.

"We're all old enough to find our own words to give thanks," Ginny said primly.

They ate in silence for a while.

"Miss, I do apologize for taking the liberty of opening your bookcase."

"Apology accepted."

"It strikes me as unusual. Out here."

"In the middle of nowhere, you mean?"

"Can't remember seeing another one on my travels."

Ginny kept her eyes on her food. "And what did you think of the contents?"

"Interesting."

Ginny frowned. Interesting in a good or bad way?

"Interesting wallpaper too."

Ginny froze. So, he had noticed it was made of newssheets.

Mary Lou was oblivious to any deeper meaning. "We did that last winter. It was so cold and Ginny had the idea of pasting up the paper to keep the bindings secure between the logs of the walls. Makes it much warmer in there now. Painting the shapes was my idea."

"I was wond'ring where you got so much newspaper."

Ginny's and Lex's eyes locked over the table. Yes, he recognized the Unionist publication, but his face gave nothing away about how he felt about it. She needed to know his allegiance, but Mary Lou spoke first.

"Papa had a huge pile of them. The newest was ten years old. I s'pose there was no point printing them once the War was won."

"And did your father fight during the War?"

Ginny shook her head. "Had this farm to run." She put down her spoon. It was time to get this out in the open. "And you?"

Lex nodded slowly. "At the end. I would've gone sooner, but my family said I wasn't old enough. For the Unionist side. In case you're wond'ring."

In case she was wondering! Of course she was damn wondering.

Ginny stabbed at a piece of chicken in her stew. "I guess you've worked out by now that the sympathies of this household were for the emancipation. But you might want to keep the side you fought for quiet, if you're thinking of staying in these parts."

Lex frowned. "I thought Missouri was a Unionist state."

"Officially maybe. And we had the Radicals toward the end. But you'll find most folk sympathized with the South. Remember, we were a slave state going into the War."

"Thank you for the warning, miss."

"There's still bad feeling around."

"I guess scars take time to heal."

Ginny gathered the empty dishes. "That's as may be. In my book, close on ten years is plenty time to let bygones be bygones."

NINE

With the meal over, they went to the parlor, where Ginny opened the stove door to heat the room. Ginny sat in one armchair, opened her sewing box and continued mending a hole in a woolen mitten. Lex sat in the other chair and Mary Lou perched on the footstool, leaning against Ginny's legs and soaking up the warmth of the fire.

"Miss, that was tasty dinner."

"You have Mary Lou to thank. She does most of the cooking."

"Well, I'm mighty grateful, Mary Lou. You are a talented cook."

Mary Lou's face lit up. "Mama showed me that a few herbs and things like frying the onions first make all the difference. Papa said she was a wonderful cook."

"Was?" Lex's eyes softened as he studied Mary Lou.

"Our mother died some years back," said Ginny.

"I'm sorry for your loss."

There was silence again.

"Is that her in the picture?" He nodded to the oil painting.

"That's right," Ginny whispered.

"She was very beautiful," Lex observed.

Mary Lou got up to study the image both of them knew so well. "Papa said she was the most beautiful woman in the world. And he fell in love the moment he saw her. She was French, you know."

Lex's eyes moved to the bookshelf. "Lucille LeRoux."

"Truth be told, it was Grandmama who was French," Ginny said. "Grandpapa's family traveled here much earlier. Mama grew up in Louisiana."

"But she spoke French, it seems. Did she teach you?"

"*Mais oui, bien sûr!*" Mary Lou made a low curtsy like a Southern belle.

"A little." Ginny's mind returned to *Madame Bovary* and heat rushed to her cheeks. She bent further over her mending.

Mary Lou strolled back to her stool, leaning in to whisper conspiratorially to Lex as she passed. "It's not true. She's completely fluent."

"And it's just you here now?" Lex asked.

"What do you mean?" Ginny's head jerked up.

"No brothers? Other family?"

"There's Papa upstairs. Of course." Ginny made a tiny cough. "He said he's sorry he's not well enough to come down and meet you. But no. No brothers. Marie-Louise and I manage fine."

Lex leaned back in the chair and fixed his eyes on Ginny. She felt the intensity of his gaze and hoped he would not notice the slight shake of her hand as she pulled a fresh strand of wool from the sewing basket.

"And the piano?"

Ginny looked back up at Lex.

"It was your mother's?"

"Uh-huh."

"But you play it?"

Ginny nodded.

"I'm surprised you have the time, what with running the farm."

"Mama told us we should never let a day go by without practicing," said Mary Lou, picking a thread from her skirt.

Lex raised an eyebrow. "And you stick to that?"

"Sometimes it's a struggle," Ginny said softly. "But it's our way of honoring her. So, yes, we try to stick to it, even at the busy times of year."

Lex lifted his right foot over his left knee. "Perhaps you could play something now?"

Ginny's skin prickled. There was an arrogance about how at ease the man found himself in their home. "There's mending to be done."

"Go on, Ginny." Mary Lou took the mitten. "I'll finish this darning. You go play."

Ginny narrowed her eyes at Lex. "Very well." She walked across and lifted the cover. "What would you like?"

"Something that lifts the spirit," Lex replied.

Ginny stretched and contracted her hands, not just to prepare for playing but to release her growing tension. He was laughing at her, and she wasn't sure why.

Ginny opened the lid of the piano seat and took out a score. "I've been trying to master this one for a while, if you don't mind a few mistakes."

She took out Chopin's Grande valse brillante and settled on the stool. The piece began with a single note repeated in a military rhythm and then the dancing tune began. Ginny's fingers ran over the keys, lightly at times and then firmly beating out the rhythmic tune. She stumbled over a particularly tricky bit, went back and tried it again. It was better, but not perfect. She reached the end of the piece with a run of notes from top to bottom and the final chords.

Silence. Ginny twisted round on the seat, hoping she had

made her point to this mocking stranger with his assumptions of what should and shouldn't be found in a homestead.

"As you can see, I haven't quite mastered all of it. As Mother said: practice."

Lex looked at her open-mouthed and then roared with laughter.

Mary Lou frowned at him, quick to her sister's defense. "Why's that funny?"

"It's not... It's just—"

Ginny closed the lid with a snap. "Maybe you need to read Tocqueville more closely, sir. What does he say? Something like: Women might be confined in the narrow circle of domestic life. But the strength of the American people is down to the superiority of the women."

He bowed his head as if acknowledging her remark, but she still wasn't sure if that smile was actually a smirk, and it made her blood boil.

TEN

Ginny harnessed her two horses to the wagon and led them from the yard to the front of the homestead. Mary Lou followed with Arion and tied him to the tailboard. The snow had melted enough to see earth beneath the hoofprints.

Under Papa's coat, Ginny wore a worsted burgundy dress and, under that, thick bloomers to keep out the cold. Her feet were chilled because she was wearing her lace-up leather boots, which she deemed more appropriate for a trip into town than her heavy farm boots. She had tucked her unruly hair into a dark bonnet secured with ribbons at her chin.

Mary Lou was also warm but smart and Ginny noted that she looked on the cusp of womanhood. She had taken off her pinafore and wore a blue homespun cape over a woolen dress. The silk flowers of her straw bonnet drooped at one side.

Ginny climbed the porch steps to the front door and unlatched it. "Ready?"

She held out his coat for him, the fabric still grimy with dirt despite Mary Lou's efforts.

Lex shrugged it on. "My Colt?"

Ginny fetched it from the kitchen.

"Papa said he was feeling too tired to come down and say goodbye."

Lex slid the pistol into its holster and buttoned it fast. He pulled his hat low over his face and limped toward the door. Ginny had fashioned an old broomstick into a crutch, which he used in the armpit of one shoulder.

Ginny grabbed her paisley shawl from the peg and swirled it round her shoulders and over her bonnet. "You want a hand?"

"Nope," he said with a slight grimace as he swung down the steps. At the wagon, he patted Arion's neck and the horse stamped its hoof in greeting.

Ginny folded down the tailboard. "Thought you'd be better sitting in the flatbed. You can stretch out that leg."

Lex glanced at Ginny and nodded. Turning his back to it, he pushed himself onto the bed of the cart with both arms. He then shuffled sideways to lean against the side of the wagon.

Ginny fastened the tailboard and made sure Arion was secure, while Mary Lou passed Lex a blanket. Mary Lou climbed up to the front bench and Ginny sat next to her. She slapped the reins once and the horses pulled away, the wagon jerking forward.

The air was sharp, but the wind had dropped. The track was not substantial enough to be called a road and undulated north through the tree-covered hills. Ginny tried to avoid deep ruts, but the cart swung back and forth nevertheless. She was aware that Lex was grasping the tailboard; it must be an uncomfortable journey with his leg not yet healed.

After about half an hour, Ginny pulled the horses to a halt at the brow of a hill.

"There's Brownsville," she called to Lex.

The small town was plotted on a grid with one main street crossed with a secondary road and minor paths leading off at right angles. A clapboard church with a stubby tower and short spire tried to assert itself over the ramshackle buildings around it. The railroad bisected the far end of town. The station was hidden behind other buildings, but telegraph wires hugged close to the track that stretched west and east.

Ginny geed the horses to move again as the track wound its way down the hill. They passed the wooden buildings at the edge of town: storage barns, small houses. Then they drove down the main road, each side with double-story buildings, most with awnings extending over the wooden sidewalk. Painted signs told them they were passing a bank, the general stores, a livery, the saloon.

"All the amenities you would expect of a modern town," said Mary Lou.

Ginny drew up outside the grandest building in the street, although it did not need much to take that accolade.

"Hofmann Hotel." She glanced over her shoulder at Lex. "Though it's more of a boarding house."

The three-story brick building had tall windows evenly spaced above the canopy, leading the eye up to the facade which hid the pitched roof.

Ginny jumped down and untied the tailboard.

"And you're sure you can afford Hofmann's?" she asked. "I could ask around and see if anyone might take you cheaper for the night."

Lex looked up at the building. The privacy of the interior was protected by net curtains at each window. "I'll manage. I'm very resourceful." Again, that one-sided grin behind his beard.

He shifted his legs over the edge and Ginny handed him the crutch.

Mary Lou looped Arion's reins to the hitching post by the stoop. "All your things are attached to the saddle."

"And you don't want me to introduce you to Mrs. Hofmann?" Ginny asked.

"As I said, I'll be fine." He stood up and handed the crutch back to Ginny.

"You keep it. It really has no use for us."

He winked. "Unless you break your ankle, falling off a horse spooked by a mountain lion."

"Let's trust that doesn't happen."

Lex made a mock bow. "Marie-Louise Snow, it's been mighty fine getting to know you."

"It's been fun! Call in any time." Mary Lou beamed.

"It's unlikely I'll be traveling that way again. But please thank your father for his hospitality. I'm sorry I didn't get to meet him. I trust he'll be better soon."

The smile froze on Mary Lou's face.

"Yes, yes, thank you," Ginny said, gently pushing Mary Lou back to the wagon. "We've got plenty of errands to run in town, so I'll say goodbye." She fastened the tailboard and put out her gloved hand.

Lex paused and looked down at her from beneath his hat. His eyes caught hers for a moment. He shook her hand firmly and the warmth that rose in Ginny's cheeks made her immediately regret the contact.

"It was nice to meet you, Miss Geneviève. Unexpected in so many ways." Despite the unruly whiskers, the smile at the edge of his mouth made Ginny's breathing uneven.

Ginny swallowed. "Unexpected seems the right word."

He adjusted his hat. "So. This is farewell."

"Indeed. Farewell, Mr.—" Ginny frowned. "I don't recall you telling us your surname."

"Don't recall I did. Not a lot of point now. Seeing our paths are unlikely to cross again."

Ginny took a step back. "No point at all. Farewell, Lex, drifter from outta state."

He laughed and turned his attention to untying his saddlebags from Arion's back.

Ginny climbed back to the driver's seat, Mary Lou by her

side. A smart tap of the reins and the horses were off down Main Street.

Don't look back, she told herself, but after a moment took a glance over her shoulder. He had been waiting, and raised his hat in acknowledgment. Ginny bit her lip and swiftly turned back to the horses, her heart beating fast, cursing herself for showing how much he intrigued her. Ginny's breathing did not return to normal until she was around the corner, at the general stores.

ELEVEN

Mrs. Bertha Hofmann eyed him with suspicion when the man knocked on her front door. Nearer vagrant than the respectable traveling salesmen she usually accommodated. But the payment he made upfront from dollars hidden in his saddlebag overcame her reservations. Still, she gave him the smallest room at the back. No point wasting one of the well-appointed rooms overlooking Main Street, especially if one of her regulars was passing through.

The first thing he asked for was a doctor to look at his leg.

She had never lost her heavy German accent. "You are wanting Bill Mack. End of the street, just beyond the Gibbes Mercantile." She jabbed her head in the direction. "He's a fine surgeon. When he's sober."

Bill Mack had a couple of rooms next to the barber. Lex tapped on the door with his broom-crutch and pushed it open. The window did a poor job of lighting the room and a lamp made a yellow pool over a wooden desk. The room smelled of castor oil and sulfur. Lex read the framed certificate near the door. MR.

WILLIAM MCCULLAR, MD, GRADUATE OF MISSOURI MEDICAL COLLEGE, CLASS OF 1852. It wouldn't have made any difference whether or not Bill Mack was qualified; there weren't any alternatives on offer.

The physician spun round on his chair at the desk and squinted through metal-rimmed spectacles. He raised a bushy eyebrow at the crutch.

"Sit yourself there and let's take a look." He waved toward the chair by the window: wooden with a back that curved forward to make the arms, with slight padding. Lex lowered himself gingerly.

Bill Mack pushed a stool in front of the leg and brought his own chair near. Lex winced as the doctor pulled off the boot.

"How you do it?"

"Horse threw me."

Bill Mack grunted and leaned forward.

"Done a good job with this bandage," he said, unwrapping it.

As the doctor prodded and squeezed the area from toes to shin, Lex studied the bald pate surrounded by a ring of wiry hair. It was shot with ginger, which suggested a once bright head of hair to match the beard, now both sadly faded to gray.

"Looks like a lucky escape to me." Bill Mack sat back in his chair. "No bones broken. You've torn some tendons, but with rest they should heal nicely. Nothing to worry about."

Lex let out a breath. Miss Snow had said much the same and had kneaded his leg with more gentleness.

Bill Mack got up and walked toward the shelves that covered the back wall, full of bottles and jars, a bronze weighing scale pushed between pestles of different sizes. On a table lay an assortment of metal instruments: a knife with a bone handle, a small saw, a spoon with a tiny bowl and long handle. Lex shuddered.

Bill Mack picked up a white jar with a stopper. "You can have this ointment to rub into it, twice a day."

"Will it do any good?"

"Who knows? Maybe, maybe not. But most folks seem to like it and you've got to buy something."

Lex nodded and eased his boot back on. "How long do I have to rest it?"

"How long since you busted it?"

"Less than a week."

Bill Mack sucked air in through his teeth. "Longer you rest it now, stronger it will be in the end. If you can keep off it another fortnight, that should do it. If you're broke and need to work sooner, you're in for a painful time." He picked up the crutch and smiled. "This shows ingenuity. Keep using it."

Lex put his leg back on the floor and pushed himself upright. He took the crutch, counted out some coins and put them on the desk.

The doctor sat down and pulled out a sheet of paper. "What name shall I make the receipt out to?"

"I don't need a receipt."

"I like to keep my paperwork in order. In case anyone wants to accuse me of anything later." Bill Mack dipped the pen into ink and suspended it over the paper.

"Mr. Carlton."

"First name?"

"Lex."

"Short for?"

"Lex Carlton is just fine."

Tucking the receipt into his jacket pocket and pulling on his hat, Lex stood on the boardwalk. He looked at the barber's next door and pushed open the glazed door. Inside, there was just the one chair, occupied by a distinguished-looking man with a mane of silver hair brushed back from his face.

The barber took one look at Lex and pursed his lips. "Take a pew."

Lex sat on the bench and waited as the man completed his work with the customer.

When it was Lex's turn, he sank into the cutting chair. It was on a pedestal and upholstered in velvet. It must have been a fine chair once, but the front seam was worn away and horsehair poked through.

Lex looked at the mirror in front and laughed out loud as he pulled his hand across the dark beard and then through his disheveled hair. Leaning forward, he could see his skin was gray with dirt. "Maybe I should've taken a bath first."

The barber snorted in a way that suggested agreement.

"But I'm here now. This raggedy beard needs to come off and my hair needs cuttin'."

The barber beat up a lather in his mug. "I like a challenge."

In the reflection, Lex noticed a Confederate flag in the corner of the room, a gray cap perched on top. He swallowed, remembering Miss Snow's advice to keep his Unionist allegiance quiet. The barber was sharpening the razor on a leather strap. Best not enter into any small talk.

Half an hour later, Lex closed his eyes as he wiped his face in a clean towel. The barber rubbed Bay Rum into his hair and Lex breathed in the smell of citrus and cloves. The face in the mirror was thinner than he was used to and certainly more weather-beaten.

"This is the life you chose," he whispered.

Returning to the Hofmann Hotel, the reception was far warmer now he was more presentable—Mrs. Hofmann seemed to think very presentable from the approving look she gave him on arrival.

"Might I trouble you for a good long bath?" said Lex.

Mrs. Hofmann smoothed her apron over her considerable girth. "That'll be extra."

"Daresay it will be worth every dime. I'm guessing laundry's extra too?"

"Indeed. I can't get nothing done today. Drawing a bath, it will take a while." She looked at his grimy clothing. "I tell you what. I have shirts left behind by previous occupants. I let you have one."

"Extra?"

"Mister, I *do* have a business to run. I can't go round giving out things for free."

"I would be most grateful, Mrs. Hofmann. Both for the bath and the clean shirt."

Mrs. Hofmann retreated to the kitchen to put water on the fire to heat, muttering to herself in German.

TWELVE

A week later, Lex was used to feeling clean and well-fed. Once laundered, the dark blue of his jacket returned. At Gibbes Mercantile, he bought a pair of ready-made pants to replace the fraying ones. He was treated politely at the store where men gathered to play checkers and complain about the price of seed, but Lex could feel the prickling of suspicion for a stranger who had arrived in their town.

Mrs. Hofmann deemed him presentable enough to be invited to her Saturday evening supper of those she considered the most respectable in their small town. Lex was anxious to make connections to find work, now his ankle was on the mend.

"This is Mr. Carlton, my new paying guest," Mrs. Hofmann announced as he entered the dining room. Now he had tidied himself up, she was rather proud of this handsome lodger. He was tall, his broad shoulders filled out that jacket and there was something about the way he spoke that suggested a cut above the itinerant cowboys who occasionally splashed out to spend a few days at the boarding house.

Mrs. Hofmann's dining room was not large, so the five guests filled up the room. Looking round, Lex realized he had met or seen all the other dinner guests over the week. Mr. and Mrs. Gibbes ran the general store. Lex was slightly surprised to see Bill Mack, given Mrs. Hofmann's tone of disapproval about his drinking. There was the silver-haired gentleman he had seen in the barbers. They nodded.

Mrs. Hofmann noticed the acknowledgment. "This is Mr. Jeremiah Tanner. This town wouldn't be able to manage without him. Banker, adviser, lawyer."

He shook Lex's hand, looking him straight in the eye as if assessing whether he could be trusted with a loan.

Mrs. Hofmann laid a hand on Lex's arm. "You sit by me." She took her place at the head of the table, so Lex sat to her right, opposite Tanner. Beside the banker was Mrs. Gibbes, with the doctor at the end of the table, leaving Mr. Gibbes on Lex's right. Gibbes sighed when he realized he would be sitting opposite his wife all evening.

The housemaid brought a china tureen of soup, which Mrs. Hofmann served at the table. It was a thin consommé—something she felt more refined than the German broth with spiced sausages that her guests were hoping for.

Over the soup, they dissected the town's comings and goings. Attention turned to Lex while they were eating their main course.

"And what is your trade, Mr. Carlton?" asked Mrs. Gibbes.

"Trade?"

"A salesman? Most of Mrs. Hofmann's guests are. You might have something you want to supply our store?"

"Oh, I see. No. Agricultural. A ranch hand. Or farming. Now my leg is mended, I'll be looking for any work I can."

Tanner coughed. "Might be able to help you out there, son. I'll introduce you to Amos Sturge. He's agent for lots of farms in the county and will know who's shorthanded."

"Thank you. I'll be much obliged."

"And what brought you to Brownsville in particular?" Mrs. Gibbes asked.

"A mountain lion, I suppose."

"A mountain lion!"

Lex wiped his lips with this napkin. "A mountain lion spooked my horse when I was traveling through the Ozarks. He threw me and that's how I busted my ankle. I was stuck out there for some time."

Mr. Gibbes raised an eyebrow. "You were lucky to make it here. Those hills are a long way off."

"The luck was being found by Marie-Louise Snow. She saw me crawling my way down the valley and took me back to the farm. Her sister fixed up my leg. A few days later, Miss Snow even found my horse and led it back."

Mrs. Gibbes' mouth fell open as she looked across at Lex. "A few *days*?"

"Maybe it was the next day. I was pretty concussed by the cold and hunger, so I couldn't tell. But, yes, she kindly took me in 'til I was stronger."

"Has that girl got no thought of her reputation?" Mrs. Gibbes looked around the table for support. "Or of her sister, who ain't a child no more. That Geneviève Snow thinking she's better than everyone, never having the good sense to ask for help. Just because she's got some kinda family history to live up to." Mrs. Gibbes speared another potato. "And now it's clear her mother brought her up without a care of what's right and what's wrong."

Mr. Gibbes shuffled in his seat at his wife's tirade.

Lex frowned. "I'm not sure what you mean, Mrs. Gibbes."

"Did she not think of her *honor*? Two young women alone in a house with a man they didn't know."

"Oh, I see," said Lex with a slight smile. "Well, it was lucky for me, because another day or so in them hills and I don't think

I would've survived. An' lucky for me they didn't assume I was a man with no morals."

"My wife didn't mean to insult you, Mr. Carlton," intervened Mr. Gibbes. "Now we've met you, we can see that you are respectable."

Lex caught Tanner's twinkling eye across the table. "Thank you, Mr. Gibbes. That's very kind." Lex took another bite of chicken. "But I don't know what the fuss is about. They weren't alone with me any way. Mr. Snow was there."

The table went silent as everyone stared at Lex. Mrs. Gibbes's fork remained halfway to her mouth. Lex looked around, aware he had said something shocking.

Tanner was the first to recover his voice. "What d'you mean, Mr. Snow was there?"

Lex opened his palms. "He was recuperating. Upstairs."

Mrs. Hofmann crossed herself and whispered a prayer in German.

Bill Mack leaned forward on to the table. "Did ya *meet* him?"

"No. But I *heard* him."

Mrs. Gibbes's fork clattered to her plate and her hand flew to the brooch at her throat.

Lex frowned. "Moving around when Ginny or Mary Lou took food upstairs to him."

Bill Mack smiled, using his knife to point at Lex. "But did you *actually* see him? Or hear his voice?"

Lex paused and pulled his hand across his chin, feeling the day's stubble and remembering being cocooned in the Snow homestead. "No. I don't suppose I did."

"But Miss Snow told you he was upstairs?"

"Yes. She explained he was poorly but would meet me soon."

Bill Mack burst into laughter. "It seems Miss Snow's respectability is unharmed, Mrs. Gibbes. Or, at least, that's how

I would see it. Given that this stranger didn't know—indeed didn't *think*—he was alone with the two young women."

"I am not understanding you, Dr. McCullar," said Mrs. Hofmann, frowning.

"Miss Snow led Mr. Carlton here to believe her father was in the house."

Lex sat back in his chair, feeling uncomfortable. He was not often confused by things and didn't like the sensation.

Tanner nodded in agreement with Bill Mack. "Mr. Snow died two years since, Mr. Carlton. The doctor here can testify to that, as he was the one who pulled the body from the lake. The Misses Snow have been struggling with that farm ever since."

Lex thought back to his time at the homestead, the stilted way Ginny and Mary Lou spoke of going upstairs, the quick glances between the young women. He felt a tightening in his stomach as his perspective shifted on what had happened during those days, annoyed that he'd been deceived. Had the sisters been making a fool of him? But his irritation passed in a moment as he remembered their kindness.

"I'm mighty grateful she *did* make up that pretense. Meant they felt able to take me in, feed me, fix up my leg. If Miss Snow had turned me away in order to retain her respectability, I'm darn sure I'd be dead by now."

Mrs. Gibbes bristled. "That's as may be. But that girl is no better than she oughta be." She adjusted the sleeves of her dress. "I can see you agree with me, Bertha. She's always been a one, with those airs and graces. There's plenty of men round here could make a go of that farm, given the chance. But, oh no. She can manage by herself, thank you very much."

Mrs. Hofmann nodded. "Foolish young woman. If I had a daughter, I'd want her to show better judgment."

Mrs. Hofmann spoke as if her pronouncement closed the matter and everyone began to eat once more.

Lex thought about what had been said. His experience of

Ginny Snow seemed so different. She had been reserved, certainly, and some might interpret that as airs and graces. But she was no fool. Nevertheless, he thought better of ruffling feathers by challenging these two older women, especially as he needed to make a good impression if he was going to pick up work in this town.

THIRTEEN

Brownsville did what it could to pretend it was a long-established town, rather than a settlement that had sprung up in the last twenty years as a fording point for Brown River, a tributary of some greater river that most of the residents could not name and did not care about. The recent railroad track had transformed the town though, bringing more change in the past five years than the previous two decades.

An important step in telling the world that Brownsville was here to stay was the Lutheran church on Main Street. Built back from the thoroughfare, the land was guarded by a low stone wall topped with a metal fence, made as if from spears, each pointing heavenwards. Inside was darker than expected. The architect had aped the gothic style and put in too few windows. Reverend Wilsher was aware that the darkness of the space and the privacy of the high-backed pews meant some of his flock were prone to sleep during the service. He countered this with a barnstorming style of oratory which had the effect of drawing a good-sized congregation, mostly of women, to admire the sermons.

The church boasted a particularly fine organ, shipped from

the east, which was rarely played to its best effect. When Reverend Wilsher had arrived in the county, he'd heard of Miss Snow's talents and went to seek her out.

The Snows had never been great churchgoers. Elijah Snow thought a loving God would not have let things turn out quite so badly for his dear wife. But fear of a judgmental God ensured occasional attendance. When Reverend Wilsher had asked Miss Snow to become the church organist, she had demurred, given the distance to drive each Sunday, but the Reverend was persistent and she was persuaded to play fortnightly.

Since the death of her father, it seemed work on the farm was never done and she had tried to give up the obligation, but Reverend Wilsher managed to get her agreement to monthly organ playing and slipped her a few coins from the collection in recompense.

It was the third Sunday in Lent and Ginny sat quietly at the organ on the left side of the church, close to the pulpit. She worked her way through the familiar hymns, trying to keep the tempo swift so the communal singing did not revert to a dirge.

She half listened to the sermon as her eyes traced the cracks creeping up the plaster wall in front of her. Ginny had long since stopped being impressed by Wilsher's flamboyant style. She thought the content questionable, using fear of damnation as a way of keeping people in their place. But she kept her views to herself.

In the half-light, she shifted her seat so her eyes could drift over the congregation; familiar faces to her, some looking up, rapt by the reverend. Most seemed lost in their own thoughts, much as she was in hers. Then her gaze snagged on a man she didn't recognize, sitting in the shadows by the wall, a few pews back. A handsome face, with a straight nose and firm jaw, his dark hair pushed back. He sat in a relaxed way, one arm stretched across the back of the pew. His expression suggested a mixture of amusement and puzzlement at the words of the sermon. She was glad to see her own thoughts reflected on someone else's face.

He turned slightly to look at her. Ginny threw her attention back to the music in front of her, embarrassed that she had been caught watching. After a few moments, though, she could not resist looking over the congregation once more. To her shock, the man's eyes were still on her. In defiance, she would not drop her gaze a second time and was surprised by the nod the man gave her, as if he were an acquaintance. Ginny frowned slightly. At that moment, a break in the clouds allowed the sun to shine more brightly in shafts across the pews. The man smiled at her very faintly, one side of his mouth rising more than the other.

Ginny hoped her gasp of recognition had not been loud enough for anyone to hear. She busied herself with the music for the next hymn.

Reverend Wilsher slowed his pace as he hammered home his final points, indicating he was reaching the end of his sermon.

"We will sing hymn number thirty-two," the reverend boomed, and Ginny pushed at the keys unusually hard. There was even a wrong note in the second verse.

She allowed herself another brief glance and saw that thankfully the man was joining the congregation in singing the final hymn. Her heart beat much faster than the rhythm of the music. Why was he still here? What had transformed the wild vagrant she'd left at the door of Hofmann Hotel into this well-turned-out churchgoer before her?

The service ended and the congregation rose. Ginny fumbled as she gathered her things, squashing her music into a cloth bag and pulling her cloak around her shoulders.

"A word," said Reverend Wilsher, bearing down on her. "You seemed rather erratic in that final song."

A heat rose in Ginny's cheeks as she swept up her bonnet.

The reverend suggested a number of hymns for the

following month. Ginny dropped her head and nodded, longing to leave and be on her way home. She wasn't sure why she wanted to avoid Lex so urgently, but she had the feeling of having revealed something intimate about her life to a man she thought she would never see again. And yet here he was. And looking so very, very different.

She stepped from the side door of the church into the March sunshine, the light dazzling her eyes for a moment. She walked to the front, hoping to slip by the knots of folk chattering. He was waiting by the gate and lifted his hat in greeting.

"Miss Geneviève Snow."

She straightened her back. "Mr.... Y'know, you never did tell me your full name."

"Carlton." Lex put out his hand.

Ginny hesitated, remembering the disconcerting effect of previous contact.

Pull yourself together, girl.

His hand was firm, as before, but she glanced down and saw that it was no longer grimed with dust. The nails were clean and neatly cut. He smelled of citrus.

"How do you do, Mr. Carlton." Ginny tried a show of confidence. "I didn't think I would meet you again."

"I'd expected to have moved on."

"Why haven't you?"

"I've taken a fancy to Brownsville." Again, there was that smile. The one that seemed to escape from half his face and made him look like he was trying not to laugh out loud. "Given me a chance to sort myself out, waitin' for my leg to be strong enough for the next job."

Lex stepped aside as a husband and wife went through the gate.

"Good morning, Carlton," said the man.

"Good morning, Mr. Gibbes." Lex tipped his hat to the woman. "Mrs. Gibbes."

She skated her eyes over Ginny, and they both moved on.

"My. You've become part of the community mighty fast."

Lex shrugged. "Where's Marie-Louise?"

"She rarely comes to church. There's always so much to do at the farm."

"As I witnessed."

"I should be getting back to her now." Ginny was eager to get away, and yet wanted to stay in his company. She pulled on her bonnet.

"And how is your father?"

Ginny froze. What could she say? She yanked the ribbons of the bonnet.

"If you've been in town for the past two weeks, I daresay you know the answer to that question." She raised her chin, glaring at his face. For the first time, there was a look of discomfort in those gray eyes.

"I didn't mean to be unkind," Lex said in a low voice. "But it did cause a stir at Mrs. Hofmann's supper party when I told them he was at the farm."

Now she felt bad at scowling at him. How did he manage to wrong-foot her so quickly?

She busied herself with her gloves. "I know it seems a strange thing to lie about. Macabre even. But I couldn't think what else to do."

"Not strange at all." His voice was still gentle. "A wild-looking man turns up on your doorstep. Many would have turned me away. You were kind enough to take me in. It was a clever way to protect you and your sister."

A memory of when she had first seen him flooded her mind, the weight of him on her shoulder as he'd struggled into her parlor, the intimacy of tending his leg. A heat prickled on the backs of her arms. It was hard to reconcile those memories with the handsome man standing in front of her.

She shook her head. "I really must be going."

Lex placed his hand on her arm as she stepped past. "Is there any way I can thank you?"

"What for?"

"Looking after me. Can I at least repay you for food?"

"Certainly not." She lifted his hand from her arm. "It was simple Christian charity. I don't know where you're from, sir, but I was not brought up to need *paying* for simply doing what's right."

"I've offended you."

Ginny pulled her cape tightly around her, hoping it hid her rapid breathing. Why was he having this effect on her? She could at least be civil.

"I'm glad you have recovered so well. I'll let Marie-Louise know. She'll be pleased. Now, it was nice meeting you, Mr. Carson—"

"—Carlton."

"Mr. Carlton. But I daresay this time it really is farewell."

Ginny hurried down the street to where her buggy was waiting. Had she managed to regain her dignity? No matter. He was a cowboy, a drifter. Even if this morning he didn't look like one, dressed up in Sunday best. He'd be moving on very soon. She wouldn't be seeing him again, so what did it matter what sort of impression she left?

FOURTEEN

Lex rode out to Amos Sturge's farm, following Tanner's directions. He'd heard that Amos Sturge acted as labor agent for most of the farms around Brownsville. Men looking for work signed up with him and farm owners relied on his seasonal workers to bolster regular hands when the agricultural year was busy. The only problem was that all the farms were busy at the same time; Amos was always looking for new labor.

Leaving town, Lex came to the railroad tracks and paused to study them. The twin bars of iron formed a gash between the trees to the west and curved out of sight to the east. Arion picked his way uncertainly across the raised wood between the rails, then back onto the road, the main route directly north to Jefferson City.

The land flattened and Lex recognized Tanner's description of the Sturge farm: a larger farmhouse than he had seen in the area, with a porch that ran all the way round, topped by a pebble-colored roof with three gables, each with a window. In the spring air, the land looked well prepared for corn and wheat.

Tanner had advised him to go to the kitchen at the back. A

woman in her forties answered the door, her face ruddy from working outside and dark hair escaping from her bonnet. A child held on to her skirts.

The woman was unsurprised by the visitor. "You'll be wanting Amos, I daresay."

She hollered for her husband and ushered Lex into the kitchen.

He removed his hat and took in the kitchen, packed full of sacks of food, shelves with jars and tins, tools for canning and grinding foodstuffs. The table was covered with papers and ledgers.

Amos Sturge ducked his head as he entered from the rest of the house. He was dressed in jeans and a thick shirt and ignored his wife's tutting at the mud on his outdoor boots. Amos motioned Lex to sit at the table.

The woman pushed a cup of coffee in front of each of the men.

"You'll have met my wife, Dinah," Amos said. He dropped heavily into his chair and pushed his long legs out to the side. "I been wondering when you'd walk through my door."

"I wanted to wait 'til my leg had healed."

Amos harrumphed. "Most of us work through injury. Hope this don't mean you're soft."

Lex's fists tightened, but he decided this comment didn't need a rebuttal.

"An' now you've run low on cash and need work."

"Something like that."

"Experience?"

Lex summarized the past two years of graft. He had experience of livestock: ranching, branding in Texas, longhorn drives to Sedalia.

Amos studied him. "Hope you weren't with those scoundrels bringing Texas fever into our state."

"I jus' drive where I'm told."

"We don't have call for that sort of work round here. More about crops and hogs."

"I can steer a pair of oxen straight, put in a long day's work in the field."

Amos picked up the pipe lying on the table and stuffed it with tobacco. "I can send you to Haggers Ranch. Big place, 'bout twenty mile north of here."

"Truth is, I already have a place in mind. Snow Farm."

Amos raised his bushy brows and returned to his pipe, striking a match and sucking until the tobacco caught. He leaned back.

"You're not the first handsome young buck to sit in that chair and say that. Now, I knew Mr. Snow and his crazy ideas. One year buying a new threshing machine, the next deciding that valley over the ridge was right for cattle. While he had his faults, deep down he was a good man. Many's the night we sat together, putting the world to rights. Now he's gone, I'm obligated to look out for his daughters."

"I'll work harder than any man you send this season."

Amos sucked on his pipe. "Betcha will. But it's not the work you're after, is it? Miss Snow is thought of as an eligible young woman in these parts."

Lex's mouth became a tight line, but he said nothing.

Amos continued. "Many a young man has worked the season, thinking he could catch a wife an' a farm all in one go. An' one like you—what my wife would call easy on the eye—probably fancy your chances."

Lex shifted in his chair. "My reason for wanting to work there is simple. Miss Snow and her sister took me in when I was injured. Being a small town, I daresay you know that. I would like to return the good deed in some way. I mentioned payment to Miss Snow, but that caused offense." Lex took a gulp of coffee. It was better than Bertha Hofmann's. "Thought if I could go as a hired hand, I'd be there to do whatever I could as extra. For free. Repairs and whatnot."

Amos snorted as he tamped down the tobacco. "I weren't born yesterday. You're hoping to catch her eye with all this stuff. Catch her eye an' turn her head. An' none of us knows the first thing about you. Where you come from, where you headed."

Lex put a hand into the slip pocket on the inside of his vest. He didn't like sharing his personal business, but it looked like he had no choice. He took out the photograph of the woman and slid it across the table.

"This is my fiancée. I keep her picture by my heart. Is that proof that my motives are honorable? I have no interest in Snow Farm. Nor Miss Snow."

Amos leaned forward and eyed the picture of the pretty woman, before nodding slightly and pushing it back. Lex tucked it inside his vest.

"As I say, Mr. Sturge, I would welcome the chance to pay my debt to Miss Snow and her sister. Nothing more."

Amos narrowed his eyes and studied him before pulling some papers from the pile. "Very well. You start Monday. There's branding and cuttin' needed for her new calves. Here's the terms."

Lex looked through the few lines and signed. "That's a lower rate of pay than I was expecting."

"Complaining?"

"Observing."

Amos smiled, showing gaps in his teeth. "Miss Snow, she ain't stupid. She knows all about the laws of supply and demand. Even read a book 'bout it and explained it to me once. While I try to protect her from the most wolfish young farmhands in the area, she knows there'll always be men willing to work for this day rate in the hope of turning her head."

Lex smiled at Ginny's unusual business acumen. Yes, that

sounded like the curious woman he had encountered. He stood to leave.

"But don't mean you can take advantage," Amos said sternly. "And I'll be there Monday to check everything."

Lex put on his hat and tipped it at Amos.

"I'll be on my very best behavior."

FIFTEEN

Ginny strode down the kitchen porch steps and into the yard. The air smelled of spring flowers and she put her face up to the morning sun. She always loved the excitement of cattle branding.

Her wide-brimmed hat was pushed back onto her shoulders, held by its strings. She wore a neat leather jacket over a cotton blouse. Her split skirt was made of soft suede, topped by a leather belt. She wore this skirt on the farm when in company, rather than her pants. Riding boots with a slight heel finished the look which said a woman who meant business.

She checked her packhorse once again for equipment: they would be gone overnight. Hearing the sound of hooves, she stepped up into the saddle of her bay mare and rode down the track to greet the cowboys Amos Sturge had hired.

To her pleasure, she saw Amos riding at the head of a group of four men, each leading a spare mount. When they came close, she called out, "Mr. Sturge, didn't realize I'd have the pleasure of your company this year."

"The pleasure's all mine, young lady." He gallantly raised his hat.

"Your wife is content for you to leave her overnight?"

"Her sister's staying over. Dinah'll enjoy having me out the way."

"Much like Mary Lou. She'll enjoy being mistress of the house."

The other men rode up.

"Saul Dunklin you know, of course."

"Always good to see you, Mr. Dunklin. How is Nancy?"

"Faring much better now, thank you. The arrival of that last babe gave us all a fright."

Amos nodded to the next two men. "Then there's Edward, Mr. Trike's youngest. He did well on Sawyers Farm last year, so I thought I'd try him branding."

Trike urged his horse close to Ginny and lifted his hat, showing hair which looked like straw had been matted through. His face was thin, but his grin broad, revealing a tooth missing at one side.

"Delighted to meet you, Miss Snow."

Ginny nodded to him and circled her horse away into its own space.

"Then this is Isiah Boone." Amos rode closer to Ginny and lowered his voice. "I figured you wouldn't have a problem with Boone."

"Course not, Amos."

"Some folks seem to think the War still hasn't settled things," said Amos with a shake of the head. "It's sometimes hard to find a place for a freed slave. An' he's a hard worker."

The final cowboy rode forward.

"An' this is Mr. Carlton, who I believe you know." Amos caught Ginny's look of surprise. "I hope that's all right. He had good experience for cattle. An' was keen to join us."

Most of Lex's face was in the shade of his hat, so she could not see his expression. She wished she was wearing her own hat to have the same benefit, as her cheeks grew hot. Ginny loosened her red neckerchief.

"If you'd rather I find someone else—" Amos began.

"No. It's fine. And we need to get going today." She sat up straighter and called out, "I hope you remember how small my farm is, Mr. Carlton. This will only be a couple of days' work. Not much earnings for you."

Lex nodded and touched his hat but said nothing.

"Well, then." Ginny turned her horse and led the way back to the farm, Amos at her side. He was just a farmhand, like many others who had worked for her. At least, that's what she told herself.

In the yard, Ginny organized the men to gather the last pieces of equipment and strap them to her two mules. Once they were ready to leave, Ginny returned to Mary Lou who was watching them from the kitchen door, dressed in her calico apron.

"Now, you remember everything I told you? Make sure you shut up everything at night—"

"Yes, I know."

"And the fire. Make sure it's—"

"Ginny, I manage the fire every day."

Ginny lowered her voice. "And Papa's gun. You know—"

"Now, shoo!" Mary Lou gave her sister a gentle push. "I'm grown up now. I'll be fine."

Ginny mounted her horse and Mary Lou stepped down to the yard. She patted Arion's side. "Good morning, Lex. Nice to see you again."

Lex lifted his hat. "You too, Miss Marie-Louise."

Ginny led the way out of the farm and toward the wooded ridge.

. . .

Snow Farm was small to middling, certainly nothing like the huge ranches which spread across the plains further west. Starting with sixty acres in 1854 when Ginny was a babe, her father had added land when he could, and it was now double that size. They owned the wood across the long ridge, where Ginny's hogs ran free for much of the year.

The horses stepped their way over branches across the steep path to the top of the ridge until a valley opened up before them. Ginny's herd of Durhams were in small groups across the spring grass.

She wheeled her horse to the left, making her way down the valley to a wooden corral. The first task was to make sure the fences and hurdles were secure for when the cattle were gathered. They tied the mules in the corral and the team then rode back up the valley where the ridge ran round like a bowl, the trees above in full leaf. Some of the cattle moved down into the valley, disturbed by the riders. A few stood their ground, still chewing as they watched them pass. They had lost a lot of weight over winter, so Ginny was relieved to see most were filling out again.

At the head of the valley, she dismounted.

"We'll take a break before we start the roundup," she called to the men.

The cowboys each dismounted and took out a canteen of water and some oatmeal biscuits. It had been a long time since breakfast.

Ginny pulled herself back into the saddle when everyone had finished. "Let's make a start. Amos, you lead the left flank, I'll go on the right, and we'll push these animals nice and calm to the corral."

She left the men to decide who would follow which lead, and couldn't work out if she was pleased or sorry that Lex went with Amos and Boone. Trike trotted close by Ginny toward the right side of the valley, Dunklin a length behind. The six riders spread out and, between yells and cracks of the rope, sent the cattle lumbering down the valley. Most females were accompanied by a steer and the task was to guide them gently to a place where they could be branded, rather than spook them into a stampede. Every so often, a steer would see a gap and think freedom lay the other side. It was the cowboys' job to react quickly and guide it back to the herd.

Looking across, Ginny was impressed by Lex's horsemanship. He was at ease in the saddle, able to keep a good seat while swooping right and left. She knew Arion was strong but willful. Lex had a deft touch with the heel which guided Arion, and was light on the bit which kept him calm. Watching him, Ginny was surprised that he had fallen so badly from his horse those weeks back. She had wondered if the story about Arion being startled by a mountain lion was to save face from being a poor rider. Now she recognized it must have taken something serious to dismount him.

Once the cattle were corralled, the business began of branding the newborn steers. Boone gathered wood and lit a fire with his flint. Lex unpacked the irons from a mule. Three letters intertwined at the end: LLR.

"Snow decided on that for his wife," Amos said to Lex. "Lucille LeRoux."

Trike was sent with a coffeepot to the stream to fetch water to boil for coffee at the same time the irons were heating.

The coffee drunk and the irons glowing, Ginny declared it was time to brand the first steer. She admired Amos's great skill with his ropework as he tethered the back leg of the nearest animal. Boone looped a second rope round the front and together they pulled it on to its right side. Dunklin positioned himself at the back end, holding the upper leg firm while fixing his left boot over the leg on the ground. Boone knelt astride the neck, holding the head still.

Ginny pulled on her leather gloves as Lex stepped toward the hot irons.

"I got this," she said. "Take the back rope from Amos so he can do the cutting."

Ginny used both arms to steady the long iron rod and pressed it firmly against the animal's hide. The beast struggled in alarm as the brand hissed and sent out a puff of smoke. Boone called to the animal, trying to calm it, while Amos knelt with his knife and expertly removed the testicles in a few sharp moves.

"Better to get that job done while they're young," Amos said. He glanced up at Lex. "You experienced with cutting?"

"Not my favorite job. But I've done it. Not got your skill with the knife, though."

Dunklin and Boone carefully released the animal so no one would get kicked by the angry steer. It pulled its way to its feet, moaning and dazed, before being pushed by Trike toward the corral to find its mother.

Amos roped the next steer and nodded to Lex. "Let's see how you do, holding this one still."

Ginny glided her eyes across, interested to know how skillful Lex was. Keeping the rear legs of the animal still took strength, but also skill to stop the animal from coming to harm. Lex rolled up the sleeves of his shirt and the muscles of his forearms flexed as he sat at the back and secured the beast. As Ginny branded this second animal, Lex easily held it firm.

After a couple more animals, the roles changed again, Amos getting to know the strengths of Edward Trike and Lex as his two new hands. Having repeated the process about twenty times, Ginny indicated they should take a breather. She stood up and arched her back, stretched and balled her fists, rolled her shoulders. She had to admit she was impressed with Lex and was glad Amos had brought him with the team.

. . .

The sun was at its height and the first roundup of newborns was complete. The cowboys looked round in satisfaction. Amos handed out some biscuits Ginny had packed for the midday break. They chewed on dried beef and washed it down with more coffee.

"Right, boys," Amos shouted, "time to saddle up again."

Everyone remounted and Ginny led the way to the lower part of the valley. They crossed the creek and then fanned out again to corral the Durhams which had settled to the east of the valley.

An hour later, a new herd of yearlings was gathered, a new fire lit, the brands burning white-hot once more.

The men had found a rhythm, each with their own skill. Lex settled to handling the animals, keeping each frightened beast as still as possible. It was hard, physical work and they were all stretched to the limit. With the tiredness toward the end of the afternoon, Trike's grip was less firm and a steer kicked its way free, the brand not fully in place. Ginny leaped back, trying to master the heavy rod so it didn't burn anyone and throwing it to the ground. The steer snorted and zigzagged, looking for an escape, pushing its way between two hurdles.

Trike cursed with annoyance.

"You watch your tongue, boy," Amos roared with a nod toward Ginny.

"If Boone had held that beast firm, it wouldn't have happened."

"Don't you go blaming others for your mistake."

Lex grabbed a rope and jumped on Arion, urging the horse to follow the errant steer. Ginny ran to the wooden hurdle and watched them, a hand to her brow to shade her eyes from the sun. She thought the steer had dodged away, but Lex threw the loop around its neck and jumped down to get the animal under control before leading it back to the corral, the slightest smile on Lex's lips.

Ginny nodded as he passed her. "You're pretty handy with the rope, then."

Lex shrugged. "Reckon I got lucky that time."

As the men got the steer back under control, Ginny came forward with the brand. "Don't cut this one, Amos. I like his spirit. Maybe he'll be a strong bull for the future."

SIXTEEN

Evening fell fast on the valley. The team set up camp by some oaks close to the river. The Snow family used the same location every year; the stone circle for the fire was mostly intact from the previous spring. Lex gathered wood and Boone showed his fire-lighting skills once more. Each man untied his bedding roll from his saddle.

Amos fixed up a bivouac for Ginny at a respectable distance from the camp. They all sat together for dinner, which was bolted down after the day's grueling activity.

"Isiah, how's about a tune?" asked Amos.

Boone fetched his mouth organ from his saddlebag and settled down to entertain the group gathered around the fire. Ginny sat on one end of a log next to Amos, with Lex on the other side. Boone worked through his repertoire of songs, the haunting tones of the harmonica stretching up through the night air.

"Here's one you can all join in," he said, and some of the men sang a few choruses.

"D'you not sing, Carlton?" Boone asked, noticing that Lex had sat silent.

"Not one of my talents. I promise it's better for everyone if I just listen."

Isiah Boone laughed and turned to Ginny. "A song, Miss Snow?"

Ginny shook her head. "You play beautifully, Mr. Boone." She was suddenly reluctant to sing in front of Lex.

"Everyone knows you're a musician," urged Trike. "Come on! Give us a song."

Ginny realized it would cause more of a fuss to continue to refuse.

"'*L'amour et la vie*?'" she asked Boone, who nodded and gave her a starting note.

Ginny sang the wistful tune with delicacy, and at the end, the men applauded.

Amos got up to tend the fire, leaving Ginny and Lex on the same log but with no one between them. Dunklin began a new pot of coffee and Boone played quietly to himself.

Lex turned to Ginny. "A song your mother taught you?"

She raised an eyebrow.

"You said your mother was French," he reminded her. "To be more accurate, your grandmother."

Ginny looked at him, the angles of his handsome face sharpened by the flames that Amos had sparked into life. "You have a good memory."

"It was a memorable time. Recuperating at your farm, I mean."

Ginny bit her lip. There were things she felt awkward about. She would not have done anything differently—a badly injured stranger had turned up at her door and she could hardly send him away into the storm. But it had led to an intimacy she felt self-conscious about. He'd glimpsed a side of her life she tried to keep hidden from others, and he knew of the daily struggle to keep everything rolling forward.

"May I ask how your parents met? Your mother was from Louisiana, as I recall."

"Yes. Papa was visiting his uncle to tell him about the death of his father. Stayed on a few days and went to the county fair. As my mother told it, she was at a stall where the prize for shooting was a lady's trinket. Her beau promised to win it but unfortunately didn't have a great aim. Papa saw the disappointment in her eyes and stepped forward to take the next shot. Of course, he won the trinket." Ginny smiled as she remembered the oft-repeated story. "He presented it to her and she was enchanted. We still have the trinket—faded and dull now 'cause it was made of tin and glass."

"The oil painting in your parlor suggested something of a Southern belle."

"Uh-huh. She was raised on one of the finest sugar plantations in the South."

"Seems strange she ended her days in Missouri, then."

Ginny plucked a long piece of grass and twirled it in her fingers. "Papa wasn't the sort of man her family considered suitable. He wasn't rich, of course. But the real problem was being an abolitionist. Active in the cause, I mean. Would write and speak about the issue. Not in Louisiana, of course. That would have got him shot most like. But he swayed Mama with his views, which I'm told got her locked up in her room."

Lex turned his body to face her and Ginny felt his gaze.

"So what happened?"

"They ran away. Eloped." Ginny stole a glance at Lex, who seemed amused. "They got married, of course. A Baptist preacher friend of Papa's, even though Mama's family were Catholic. The story goes that Mama packed as many jewels as she could and they hightailed it up the Mississippi."

"Until they settled at Sainte Geneviève."

"And I thought you were pretty much unconscious most of the time in my parlor."

He grinned and Ginny felt her stomach tighten in a way she had not experienced before.

"And it's a happily-ever-after story?"

Ginny threw down the blade of grass. "Not really, truth to tell. Mama's family disavowed her. Grandmother never got over it. She died the next New Year's Day, having caught a chill driving back from mass. Marie-Therèse. Mary Lou is part named for her."

"But your parents were together."

"True. It often felt like them against the world. Honestly, I think Mama sometimes missed her old life. You can see it in the how she brought up me and Mary Lou. We've a wardrobe of pretty but completely impractical dresses."

"And she taught you French."

Ginny laughed. "You see? Southern belle priorities."

"Playing the piano."

"I mean, who needs that in deepest Missouri? Although... that's something I *am* grateful for. It connects me with Mama's spirit. I can't remember a time I didn't play. Whenever I can afford it, I send off in the catalog for a new score. Won't rest until I've mastered it."

"Did the LeRoux family ever relent?"

Ginny looked into the fire, where Amos had tossed another log, throwing sparks into the air. "They were forever hopeful Grandfather might. Papa worked so hard, trying to build up this farm. I think he hoped to prove to her family that Mama hadn't married beneath her. And Mama hoped Grandfather might soften when Mary Lou and I came along. But once the War started, there was no way back."

"Different sides?"

"Very much so." She went to take a sip of her coffee but found the mug empty.

Lex, watching her, took it from her hand. "Let me get that filled for you."

He returned with a fresh mug and sat a little closer on the log, stretching out his legs to the fire. The smell of the woodsmoke was comforting.

"So, you have no family?"

Ginny smiled. "You don't need to take pity on me, Mr. Carlton. I've an aunt and uncle, a cousin. Aunt Josephine is Mama's younger sister. I'm told she was heartbroken by what happened. She secretly sent letters whenever she could. Even managed to get some of Mama's belongings shipped out once she'd settled. That's why we have the oil painting and bits of furniture, the dresses and whatnot." Ginny took a gulp of coffee. "Aunt Josephine didn't make the same mistakes as Mama, though. She knew she needed to marry well, though I daresay her prospects had been damaged by the scandal. She bided her time and found a wealthy businessman. Lives in Jefferson City."

Lex raised his eyebrows. "So close?"

"I'm sure moving to Missouri was part of the attraction for Aunt. Away from the sadness in Louisiana. Her sister nearby once more."

"Do you see much of your aunt?"

"When I was little, we would visit a couple of times a year. It was like entering another world. My mother would take out the pretty dresses and I would learn a new piano piece to show off. Some years even Pa would come, if we could afford cover at the farm. Uncle and Aunt were always kind to him. And Madeleine—that's my cousin—we're near the same age. She's like a ray of sunshine. The kindest soul."

Ginny paused for a moment as memories swept over her.

"And you still visit?"

"It's the big treat of the year. Every Thanksgiving if we can manage it." Ginny smiled and glanced over at Lex, who was watching her with earnest gray eyes.

"So you've never left Missouri?"

"Furthest I've been is St. Louis. Five years ago, when the

railroad first came through this county. Couple of years after Mama died. Papa got some crazy notion into his head about a new piece of farm machinery. I felt I needed to look after him."

"What did you think of the train journey?"

"Oh my! I loved it. I was sixteen and it was the most exciting thing I've ever done. Papa had to stop me spending the whole time with my head out the window to feel the wind rushing by."

Lex chuckled. "I'd have liked to see that."

She studied the fire which was beginning to fall into embers.

"You now know more about me than all these men put together," Ginny said quietly. "Except perhaps Amos."

"A warm fire under the stars turns us all into storytellers."

She looked at him, curious. "Except you've said nothing of your story."

Lex looked up at the sky, where stars had lit up one by one. The darkness had gathered around them as they had sat together. "A little late now."

"Your turn next time." Ginny rose to her feet.

She walked through the damp grass to the canvas bivouac and crept in. Once under her blanket, she could not get comfortable, even though she was dog-tired. Her mind would not be quiet as it filled with images of Lex, of him moving at one with his horse, of his arms pulling the rope taut, of the stubble on his jaw lit by the evening fire.

She chided herself for telling him so much. She'd never done that before—told a stranger her personal story. She didn't want people's pity, or for them to think she was dissatisfied with what life had dealt her. She could manage by herself.

But there was something in the way Lex had listened that had drawn her story from her, the way his eyes settled on her with his full attention.

She resolved to be more guarded next time. And then she resolved to keep her distance and make sure "next time" never happened.

SEVENTEEN

Lex struggled to sleep under the stars, a blanket wrapped tight around him. The Milky Way stretched across the Missouri sky like a pale silk scarf. As dawn approached, the eastern sky turned sapphire blue and then salmon pink as the sun rose. Lex's shoulder muscles ached from the day before, but there was no point lying on the hard earth in the hope that sleep would return.

He fetched water from the stream and blew the embers of the fire into flames. The smell of coffee soon roused the rest of the men. Amos got out the frying pan and threw in generous cuts of cured bacon.

Lex glanced over and his skin tingled as Ginny emerged from the bivouac tent that Amos had strung up using the branch of a tree. She was in the same split skirt, her blouse cinched in by the belt, showing her neat waist. Her hair was loose across her shoulders, the sun catching the tumbling curls and making them appear a copper-gold. She picked her way through the grass to the stream and splashed her face with the cold water. Running her hands through her hair, she pushed it back off her face and looped it into some order.

Breathing deeply and pulling his attention back to making coffee, Lex realized he was not the only person to be captured by her femininity. Edward Trike was staring at her, his mouth slightly open. Lex frowned and wondered if he had looked equally lascivious. He scooped a couple of rashers from the pan, feeling uneasy with his own reaction.

"Here." Amos spoke sharply to Trike. "Eat your breakfast."

Trike reddened and said something under his breath.

"I got my eye on you," Amos growled.

Ginny came over to the camp and sat on a rock, nodding good morning to each man. She braided her hair, and having tied the end, she circled the thick rope and pinned it at her nape.

Amos handed her a plate.

"That looks good," she said.

Ginny enthusiastically ate two rashers, washed down with the black coffee Lex gave her. When finished, she cleared her throat.

"We'll be repairing the fences at the northeast boundary. We'll need some wood from that thicket. There's also a tree fallen across Bran Creek. Debris has gathered and it's making the land around waterlogged."

Camp was struck quickly, Boone throwing earth on top of the embers to make sure the fire was out. Dunklin rinsed dishes in the stream, while Ginny folded the canvas bivouac. Lex went over and began to untie the rope from a higher branch.

"I can untie knots, Mr. Carlton."

With her sharp tone, Lex wondered if she had caught him watching her. He felt a heat around his neck and avoided looking at her. "Don't doubt it. Just helping out with the higher one."

The men saddled up, spare horses tied behind, and Ginny led the way on her bay mare. Dunklin fell in beside Lex.

"Should've been born a boy," Dunklin said, nodding ahead. "Could really make something of this land."

"She seems to be doing fine as she is," Lex replied, and adjusted his hat as they turned into the rising sun.

Lex looked forward to the hard day's work ahead. It would take him away from the thoughts that had coiled through his mind during the night, keeping him from sleep. He'd been traveling for two years now, each job building his knowledge or honing his skills. Perhaps the time for a decision was near. It was unreasonable and selfish to expect his fiancée to wait so long.

But, damn it, Ginny intrigued him. He'd never met a woman who combined femininity with a determination he'd previously only seen in men. And there was the debt to repay to both the Snow sisters. He'd be dead without them, no doubt about it. So he'd return home soon. Home to a patient but puzzled fiancée, to a disappointed father and a mother dismayed by the choices he'd made. Just not quite yet.

EIGHTEEN

Ginny rode into the yard ahead of the men as Mary Lou ran out to greet them.

"I made plenty of coffee," Mary Lou called. "An' there's food on the table."

The men tied up their horses and gratefully crammed into the kitchen. Having scanned the yard, Ginny followed them in. Again, she cast her gaze around: everything was in order, chores completed.

She caught Mary Lou's eye. "You done a good job, sister."

Mary Lou beamed and all but skipped as she fetched a couple more chairs so everyone could sit.

"D'you want us to take our boots off?" Saul Dunklin asked.

Mary Lou batted away the question. "You're fine here. As long as you're not going into the parlor." She went round filling tin mugs. "How was it?"

"Everything just dandy, as usual," Amos assured her.

After a second coffee, Amos heard the clock chiming in the parlor. "Better be making our way. We'll get the gear tidied up first, though." He went back into the yard, followed by the men and Ginny.

"Amos, don't you worry about that. You need to get back to Dinah quick as you can. Tell her I'm grateful to her for letting you come out branding again this year. You too, Saul. Nancy'll be waiting for you with a big meal, I daresay."

The two men rode off in the direction of the town.

Ginny stood with her hands on her hips and looked round at her farm, feeling the spring air on her cheek, pleased to be home. She called to the three remaining men.

"There's not a lot to do here. You folks get back to town as well, now."

Ginny led her mare to the crib barn and into its stable on the right. She hauled the saddle down, unbuckled the bridle and bit and hung them on the peg. Taking an armful of hay, she dumped it in a pile in the corner and her mare gave it her full attention.

Ginny took a pail through the breezeway running down the center of the barn to the water butt at the back and heard hooves fading into the distance. The rest of the men were riding to town. Her shoulders sank; it felt good to have the farm back to just her and Mary Lou. Ginny swung the full pail back beside her mare. She pulled the colored blanket off its back and fetched a couple of brushes from the tack room to clear the mud from the chestnut body and black fetlocks.

Returning to the stable, she stopped dead, brushes in hand, at the sight of Edward Trike beside her horse.

She swallowed and found her voice. "Thought you had all set off for Brownsville, like I said."

"Reckoned I'd make sure the branding equipment was sorted first." He put a hand to the mare's neck.

"Thank you. That was kind." Ginny wanted to get on with brushing down her horse but resisted taking a step nearer Trike.

"I could be kind in other ways too." His voice was quieter than before.

The skin on Ginny's neck prickled. "I manage perfectly well, thank you."

"For now, maybe. But you ain't gonna be by yourself forever."

Her horse stamped and shook its head, seeming to be aware of the tension in the air. Ginny cleared her throat. "Mr. Sturge knows when I need hands. If you want more work, then speak to him."

Trike laughed. "I was thinking of a more permanent arrangement. There's plenty of girls round here think me quite a catch."

Ginny's mouth went dry. "Oh. I see." Her voice was soft. "Well. I think, Mr. Trike, I should be clear. At some point, I may take a husband. But the time is not now."

"The name's Edward." He turned fully toward her.

Ginny clutched the brushes harder. "And, Mr. Trike, if the time comes, it wouldn't be you."

Trike took a step nearer. "Now you're just hurtin' my feelings."

"I'm sorry. I didn't mean to be rude. I thought it best to be clear."

Trike laughed again, showing the gap in his teeth. "I'm jus' messin' with you! I know that's what you think you should say. I'm told your mama brought you up to be prim and proper. But I know how you feel about me."

"Pardon me?"

"That show you put on for me this morning. Making sure I saw what a womanly figure you got. Shaking that fine head of hair so I'd notice."

A hot flush of blood came to Ginny's cheeks and she dropped her eyes to the ground. Had she been too unguarded this morning?

Trike grinned. "See? I can tell by the color in your cheeks

you felt it too. Come on, how 'bout a little kiss to seal what you've started."

The taste of bile came into her mouth. Ginny looked up at him, pulling herself as tall as possible, setting her shoulders. "Mr. Trike, you should leave. Now."

"Not 'til I got a down payment on my offer." His brows lowered as he stepped nearer.

Ginny threw a horse brush at him, then the other. Trike batted them away and roared with laughter. She turned and ran out of the stall and into the breezeway of the barn. She headed to the opening, where the double doors stood wide, but Trike was quicker. He grabbed her arm with a tight fist that made her gasp. As he pulled her against him, she ducked away from the smell of sweat and the stench of chewing tobacco. His fingers dug into her upper arms as he leaned in to kiss her.

Ginny twisted her arms and torso. "Trike, stop this."

He paused and looked at her, his eyes black, a line between his brows.

"So. *That's* the sort of girl you are. Think you can toy with a man. Make promises you've no plan of keeping." He threw her back and she stumbled, then he circled so he stood between her and the barn opening.

Ginny's heart thumped so hard it hurt. She could see the house the other side of the yard and tried to think how to escape. Maybe if she soothed him.

"Mr. Trike—Edward—I'm truly sorry if my behavior suggested I had feelings for you—"

"Oh, no. You don't get round this with fancy words. Think you're better'n me? It's high time you were taken down a peg or two."

He grabbed the long carriage whip hanging on a peg by the stable. Ginny dashed for the opening, but the whip cracked across her back. She screamed in shock and pain, and spun round to face him once more. He strode toward her, now grinning, cracking the whip through the air. He raised his arm to strike her again, and she put up her left hand and stumbled to the barn floor. The leather caught her forearm with a sharp pain, like being slashed with a knife. Shrieking out again, she balled herself up on the ground, eyes awash with tears.

Trike took a step toward her, but she heard another set of boots and suddenly Trike lay sprawling on the other side of the barn.

Ginny raised her head to see the man drag Trike up by his shirt and send him reeling from a punch to his jaw.

"You want more?" Lex roared.

Trike put a hand up in submission, the other hand to his mouth. He looked at the teeth and blood from his broken jaw.

Lex turned and strode to where Ginny was lying; he squatted down beside her. Relief flooded through her as she cradled her arm. The jacket fabric was ripped and a cherry-red line of blood seeped through.

Lex glanced over to Trike, then back at Ginny. He unhooked a rope from a peg and strode over to where the man was crouched on the ground. Lex circled it round Trike's arms and torso and pulled a knot. "Don't you dare move!" Lex hurried back to Ginny. "Let's get you to the house." His voice was as soft and comforting as molasses. He put his arm around to help her up, but Ginny flinched and cried out in pain.

"My back," she whispered, struggling to her feet. "He caught my back."

Lex draped Ginny's arm over his shoulder and put his arm round her waist to support her. Ginny was breathless with pain but stumbled out of the barn into the evening light.

The kitchen door banged and Mary Lou jumped down the steps.

"What happened?"

"Not sure. She was attacked. Trike."

At that moment, hooves clattered behind them and Trike urged his horse to the road as fast as he could.

Lex swore under his breath as the man disappeared, a cloud of dust kicked up behind him. He turned his attention to Ginny who was pale and like a ragdoll. He all but lifted her up the steps and into the kitchen.

"Can you carry her to her room?" Mary Lou asked.

Lex nodded and he picked her up, soft in his arms, but she seemed unaware of her surroundings. Mary Lou led the way up the narrow stairs and opened the door on the right, above the parlor. Lex sat Ginny gently on the bed. He stood for a moment, running his hand through his hair, uncertain what to do next, desperate to make things better. Ginny's eyes were dry of tears but focused somewhere beyond the window. His chest tightened and he knelt down to unlace one boot and then the other.

Mary Lou started to take off the jacket. "Ginny, sweetheart. Can I slip this off?"

Ginny made no response.

By maneuvering the jacket off her right arm, Mary Lou was able to slide it down over the injured left arm. Blood seeped through Ginny's blouse, both on her back and arm.

A pulse quickened in Lex's jaw as anger rose in him. Thank God he had stayed to talk with Mary Lou in the kitchen. He closed his eyes to keep out thoughts of what might have happened had he left for town with the others. "I'll get the medicine box. It was in the other room, wasn't it?"

When he returned, Mary Lou had removed the cotton blouse, leaving Ginny in her camisole. Much of her hair had escaped the twist at the back of her head and fell around her shoulders. Mary Lou dipped a cloth in water from the jug on the dressing table and wiped at the blood on her back and arm.

Lex put the box on the bedside table.

"The cut on her arm is deeper," Mary Lou whispered,

looking up at Lex with wide eyes. "But I'm not sure how to bandage her back. And she won't speak."

Lex paced to the window and looked out across the valley in front of the house, the lake barely visible in the evening light. "I'm going to get help. You can't be expected to manage this on your own."

Mary Lou's eyes brimmed with tears. "Can't you stay?"

Lex shook his head.

"Why isn't she saying anything?" Mary Lou dabbed at her arm.

"I don't know. Keep talking to her. But you need a doctor. Sooner I ride to town, sooner I'll bring Doc McCullar back."

Mary Lou bit her lower lip and frowned. "What about the man who did this?"

Lex's gut tightened. "Trike?"

"Yes. What if he comes back?"

"He's not going to do that. He's a miserable coward." Lex put a hand on Mary Lou's shoulder for a moment. "I'll be quick as I can. I promise."

He rushed down the stairs, took his hat from the kitchen table and galloped toward Brownsville. Part of him wanted to chase after Trike and make him pay for what he had done. But caring for Ginny was the most important thing now, and that meant bringing the doctor as fast as he could.

NINETEEN

Lex banged on Bill Mack's door. He waited a moment and banged some more, then peered through the window, but could see nothing through the dirt.

"He's in the saloon," said the barber, emerging from next door.

Lex hurried up Main Street, silently praying that the doctor wouldn't be the worse for wear. Pushing his way into the bar, he saw Bill Mack in a corner, an empty glass in front of him. Lex sat down and quickly explained what had happened. Bill Mack sighed and struggled to his feet, looking regretfully at the glass.

"How many you had?" asked Lex.

"Not so many that I can't do my job, son." The doctor made his way onto the street. "But I'd be better in my buggy. Can you drive it?"

Lex nodded. "Sooner you attend Miss Snow, the better."

It was nearly dark as Lex urged the horse up the slight hill to Snow Farm. The fresh air had sobered up the doctor. He clambered down from the buggy, complaining about his old bones, and Lex passed him the leather traveling bag containing medicines.

Mary Lou heard the carriage and opened the front door. She led Bill Mack down the passage and upstairs.

Lex paced the narrow space and could hear footsteps above, the floorboards creaking. He couldn't stand idle, so went outside to tend to Bill Mack's horse. He brought a pail of water, which the horse had lapped up by the time Lex returned with an armful of hay. He checked on Ginny's two horses. The bay had wandered from its open stable and into the corn crib. Lex led the mare back and secured her for the night.

Leaping the steps up the porch, Lex let himself in through the front door again. Bill Mack was still upstairs. Lex slipped into the parlor, where low voices seeped through the floor, the words muffled. Eying the room, he decided to light the stove. He then used a taper to light the wicks of two oil lamps. Slotting in the decorative glass chimneys, the lamps gave the room a honeyed glow. The room was ordered, like the whole farm, even though it was just the sisters; kindling and larger logs by the fire so it could be lit quickly, lamps full with oil and tapers trimmed.

Lex's stomach growled and he realized he hadn't eaten for hours. He went into the kitchen at the back of the house. Surely they wouldn't mind if he found something to keep hunger at bay. The stove was out, but he lifted the lid on the large pan and smelled the meat and vegetable stew. Having ladled some into an earthenware bowl, he sat at the table. The stew was still warm and a wonderful mix of flavors.

Hearing footsteps on the stairs, Lex leaped to his feet. Bill Mack came into the kitchen.

"Well?"

"Not as bad as it looks. A lot of blood. I've put in a couple of stitches where the cuts are deepest. Help the flesh to knit together."

"That sounds pretty bad to me, Doc."

"Her spirit is chastened by the experience. She has drawn into herself. A quietness often comes after something frightening has happened. But it meant I could put in those stitches with Miss Snow barely noticing."

Lex shook his head; that a woman as vibrant as Ginny could be laid so low. His jaw tightened as Trike came to his mind again. "What next?"

Bill Mack unhooked his wire spectacles and wiped them with his shirttail. "I'm not quite sure. It will take a few weeks for Miss Snow to be strong again. God knows what will happen to the farm. Cows and goats don't milk themselves."

"Won't the community help? I thought the West prided itself on its neighborly spirit."

Bill Mack grunted. "Not sure where you heard that, son. And even if it were true, the Snows aren't particularly liked by some in this area."

Lex raised an eyebrow.

The doctor sighed. "Elijah Snow was very clear what side he took in the War. Some folks haven't forgotten what the Radicals did immediately after, taking farms from anyone who supported the South."

"But Mr. Snow is dead and buried."

"True, but Ginny Snow never made much effort to build bridges."

Lex thought of the sisters trying to manage alone. He had seen enough to know it was a struggle at the best of times.

"I'm prepared to help," said Lex. "Surely others will."

"Maybe they will. Maybe they won't."

Lex heard the latch lifting on a door upstairs and Mary Lou came down to the kitchen, her face pale and eyes reddened.

"Thank you both for everything you've done. Ginny's sleeping now. I'll make you some supper."

"I'm afraid I've already helped myself."

Mary Lou threw him a weak smile and put out more bowls.

She looked at the black sky outside the window. "It's too late for you to drive back to town."

Lex was relieved when Bill Mack nodded. They would both be here to help through the night, if needed.

"I'll bring down some blankets," said Mary Lou. "Are you happy to camp in the parlor?"

The early-morning sun crept through a crack in the shutters where Lex had failed to close them fully. He had not slept well. Dr. McCullar's wheezy breathing and occasional snorts had led to a fitful night. Lex had spent some of the night thinking of ways to help. Farm life was precarious. Ginny and Mary Lou just about kept their heads above water, with hired help. One unexpected catastrophe had left them with no one to lean on. How could it have come to this? They had been generous in his time of need. Would the town really abandon the sisters?

He could stay and help. But Lex had learned enough in his short time in Brownsville to know Ginny's reputation would be damaged. And he could see—as could the town's gossips—that what Ginny really needed was a husband. A blemished reputation would make that harder. He could not understand why she was still unmarried. Ginny was uncommonly beautiful, added to which she brought wit and determination. She needed someone to share the burden and make a success of this small ranch that she seemed to care for so deeply.

Giving up on the prospect of more sleep, Lex dressed and went to the kitchen to heat up some coffee. After a few sips, he pushed open the back door to study the yard in the watery dawn light.

What would Ginny do? Where would she start?

Water. That was the first thing.

He took to the water pump and filled the large oak barrels. Then wood: make sure there was fuel for cooking and heat.

After an hour of physical activity, Lex heard the kitchen door bang.

"Would you like some breakfast, Mr. Carlton?" Mary Lou called.

Lex returned to the kitchen, gratefully remembering how good Mary Lou's breakfasts were. She spooned two fried eggs and some beans on to a plate for him and went back upstairs to sit with Ginny. The doctor was up and warming his hands on a tin mug of coffee.

"I'll need to be getting back to town now, son. Other patients to see."

"I'll cover your fees for tending to Miss Snow."

Bill Mack cocked a shaggy eyebrow. "Now, why would you do a thing like that? And where d'you get the money from?"

"I've got enough from my work. Live simply. And as for why: Remember how the sisters looked after me?"

The doctor eyed him intently as if sizing up the offer. "Very well. Someone has to pay me. I'd rather take your money than poor Miss Snow's. She's gonna need every dime."

They finished their breakfasts.

"May I say goodbye to the patient?" Lex asked.

Bill Mack shrugged. "Don't take long."

He went upstairs and tapped on the bedroom door. Mary Lou opened it.

"I thought I'd say farewell."

Mary Lou stepped to one side. Ginny lay on the bed, propped up on the pillows and looking out of the window at the far distance. Her hair was loose. She glanced at Lex, uncertainty in her eyes.

"I need to fetch some fresh water," Mary Lou said, and Lex found himself alone with Ginny. He took a chair and set it by the bedside.

"The doctor and I are going back to town now."

"Yes. Of course." Her voice was faint.

"How you feeling?"

"I'm fine, thank you, Mr. Carlton."

"No, I mean it. How are you feeling?" Lex gazed at Ginny's face. He could see tiny salt crystals on her cheeks from where she'd been crying.

"There's a pain. That comes and goes in waves. Bill Mack has left those tinctures on the dresser if I can't sleep."

Lex saw the brown bottles and waited for Ginny to say more.

Her chin trembled and she bit her lower lip, trying to control her response. "I'm afraid."

Lex nodded.

"Afraid of so many things." Ginny raised her arm. "Little things, like will I still be able to play the piano." She tried a weak smile. "And big things. Like how in God's name can I keep the farm going. A roof over Mary Lou's head."

Lex leaned forward. "For the moment, you don't need to worry about that. I'll come back and I'm sure the townsfolk will help."

Ginny waved a hand to dismiss the idea and stifled a sob. "But what I'm really afraid of... I keep thinking about what happened. What did I do wrong?"

"You did nothing wrong." Lex took her hand. It was fragile in his palm.

"If you hadn't been there... if you hadn't stayed to talk to Mary Lou... hadn't come out to the yard at that moment—" The gasp escaped into tears.

Lex sat on the side of the bed, reaching his arms around her. What could he say? He had had been troubled by the same thoughts himself. She buried her head into his shoulder as she gulped the tears. He gently rocked her, trying to soothe the moans. In time, they subsided.

"The thing is," Lex whispered in her hair, "I *was* there. So nothing happened. You're safe. You can't let one man, even one as vile as Trike, change your life. You are still the strong, bold woman you were yesterday morning."

Ginny disentangled herself and sat back. She reached for a lawn handkerchief.

"I must look a sight," she said, blowing her nose.

Lex brushed a lash from her cheek.

"You look beautiful."

Their eyes met. The air in the room had become still. Lex got to his feet, fearful the moment would develop into something else, and embarrassed he had let his feelings show at a moment of such vulnerability. He picked up his hat and made his way to the door.

"I'm driving the doctor back to town now. In the buggy."

"Yes. Yes, of course."

"But I'll be back later to help."

Lex gently closed the door and stood a moment, confused by the depth of feeling for a woman he barely knew. He was affianced elsewhere; what was he doing promising to return here?

Lex went back downstairs to find the doctor waiting impatiently.

TWENTY

Ginny made a good recovery. She used Bill Mack's tinctures to help her sleep the first few nights but hated the addled feeling the next morning. Unable to sleep on her back or left side while the wounds healed, she trained herself to sleep facing the dresser and gable-end window.

She listened to the familiar sounds of the farm. The cockerels in the morning, goats bleating while being gathered for milking, the kitchen screen door banging shut. *Mary Lou must be exhausted.*

Within two days, Ginny crept downstairs to see what could be done, only to be chided by her younger sister.

"The more you rest now, the sooner you'll be back to normal," said Mary Lou with a stern look in her eye.

"I can't leave you doing everything yourself."

"I'm not doing everything. I got help."

Mrs. Hofmann appeared, carrying a broom. "*Du lieber Himmel!* Your sister, she is right. You shouldn't be down here."

"Mrs. Hofmann!"

She started to sweep the floor. "I don't know why you are so surprised. I am just doing my bit to help young Mary Lou."

"Thank you, that is kind. But Mary Lou and me have learned to manage by ourselves."

Mrs. Hofmann huffed. "I took a look in that dining room. I'm not so sure."

Ginny flinched at the criticism and opened her mouth to protest but caught the significant look from Mary Lou.

"How did you get here, Mrs. Hofmann?"

"Borrowed Bill Mack's buggy. Mr. Carlton was driving me. Now, shoo! Off you go upstairs."

Back in her bedroom, Ginny's stomach fluttered as if there was a spring bird in there. If Lex had driven Mrs. Hofmann to the farm, he might still be here. She had a dreamlike memory of his kindness, of feeling safe in his arms.

From her room, she heard an ax swoosh and bang on wood, then again in a steady rhythm, sometimes with the crackle of a log spitting. Ginny padded to the window overlooking the yard and took in a breath. There he was, standing firm, as he used both arms to swing the long-handled ax around in an arc and heavily down on the piece of tree trunk poised on the cutting block. There was a splitting sound and then Lex pulled the last fibers of wood apart with his hands and pushed the two pieces to the earth, where he kicked them toward the pile.

He bent down to pick up the next log, placing it upright on the block. As he swung the ax around and above, Ginny could see the dark line of sweat in the middle of the back of his shirt. The wood broke clean. Lex gathered the pieces into a large basket and carried them behind the barn, where he disappeared from sight.

A few minutes later, he returned from the log shed, empty basket in one hand. With the other hand, he ran his fingers through his dark hair, pushing it back off his face. He wiped his arm across his brow to remove the sweat.

Throwing his basket to the ground by the block, he stood up tall and pulled his shirt free from his trouser belt. Undoing the top few buttons, he tugged the shirt over his head and tossed it to one side.

Ginny held her breath and stepped back from the window, fearful of being seen. Unable to help herself, she stole forward again, close to the side of the window, her heart beating like a runaway horse.

Lex picked up the ax. He had dark hair across his chest and a line of hair down his solid abdomen, to where it disappeared into his suede pants. His well-defined chest glistened from sweat. He turned round to continue with his task. Ginny watched the muscles on his back ripple and tense as he swung the ax once more. His shoulders were more muscular than she had expected. The lower part of his forearm was a darker shade where the sun had caught it.

Ginny felt she was intruding, that she was observing a masculine ritual. But she couldn't pull herself away. She leaned her brow against the side of the window casement and let her eyes follow the movements as if watching a dance, as Lex methodically worked through his task. She let her fingers trace his outline on the glass.

The kitchen door banged, her sister's voice calling. Something about coffee. Lex grabbed the blue cotton shirt, and pulled it over his head, covering his chest.

"Almost done." His familiar voice was like dark velvet.

He filled the basket with small split logs and took them to the log shed. Ginny remained at the window, hidden by the curtain, longing for one last look. Lex returned and, with long strides, crossed the yard to the kitchen door. Ginny heard it slam. She caught sight of herself in the mirror on the dresser. Her face was flushed.

She closed her eyes against the foolishness of these feelings. What on earth had come over her? She had no idea who this man was, where he had come from. He could be on the run from the law, for all she knew. Probably was, given he seemed to be hiding something from his past.

Although, he *had* revealed something. There was a woman somewhere he cared for. Ginny could not forget the photograph of a beautiful lady, knowing Lex carried it by his heart. She climbed back into her bed, aware of an ache inside, very different to the pain of her arm and back.

TWENTY-ONE

Ginny was out of bed and getting dressed by the time Mary Lou brought coffee first thing the next morning. Mary Lou opened her mouth to protest.

"No, Marie-Louise. Lying abed can make the body more feeble, not stronger."

Mary Lou sighed. "Could you at least do the lighter chores? Each day a man from the town comes to help with the heavier work."

Ginny slammed the coffee cup on the dresser. "I've told you before. We don't need their pity. We don't need their help."

Mary Lou pulled a cloth from her apron pocket to wipe the spilt coffee. "I don't know about that. And it's done now."

Ginny was chastened and knew that memories of yesterday were making her irritable. "I'm sorry, Mary Lou. But how on God's earth did you fix help? Is this Amos trying to get us to sign up to the Grange?" She knew her Pa had toyed with joining this new movement to band farmers together, but Ginny just couldn't find the time for all their meetings and rituals.

Mary Lou shook her head. "Mr. Carlton made a list. He's been here every other day and has gotten one of the men to do in between. Says that's how we'll run it 'til you're better. It's just the outdoors chores, I promise you. They only come in the house for coffee and a bite to eat."

Ginny put both palms to her temples. "How are we *ever* gonna pay for all this labor? I hadn't planned for it. Oh, Mary Lou, it's going to eat up any profit from this year's steerage sale."

Mary Lou bit her lip and frowned. "I hadn't thought of that."

"Is he here today? Mr. Carlton, I mean."

"No. Today it's Isiah Boone. He's been real nice. Said he could teach me the harmonica. Mr. Carlton said he'd be here tomorrow."

Ginny turned to the mirror and pinned up her hair. She didn't know if she was disappointed or relieved. "I'll find out how strong I feel today. Then we'll see if we can end the help from town."

Ginny marched downstairs, her sister following in her wake.

"And, Mary Lou. Can you ask Mr. Carlton to come and see me tomorrow? As soon as he arrives."

If Ginny had dared to turn round, she was sure she would have seen Mary Lou rolling her eyes.

Although every muscle in her body ached from her first day back on the farm, Ginny made sure she was up early the next morning. She was milking the cows when she heard Lex's horse trotting into the yard. She considered going to meet him but decided it would look better if he could see her at work.

She heard him call Mary Lou and the storm door to the kitchen bang shut. They seemed to have become firm friends whilst she'd been unwell. A minute later, his footsteps came across the yard and he entered the milking parlor. Her heart thumped.

"Mary Lou said you wanted to speak to me."

His deep voice made Ginny's stomach turn over. She remembered the last time they were together, the moment when he had gazed straight into her eyes.

She kept her head turned away, her cheek to the cow's side. "Yes. Can you give me a moment? I just want to be sure old Betsy here is finished."

Ginny gave a few last tugs on the teats, then wiped down the udder and moved away the pail. She stole a glance: Lex was leaning against the doorjamb, arms folded, watching her every movement.

"It's good to see you up already, Miss Snow."

"I'm feeling much better." She stood and moved the stool to the side of the parlor.

"Even though you're favoring your right arm."

Ginny flashed him a look, surprised he had noticed.

She straightened her back. "I want to thank you for everything you've done."

Lex's eyes narrowed. "But?"

Ginny frowned.

A smile escaped from the side of Lex's mouth. "I can sense a 'but' coming."

"But... it needs to stop."

"May I ask why?"

"As you can see, I'm back to usual now."

Lex paused. "I can see you're up and working. But I doubt you're back to usual."

"Near enough. So please thank Isiah Boone and any of the other men, but they are not needed now."

"Have you discussed this with Mary Lou? Seems pretty hard on her."

Ginny's hands clenched into fists. "What d'you mean?"

"We're helping the both of you. She's working every moment of the day, to get you rested."

She ground her molars together, furious he should be interfering in their lives, but even more, that he had seen them struggling. She turned back to the pails of milk and went to pick up the pair before being frustrated that she could only lift one at a time.

"All the same," she said, "you need to stop coming here."

Lex did not move. "What aren't you telling me?"

Ginny sighed and put the pail down. "It's obvious, isn't it? Do I have to spell it out? I'm only just holding on to this farm by my fingertips. I plan down to every last dime. I know how much help I can hire in. I need cowboys like you to get the branding done, and to move the steers to town for the annual sale. But I can't afford extra help now. There isn't the money."

Lex went to speak, but Ginny put up her hand.

"An' I know I pay less than the going day rate. I *know* why some men will sign up for my farm with Mr. Sturge. Don't think it's not humiliating. But I thought I could play the game. Now, I've had a lot of time lying upstairs in that homestead thinking 'bout it. And what happened with Trike last week shows just how stupid I've been."

He continued to stare intently at her. "Edward Trike has gone. You have neighbors who are happy to help. *I'm* happy to help."

She shook her head angrily. "Where were they when my papa needed help? When he'd lost the love of his life? When he was so sad, he could hardly drag himself out of bed? I don't remember any visitors coming round to help *then*."

Lex took a step backwards, his face unreadable. Yet again, she was telling him things she had never revealed to anyone. Not even Amos.

Ginny turned away and swiftly wiped a tear from her cheek with the back of her hand. *Don't cry. You are not going to cry.*

She settled her breathing and turned back to look up at him.

"Mr. Carlton, I don't want your pity. Nor anyone else's in

this county. And I've decided I have to pay the going rate in future. I have my pride. I *have* to pay you an' all the other men for the work you've been doing. And that's gonna wipe out all this year's profit."

Ginny looked at the house framed through the wide opening of the barn's breezeway. Every wooden plank nailed there by her father, every curtain hung by her mother. "This farm is the only thing we've got left of Mama and Papa. It's how Mary Lou and I keep connected with them. I can't let it slip away."

Lex stood beside her shoulder, looking at the same view. She resisted the temptation to glance at him.

"Miss Snow. Ginny. Do you remember what you said to me in the churchyard? When I tried to pay you for looking after me with my busted ankle. You said people didn't need paying to do what's right."

Ginny felt exhausted by the emotions flowing through her. She leaned against the milking parlor wall.

"We've all got a living to make," Lex said. "But we also have a life to *give*. I saw that on the battlefield. It was hell on earth, but men stood by each other. I've been traveling a couple of years now, and d'you know something strange I've learned? There is a joy in giving. But for someone to experience that joy, someone else has to accept the gift."

Ginny laughed. "My goodness, Mr. Carlton. You would do a better job in the pulpit at that church than the present incumbent."

This time, his smile was broad. "It's true, though. Your neighbors, they *like* to give something. So let them. Let *me*, just for a little longer. Just until you're completely better. Accept it with a kinda grace."

Ginny looked at him and swallowed. She couldn't trust herself to speak. She had started out, determined to settle up what was owing and send him away. But here she was, charmed into accepting more help.

"So, if it's all the same to you, Miss Geneviève, I'll start by taking those pails through to the creamery and we'll see what else needs doing today."

TWENTY-TWO

A week later, Lex sat at the wooden table in the kitchen, finishing the meal Mary Lou had cooked for him. He had reluctantly agreed it would be his last day, that Ginny was strong enough to run the farm by herself. Mary Lou watched him eat.

"You're making me nervous," Lex grinned.

"Just checking you eat it all up."

"You sound like the woman who looked after me when I was a kid."

"Not your mother?"

Lex paused. "No. My mother always seemed to have something else to do at mealtimes."

"Probably tidying up the kitchen."

Lex smiled. Mary Lou's life had narrow boundaries. She ran the home with the skill of an experienced housekeeper, always thinking about the next meal, about how to make today's meal stretch to tomorrow. Everything the farm produced was put to use. There were jars of fruit from the apple trees, a haunch of pig hanging in the smoke to dry for winter. It was quite a burden to be placed on such young shoulders. Mary Lou seemed to have missed out on the wider view of the world that

Ginny experienced. But Lex could not think of a more cheerful fourteen-year-old—he had a number of cousins that age and they seemed to be constantly fretting over nonsense.

Character-building. That's what Lex's father would say about the hardship faced by the Snow sisters. There weren't many things he agreed with his father about, but perhaps this was true. They both had such striking characters. But did life have to be so darn hard for this sweet girl and her beautiful sister?

Mary Lou took the plate away. "I'm gonna miss you," she said, her attention on the plates she was washing.

The words hung in the air.

Lex looked around the kitchen and felt the same way. He was going to miss Mary Lou's chatter as she served up wholesome food, the rough wood of the table, the bang of the kitchen door as Ginny came in from the farm. But he had to move on.

He got to his feet. "Time to saddle up."

Lex took the steps down from the kitchen quicker than usual, and strode across the yard and into the stable where Arion was waiting. Ginny was tightening the girth under the saddle.

"Thought I'd get him ready for you."

Lex nodded his thanks and checked the length of the stirrups to hide his quickened breathing. He hooked a water canteen on the side.

"Well—"

"I wanted to—"

They both paused.

"You first," Lex said.

"I want to thank you for everything you've done over the past couple of weeks." Lex opened his mouth, but Ginny continued. "No, don't say 'It was nothing.' I know you could have been earning a wage on some other ranch every day you've been coming here."

Lex shrugged. "Money isn't everything."

"That's usually said by people who have plenty of it."

Lex laughed and ran his fingers round the rim of his hat. "I can stay a couple of days more, if you need me."

"No, no. I'm fine now. Look, all healed up." Ginny held out her arm and pushed up the cotton sleeve. The mark was still there, a red line against the cream of her skin. But it was not inflamed. The arm was smooth.

Lex reached out and took her hand. She breathed as if she had touched a wood nettle. But she did not pull away.

"It hasn't changed your piano playing?" He turned over her palm.

"Not in the least. I have started practicing in the evenings."

"Maybe I'll hear you play again. One day."

She looked up into his face. "I'd like that," she whispered.

He raised her hand and kissed the open palm. Ginny gasped. He looked at her face, at those long lashes and directly into those dark brown eyes. Did she feel the same way? A heart thumping as if he'd run across a whole field? Her lips were slightly parted and he leaned down, gently brushing his lips against hers. The softness made his skin tingle.

Ginny pulled her hand away and stepped back, breaking the spell.

What complete madness had come over him? He turned quickly and pushed his hat on, shadowing his brow so she wouldn't see his eyes. He put his left leg into the stirrup and swung his right leg over the saddle. Pulling at the reins, Arion circled toward the barn entrance. Lex ducked as they walked out into the yard. The feelings that had been threatening to overcome him for weeks now bubbled to the surface. He must get away from her.

"Wait a moment," Ginny called, and ran out into the yard. She looked up at him, her eyes bright. "What would you want to hear me play?"

Lex tried to think of the woman who had promised to wait for him, whose picture he carried. But instead, his mind was filled with the memory of Ginny at the piano, playing with energy and abandonment.

"That piece when you rescued me."

"The Chopin Grande valse? Very well."

Lex nodded. "Until then."

He took off down the track. Once on the road to Brownville, Lex kicked at Arion to spur him to a full gallop. He knew he had to leave. Now. Return to his family and what was expected of him. To duty.

But all he could think of was the softness of Ginny's palm, of her lips like the skin of a peach.

PART 2

TWENTY-THREE

JEFFERSON CITY, MISSOURI—NOVEMBER 1874

"There it is, Mary Lou. Jefferson City. We'll be at Aunt Josephine's very soon."

Ginny felt Mary Lou shift her head from where she had been resting it on Ginny's shoulder, drifting in and out of sleep from the rhythmical rocking of the buggy.

"You cold?" asked Ginny.

"A little."

With one hand, Ginny adjusted the blanket tucked round them, while keeping hold of the reins with the other hand. The seventy-mile journey had given Ginny plenty of time to think about the past six months; it had not been a happy time. But now she shook those thoughts away. She needed to think of the future.

Jefferson City was laid out on a grid before them. The capitol building rose on a bluff above the Missouri and the wide, leaden ribbon of the river stretched out northwest and east. The railroad ran by the river edge. A paddle steamer was pushing its way upstream. Beyond the river were rolling hills, patchworked with tobacco and hemp plantations. On upper ground to the east, the state penitentiary loomed: a huge, stone building which kept a brooding eye over the city.

"We need Washington Street. Aunt Josephine's directions were clear."

Ginny had tried to cry off joining her aunt, uncle and cousin Madeleine for Thanksgiving. She worried about leaving the farm for five days: two days journey to Jefferson City, two days back, seemed a lot for a single day of celebration. But when Aunt Josephine had sent enough money to pay Sturge to supply a man to keep an eye on the farm, she'd felt unable to refuse.

It was kind of Aunt Josephine to do so much to keep them close. Ginny knew her aunt didn't hold with Thanksgiving, associating it with Abraham Lincoln and Northern Yankees. And the chance to see Cousin Maddie was always treasured.

As Ginny guided her horse and buggy down the straight streets, she eyed the houses on either side. Some were in an early stage of construction, others were near complete. So much building work.

Thomas and Josephine Critten's house was newly finished and Ginny had not visited it before.

"Bellevue," Ginny whispered to Mary Lou. "Somewhere on the right." She read the name on the brick gatepost.

"Oh my!" said Mary Lou.

"Oh my, indeed," echoed Ginny.

She gazed up at the house. It was a fantastical mix of styles and textures. Peach-colored painted brickwork, windows outlined in dark green. A steep flight of steps led to the double front door with a square porch. On top of the porch, a balcony. Above that, twin arched windows. Ginny leaned back: the house was topped with a cupola with windows on each side.

"It's like a fairy castle," said Mary Lou.

"Sure is something else."

A curtain moved in the bow window to the right of the front

door. To the left, a covered porch led to a veranda, jutting out as if a boat was going to glide up and moor beside it.

Ginny geed the horse onto the sweeping path to the house.

The door banged and Maddie flew down the steps, lifting the skirts of her sky-blue dress. "I've been watching for you most of the afternoon."

Mary Lou jumped down before Ginny pulled the buggy to a halt and ran to hug her cousin. Ginny climbed down as fast as she could and joined the embrace.

"Oh, Maddie. It's so good to see you." Ginny was a little taller than her cousin, who threw her arms around her. Ginny felt Maddie's blonde hair against her cheek and tears pricked at her eyes. It was good to be here, to put worries about the farm to one side for a day, to feel the balm of a loving family.

"Geneviève, Marie-Louise. You have arrived safely."

Ginny looked up to see her aunt standing in the porch and she ran up the steps to kiss her on both cheeks, as she had been brought up to do. Aunt Josephine looked fragile; the same light hair as her daughter, her skin was drawn over her cheeks like paper. Uncle Thomas stood behind. Ginny shook his hand.

"Uncle."

"Let's get you girls inside, in the warm." He gestured to a manservant to bring in the traveling trunk. "One of my boys will stable your horse."

Uncle Thomas was tall with sunken cheeks which made his eyes more piercing. His tapering beard emphasized the narrowness of his face. He was used to being in charge.

Maddie stepped between Ginny and Mary Lou, catching a hand each. "I can't wait to show you the new house."

"It's mighty fine, I must say."

"Five floors, counting the solarium in the cupola. Can you imagine? Five floors!"

Inside was warm, with opulent furnishings glowing from the gas lights.

"Morning room." Maddie gestured to her left. "Opens onto the veranda. Parlor." She waved her hand to the right and twirled to Ginny. "With a new piano. We're expecting plenty of music from both of you." Turning back, she pointed to the right. "The library is down there. Although Father insists on calling it his study. The name hasn't quite settled yet." She began to climb the curved staircase. "Now, I want to show you your rooms."

"We're dying to see them." Ginny and Mary Lou followed her up the stairs.

Maddie gave a dimpled smile and led the way. She opened the door to a room which looked like spring had blossomed overnight. Floral wallpaper, swags of fabric at the windows, pretty upholstered chairs, more flowers on the coverlet across the bed.

"Mother let me choose everything for my room."

"As I can see," Ginny said. She took in the mess of clothing among the floral ruches, hair accessories spread across the dresser, shoes scattered on the carpet. "You haven't changed one bit."

"Mother despairs of me. But Nancy knows I like it like this and wouldn't dream of tidying it for me." Nancy had been with the family as long as Ginny could remember and doted on Maddie.

Maddie's bed commanded the room, but a smaller bed was tucked by the window.

"I thought it would be fun for you to be in with me, Ginny. Like old times. But you can have your own room if you prefer."

Ginny gave her a squeeze round the waist. "Sharing with you will be lovely."

Maddie turned and led the way up the next set of stairs. "And I thought you could have this room at the front, Mary Lou." It was the room with the twin windows, above the balcony and looking out on the street. "Unless you would prefer to be further down."

"I love it!" said Mary Lou, already drawn to the window.

"I will show you the solarium tomorrow. It really needs to be seen in daylight, and evening is drawing in." Maddie went back to the staircase. "Right. As soon as you've freshened up, it's down to the dining room and we'll get you fed."

After dinner, Ginny asked her uncle if she could speak to him in private. He led the way to the study. Ginny's eyes ran over the wooden shelves, stacked with leather-bound books.

"A wonderful collection, Uncle Thomas."

He grunted. "Truth is, it's mostly for show. The books I'm interested in are business ledgers. Not"—he went to the nearest shelf and used a finger to prize out a green-backed book—"*The History of the Decline And Fall Of the Roman Empire*." He slotted it back in place. "Now, sit yourself down and tell me what's troubling you." He gestured to the high-backed armchair the other side of the fireplace as he busied himself with cutting and lighting a cigar.

Ginny sat with a leather case on her lap.

"I have a favor to ask. Would you sell these jewels for me?"

He put out his hand and Ginny passed over the case. Uncle Thomas pushed the brass lock with his thumb and looked at the necklace and earrings on a velvet mount. "Your mother's?"

Ginny nodded, struggling to keep her emotions hidden, and took a bag from the pocket in her skirt. "Also, this. There are some brooches. Two rings."

Uncle Thomas sighed and closed the box. "Surely things can't be bad as all that?"

She tried a nonchalant shrug. "They are just pieces of pretty glass in the end."

"Geneviève, we both know that ain't true. These are memories of your mother. Is there nothing else you can do?"

"I can't go to the bank. Mr. Tanner has been clear that Missouri Farmers Bank can't extend any more credit."

Uncle Thomas shook his head. "How did it come to this?"

Ginny lowered her eyes. Local folk had whispered that she wouldn't be able to manage the farm and recently they'd been proved right. Her sense of failure felt heavy on her shoulders. "Thing is, it's been a bad summer. The cattle got Texas fever. Heaven knows how. It was awful to see. Healthy cattle and in no time they were a bag of bones."

"You lost them all?" Her uncle's eyes were kind and that just made it harder to keep her own eyes dry.

"About half. I'm hoping the money from the jewels will take us through winter. Then I can try to start building up the herd again. Mary Lou's butter does well. We sell that in Brownsville."

"Are your crops all right?"

Ginny nodded.

"I heard about the grasshopper plague."

"That was further west, thank the Almighty. Although Lord knows how those poor farmers have managed."

Uncle Thomas drew on his cigar. "I heard the swarm came down from the north, like something biblical. Picked everything clean."

Ginny shivered. How helpless those croppers must have felt. "No matter how bad things are, there's always someone worse off. So I am really not complaining."

Uncle Thomas tapped the top of the box. "When would you want them exchanged?"

"Ideally tomorrow. I could take the cash back with me."

"Might be hard to find a buyer tomorrow, it being Thanksgiving."

Ginny bit her lip; stupidly, she hadn't thought of this.

Uncle Thomas leaned forward. "But if I can't, I'll advance you the cash and sell them after. I'll send on any difference, if they make more than expected. Those LeRoux sisters had mighty fine jewels." He tapped the end of the cigar into a dish. "I've said it before, but your grandparents were overly harsh with your mother, in my opinion. Blood is thicker than water. Although, at the time, I doubt Lucille could have run off with anyone worse than an abolitionist. I don't mean to speak ill of your father, but there it is."

"It's ancient history now, Uncle. About as dead as the Romans in that there book."

TWENTY-FOUR

The family went to church in the morning and then took a turn around the streets, admiring the new buildings. Back at the house, Maddie and Ginny retreated to her bedroom while Mary Lou took a nap.

Ginny brought out her evening gown from the closet and showed it to her cousin. "I have this for tonight."

"That's very pretty."

The dress was silk, the color of opal; not quite blue, not quite pink. The sleeves were short and puffed with ribbons and lace. The neckline scooped low.

"It was my mama's. You don't reckon it's too flouncy?"

"If you can't flounce on Thanksgiving, then I don't know when."

"I need some hoops to thread through. Would you have a set?"

A line of a frown briefly settled on Maddie's brow. "I'll send the maid to see what we have. But are you sure you couldn't wear it over a bustle? Pull the skirt round to the back?"

Ginny eyed Maddie's fashionable dress, the elegant shape

with a flattened front and drapery over her rear. She shook her head. "It wouldn't work. This skirt needs to be a bell."

When the maid returned, Ginny was soon threading thin metal through the hoops of the petticoat, inwardly cursing the impracticalities of women's dress.

Maddie sent away her maid so they could help each other dress, rebuilding bonds from previous years. Ginny watched her cousin, noting the changes since she'd seen her last. Maddie shone brightly in every way. Not just the glint from her blonde hair or the glimmer from her silk dress. It was her good spirits, her desire that everyone around her should enjoy life as much as she did. Ginny realized she had let the troubles of the year oppress her spirit. It was not just the farm that was failing. Her heart had been hurt and she had struggled to recover her usual optimism.

Ginny stood in front of the full-length mirror, smoothing down the silk skirt. "I know it's hopelessly old-fashioned. But it's special to me. It was among the things Aunt Josephine sent, after Grandmother died. Mama used to wear it when she was going out into society. Or so I've been told."

"It's a beautiful gown," Maddie said, patting and shaping the fullness of the sleeves. "Something like this never goes out of fashion."

Ginny smiled: it was so typical of Maddie to try to make her feel better. She ran her fingers over the red scar on her forearm, as if that would make it disappear. Maddie didn't seem to have noticed it, at least. She tugged at the lace hanging from the sleeve in the hope of covering the mark.

Maddie looped a braid on top of Ginny's head and pinned it securely. "You are so lucky to have such thick hair."

"I can never keep it under control."

"The wildness is what makes it so perfect. The wisps escaping and framing your face."

Maddie made some finishing touches: a flower tucked in Ginny's hair, a touch of rouge on her cheek bones.

"Perfect."

The two women entered the parlor arm in arm. Mary Lou was already there with her aunt and uncle.

Aunt Josephine gasped as she saw Ginny; her hand flew to her mouth and trembled.

"Your mother was the most beautiful young woman in the whole of Louisiana. Everybody said so. You are the absolute image of her."

Ginny dropped her eyes to the carpet. "I'm sorry, Aunt, if this frock... I can change—"

"No, *chérie*. It's wonderful to feel my sister's presence here again." Aunt Josephine took Ginny's hands and kissed them. She drew her into the room. "This is Mr. and Mrs. Price. My other niece, Geneviève."

Ginny dropped a curtsy at the man and his wife.

"Uncle Thomas says you are his business partner," she said.

Mr. Price nodded. "My son: Frederick."

She bobbed again to the man by the window. He was about her age, thin with curly brown hair and the beginnings of a mustache.

"Good evening," he said, but his attention slid past Ginny and on to her cousin.

Glancing at Maddie, Ginny saw pinkness rise in her cheeks.

Aunt Josephine led the way into the dining room. She may have considered Thanksgiving a Yankee tradition, but that was not going to stop her putting on a spread. Especially in her new dining room.

The mahogany dining table had been extended to its full length. It was laid with porcelain and silver and glass. Candles made the light glitter from the tableware, and the ornate sideboard was laden with dishes ready to be served.

Uncle Thomas sat at the head of the table, Mrs. Price on his right and Frederick to his left. At the far end of the table, past the candelabras and bouquets of greenery, Aunt Josephine settled Mr. Price at her right hand, Ginny on her left, with Mary Lou tucked in between Ginny and Mrs. Price.

Frederick pulled out the chair for Maddie beside him. "A rose between two thorns," he joked.

Not the most original of comments, but Ginny was pleased to see the dimples in Maddie's cheeks.

A servant placed an enormous turkey before Uncle Thomas. He stood and led prayers: thankfulness for food, for family, for friendship. The amen rippled around the table and Uncle set about his carving.

"And what are we all thankful for?" asked Aunt Josephine in a lull in the conversation. "Madeleine, why don't you start, given you always have something to say."

"There's so much, mother. My heart feels full. Moving to this house. Having Geneviève and Marie-Louise with us. And the Price family, of course." The blush came back to Maddie's cheeks.

"Husband, dear," continued Aunt Josephine. "What makes you thankful?"

"Business is on the up, I'm thankful for that. Trade. The railroad. Feels like this state is truly making its way after the devastation of the War."

"Amen to that," said Mr. Price. "I was speaking to the Governor only last week and he said much the same."

Aunt Josephine put her hand over Ginny's. "And you, Geneviève. I hope you have things to be thankful for this year."

Ginny swallowed and forced away anxious thoughts of Mary Lou's future and her own. "I am thankful for family. For you welcoming us into your home once more. Most of all, I'm thankful for my sister, Marie-Louise, who gets up each day and finds joy in life."

Mary Lou glanced up and gave her a bashful smile before looking down again and drawing a circle on the table with her finger, not used to praise in public.

Aunt Josephine looked affectionately at her nieces. "And Marie-Louise? What do you say?"

"Oh, I'm thankful right back. I couldn't imagine one day without my sister. I don't know where she gets the strength from."

After Mrs. Price had taken her turn, Aunt Josephine finally turned to Frederick. He loosened the collar of his shirt where it dug into his neck.

"I'm thankful this year for my father for letting me show him I can manage the business. Or at least part of it."

"All in good time, son."

"And thankful for being here, Mrs. Critten. We're not family, but you sure have made us feel like it."

Maddie flashed him a shy glance and the redness around his collar increased.

At the end of the meal, the ladies moved back to the parlor, where they were joined by the men once they had finished smoking.

"I don't think I need eat another thing 'til Christmas," said Uncle Thomas, collapsing into an upholstered leather chair. Aunt Josephine sat on a sofa near the fire and everyone else gathered round.

"Then Lord be praised that I asked my nieces to give a piano recital to help our digestion."

Mary Lou settled down to play first, Ginny sitting next to her to turn the pages on the scores they had brought with them. Ginny could feel a slight trembling from her sister.

"You'll be fine," she whispered.

The notes filled the room and there was praise and applause at the end. Ginny glowed with pride for Mary Lou as the sisters changed places.

"You show 'em," Mary Lou breathed.

Ginny winked and launched into Chopin's sparkling Grande valse, remembering playing it when the stranger had turned up at her farm. She had mastered some of the trickier parts now. She softened the mood with a wistful nocturne before completing the set with a deeply romantic waltz, with a melody that matched her emotions.

The applause was enthusiastic. Frederick leaped to his feet.

"My goodness, Mrs. Critten," said Mrs. Price, "your niece really *is* something special."

A smile came to Aunt Josephine's lips, but her eyes were damp. "She takes after my sister, Lucille, in so many ways. It's like having her in the room." She dabbed her lashes with a handkerchief. "Although Geneviève's ability is even finer. I've always said she was a prodigy."

"Bravo," said Mr. Price. "You know, the Governor has recently taken possession of a grand piano. Had it shipped out from the East. I think Miss Snow would be able to entertain the Governor with such playing."

Ginny gracefully curtsied to accept the applause and took her seat once more. Although the farm might be struggling, at least there was one thing she could do properly to honor her mother.

TWENTY-FIVE

Ginny lay in her narrow bed watching a couple of stars twinkling through a crack in the curtains. The floral design had faded into black and gray.

"Are you asleep?" Maddie whispered

"Yes. Can't you tell?"

Maddie giggled. "D'you want to come over and talk like we used to, when we were little?"

Ginny's bare feet padded across the rug and she folded back the coverlet to slip in next to her cousin, their heads facing each other on the pillows.

"So, what's keeping you awake?" Ginny asked.

"I don't know."

Ginny gently dug her with her elbow. "I'm joking. I know *exactly* why you can't sleep."

"Oh?"

"Frederick."

Maddie suppressed a squeal. "Is it that obvious?"

"It's kinda hard to miss."

"What d'you think of him?"

"Seems sensible enough. He might be under his father's thumb. But sounds like he's got a good business head."

"He's handsome, isn't he? You didn't mention that."

"Yes, I grant you that too. Very handsome. But, most importantly, he likes you and that makes him the most sensible man in the state."

Maddie's eyes flashed in the starlight. "D'you think he likes me?"

"Hasn't he spoken to you?"

"No, not yet."

"Then I take back what I said about him being sensible. Anyone can see you're right for each other. He needs to speak to you properly. And soon. Take you to a dance. Do they do that here?"

"The Governor hosts dances all the time."

"Ah, yes. The Governor. Mr. Price did mention him. Once or twice."

Maddie tutted. "Mr. Price's contacts are important to Daddy's business. They've done very well together since the end of the War."

"And I'm sure Uncle and Aunt will be very pleased with the match. So you have every reason to lie awake at night and think about him."

"And what about you?" Maddie asked.

"Me?"

"There's a sadness to you this year. Something's happened."

Ginny sighed. "It's not been a good year for the farm. In fact, I can't remember a good year for the farm."

"Why don't you sell it? You and Mary Lou could move here."

Ginny took a slow breath. "There's so much debt. I don't know what I'd get for it. But, more than that, it's all we've got left of Papa and Mama. I look at the gate and remember Papa leaning on it. Mary Lou will cook a dish and the kitchen smells just as it did when Mama was alive."

Maddie reached out and found Ginny's hand. "You need a Freddie."

"I think you got the only one, Maddie."

"You know what I'm saying."

Ginny rolled over onto her back.

"What is it, Ginny? It's more than the farm, isn't it? It's like there's a thorn in your foot and it hurts every time you step on it."

Ginny searched for the words. "There was someone. Someone I had feelings for. I thought he felt the same. But I was wrong."

"Dear Ginny, I'm so sorry. How were you introduced?"

"Introduced?" Ginny laughed. "A storm blew him to us. Just showed up. Made things a whole lot better for a while. Then moved on. I'm guessing to another farm. Another state. My agent started to tell me, but, to be honest, I was too heartsick to listen. And I can't go back now and say, 'Mr. Sturge, remember that cowboy? What did he say about leaving? Where was he heading?'"

"A cowboy?"

Ginny knew that if she could see Maddie's face clearly, it would show her disapproval.

"I have a farm, Maddie. He was more of a farm laborer. Although he always seemed a cut above. Seemed to have enough money to see him through without working too hard. I never asked him where it came from. Too scared I might not like the answer, truth to tell."

"An itinerant farm worker is not what I'm picturing for you. With all your brains, you need someone clever. Like a rich businessman. Or a successful lawyer."

"Not many of those in Brownsville."

"So tell me more about your cowboy."

Ginny paused to picture him. She had difficulty bringing his whole face to her mind's eye. It swam around, hard to fix. She thought of the individual features.

"He had gray eyes which glistened when something made him laugh. And tiny lines around his eyes. He laughed a lot. Things seemed to amuse him..."

"Go on."

"He's taller than most. Good shoulders. But not in that heavy way of some farmhands. His hands were rough, like he'd been handling rope too long. One time, I happened to see his back, the muscles moving as he worked, a sheen on them from his laboring. I thought I was gonna stop breathing."

"Oh my!" Maddie giggled. "So. Light-haired like my Freddie?"

"No. Dark. Straight hair that he would push back out of his eyes. Sometimes I had to sit on my hands to stop myself from doing it for him, just to find out what it felt like."

"Handsome, then."

"Maddie, like no one I ever seen." Ginny sighed. "An' if you *ever* breathe a word of this, I'll kill you with my bare hands."

Maddie laughed. "So, good with the farm. Handsome. Maybe not a lost cause. You could do something to get him back? What about his family? Where did he come from?"

"Absolutely no idea."

Maddie propped herself up. "What d'you mean? He must have come from some place."

"He never said a word. I tried asking sometimes but got nowhere. But—and this is why I feel so damned stupid—I knew there was a woman special to him. Right from the start."

Maddie's eyes widened. "How?"

"A photograph fell from his pocket."

Maddie lay back on the pillow and stared at the ceiling. Eventually, she spoke.

"Oh, Ginny, my dear Ginny. I think you had a lucky escape."

Ginny rolled back to face her. "How so?"

"A man who turns up out of nowhere. Disappears suddenly. You said he had money without working. I'm sorry, Ginny, but most likely he was on the run. An outlaw. Men have started robbing trains. Put things on the tracks and hold up the engine-men. Father thinks I don't read the papers, but I do. Did he have a gun?"

"All men traveling round like that carry a gun." But Ginny recalled how large the pistol was, how new, with an expensive mechanism she hadn't seen before. She screwed her eyes up tight and wished she could block her ears. Because Maddie was voicing thoughts she had had many times herself.

"If he's already got a sweetheart elsewhere. And then goes turning your head. He's dishonorable in every way. A lucky escape, Ginny. You mark my words."

A tear squeezed its way between Ginny's lids.

She knew. Oh, how she knew. So why did it hurt so much? Why even now, six months on, did it feel like there was a stone lodged beneath her ribs?

The weather had turned colder as Ginny urged her horse up the slight hill out of Jefferson City the next morning. She pulled on her father's overcoat now they were leaving the city. Mary Lou was tucked in close, chatting away; already planning how she would spend the winter unpicking skirts and sewing them up into the fashionable style. No longer a girl happy to be in hand-me-downs or skirts above the ankle; she was becoming a woman, aware of her silhouette.

Ginny frowned at the road in front. The trunk was securely tied at the back of the buggy. Papa's pistol was tucked into the pocket of her overcoat. All that talk of outlaws last night had unnerved her. Inside the trunk was an envelope with enough cash to take them through the winter. Maybe even buy some fabric for a new dress each. Uncle Thomas had given her an advance, confident of getting a good price for the jewelry. But if things didn't change, Ginny was not sure how much more she could sell, how much longer she could keep a roof over Mary Lou's head.

TWENTY-SIX

SNOW FARM, BROWNSVILLE, MISSOURI —APRIL 1875

For Mr. Tanner to have made the effort to send a boy out to Snow Farm, there must be something serious about money to discuss.

Ginny looked at the note again and feared the worst. *Please visit me at the bank at your earliest convenience.* Not something that could wait for the fortnightly visit to Brownsville for provisions. Something more formal than could be discussed after church when she was next on hymn-accompanying duties.

"Tell Mr. Tanner I'll be with him this afternoon," she said to the boy, who trotted back toward town on his pony. She had urgent chores to complete: the animals could not wait. April was a busy month on any farm, even more so one run by just two young women. But this afternoon's tasks would be put off to another day.

Mary Lou saw the shadow of concern pass over Ginny's face. "Shall I come with you?"

"No, better you stay here. If I take the horse, I can be there and back in a couple of hours."

Having eaten an early lunch, Ginny washed the dust from her hair; she would let it dry during the ride and pin it up just before reaching town. She put on a clean cotton blouse, one with feminine ruffles at the wrists, and buttoned up her neat burgundy jacket with delicate stitching. The peplum fanned out over the matching split-skirt. She fastened her best boots. Standing tall, she looked in the mirror. However bad this meeting was going to be, she would face it as her Mama would want: with her head held high.

The dogwoods and oaks by the road glowed green as fresh new leaves unfurled. The fields to the left were coming to life after a long, hard winter. The weather still had a nip and Ginny was glad of the woolen cloak around her shoulders.

The road improved as she reached Brownsville. The town had grown rapidly since the railroad station was built at the far end of town and the buildings pushed and overlapped each other like too many teeth in a mouth. False fronts made modest buildings look more substantial. Wood was being replaced with brick. Ginny thought that every visit seemed to bring a new sign, jostling for attention: the post office, the ironmongers, the tobacconist.

Men hurried along the sidewalk under the awnings extended from each building. She could hear work continuing behind barn doors: the rhythmic metallic thump of the farrier banging iron in his forge. Somewhere, a mule brayed, complaining of the weight of its burden. Music trickled from the saloon as she rode past.

She pulled up her horse outside the bank and dismounted at the block. The building stood detached from those on either side, as if trying to assert its independence. Folding her cloak over her arm and peeling back her riding gloves, Ginny took a deep breath and pushed the door open. Her eyes adjusted to the murky light. The bank had the grandest interior of all the buildings on Brownsville Main Street. The space was divided: the right side was for the public, the left for bank staff, and between was a wooden counter to waist height, then a series of panels and ornately curved iron bars. Above, a carved wooden sill ran the length. Unlike so many buildings in Brownsville which had been thrown up as quickly as possible, this one displayed care and craftsmanship. The fact that many carpenters and metalworkers were paid to create the ornate interior was designed to tell the customer: this is where your money is safe.

Ginny stepped up to the counter and the teller got to his feet as fast as he could and came over, his body swinging like a pendulum. Bob Stone had worked as Tanner's teller for around ten years. He had lost the lower half of his right leg in the Battle of Wilson's Creek and people had praised Tanner for giving him a job. "Brains are more valuable to me than brawn," Tanner had replied, "so try your flattering phrases elsewhere."

"Miss Snow, I'll let Mr. Tanner know you're here."

Ginny noted the nervous blinking in Mr. Stone's eye and the hollow feeling deepened in her stomach. She only had to wait a minute.

"Good of you to come so soon." Tanner's voice was slow and gravelly. "Let's go through to my office. Somewhere more private."

He opened the door in the counter and let Ginny through to the business side of the bank. She followed him into the back office. The room was dominated by a navy-blue safe. Ginny tried to steady her breathing. This must be something serious to be invited into the inner sanctum.

Tanner took her cloak and indicated to one of the upholstered chairs in front of a desk covered in ledgers and papers. The cedarwood paneling below the dado gave the room a woodland smell. There were twin sash windows which looked like they had never been opened, vertical bars obscuring the view of the small yard beyond. Ginny had sat in this chair once before: for the reading of her father's will.

"Can I get you anything to drink?"

Before Ginny could reply, Tanner called to Bob to bring through some water. He sat in the leather chair opposite and took out a large handkerchief to wipe the sweat from his palms. Ginny wished Tanner would just get on with whatever he had to say.

Bob set down the glass and water carafe but this time avoided Ginny's eye and left quickly.

"And how is Marie-Louise?"

"She is well enough." Ginny took a sip of water for form's sake, her hand trembling slightly. "Whatever it is you need to say to me, Mr. Tanner, I would appreciate you saying it quickly."

He moved the handkerchief to his brow and then tucked it in his pocket.

"Yes. Quite." Tanner cleared his throat. "As we both know, the farm has struggled with debts since before your father's untimely passing. I won't go into the whys and wherefores of some of your father's purchases."

"Farming is always a lottery. Papa was a visionary. Some of his experiments might have paid off."

"But the sad truth is they didn't. You managed to get through this last winter without asking for further credit, I appreciate that."

Ginny could sense him moving to the crux and she struggled to keep her leg from tapping.

"I'm afraid Missouri Farmers Bank has decided to call in the loans."

Ginny near stopped breathing. "But how am I supposed to pay them back?"

Tanner pushed his hand through his mane of silver hair. "I see no option but to sell the farm."

Ginny felt like she had been punched in the belly.

"But why? I've been keeping up with the interest payments."

She looked at the lines on the banker's face across the desk. He was suddenly far older than his sixty-odd years.

"I have some money; I can make a bigger payment this month," Ginny said. "I have things at the farm I can sell."

"Such as?"

"There's a couple of silk dresses of Mama's that I'll never wear. One or two pieces of jewelry left. And paintings. Some of the newcomers round here, they might like a fine oil painting, one that once graced the parlor of the largest sugar plantation in the South."

Tanner shook his head sadly.

Ginny moved to the edge of her seat. "And there's the piano. A few bits of furniture, all quality-made."

"Miss Snow, those things will hardly scratch the surface of what is owed."

Her mind was racing. What could she do to stop this? "But if the bank could just give me a bit more time. If things go well this year, I could build up the herd again. I can turn things around."

Tanner leaned forward across the desk. "The truth is, Miss Snow, this has little to do with your farm, and whether you are a good farmer and have plans to turn it around. It's to do with the health of the Missouri Farmers Bank as a whole. Last summer, the west side of the state was badly hit by the grasshopper plague. Never seen nothing like it. That has weakened the bank, a situation that can't be allowed to continue. The shareholders have decided to liquidize any assets they can. They've had a look at farms with debts that can be called in. Yours is on the list. I argued your case, heaven knows I did." He shook his head sadly. "But that's all there is to it."

Ginny sat back in her chair. A fly crawled over the window behind Tanner, trying to find a way out. It buzzed and settled elsewhere and continued its search. A metallic taste flooded her mouth. This was it. She had failed. She had lost everything that had belonged to her family.

"How soon will it happen?"

"As soon as possible. The next fortnight, most like."

Ginny gasped. "That soon? Do you have a buyer in mind?"

Tanner shook his head. "It will go to auction. Here in Brownsville, so any prospective buyers can survey the property and land."

"So all the town will know my business."

"That cannot be avoided."

"And at the end of it, Mary Lou and I will be homeless."

Tanner dipped his head. "With luck, there should be something left over from the sale that would be yours. Enough to tide you over."

Ginny leaned back and pulled both palms across her head. Her whole life, changed in a moment. What was she going to tell Mary Lou? How would she keep Mary Lou safe?

"What next?"

"I'll start making arrangements for the auction." Tanner sighed. "I'm so sorry, Miss Snow. If there was anything I could do to change this, I would. It's desperate times. My hands are tied."

Ginny stood up and swayed whilst getting her balance.

"Do you want to rest here awhile? You've had a shock."

"That is kind, Mr. Tanner. But I want to get back to the farm. Think how I'm going to tell Mary Lou." She picked up her cloak and walked back through the bank's office area. She caught Bob Stone's eye and he looked away, telling her that he already knew of her predicament.

Tanner shook her hand at the door. "Might you come back in a couple of days so we can discuss arrangements for the auction?"

"Wednesday?"

"That would be kind, Miss Snow. Take care riding home."

Ginny stepped out onto Main Street, fighting back the tears. When she had stood here less than an hour before, she still had hope. Now she had none. She had lost the last link to her papa and mama, failed them utterly, and now she and Mary Lou were facing an uncertain future.

TWENTY-SEVEN

Ginny finished the bowl of grits and gave Mary Lou a weak smile across the kitchen table. It had been a week since Tanner's shocking news and she was yet to have a good night's sleep. Ginny was dressed in her kid-leather breeches, a full white shirt that had belonged to their father and a jacket. She buckled up her working boots, then got up and tucked her gloves into her belt and lifted her wide-brimmed hat from its hook.

"It'll take a few hours. I haven't been down Cattail Lake in a while. But the jetty needs fixing before the sale."

"I'll finish sorting the dining room today. I don't know how we managed to gather so many things."

"Pa liked keeping reminders of the past. And now—" Ginny put her hand to her mouth to stifle a sob.

Mary Lou came round the table and gave Ginny a hug. "It'll all work out in the end. Things always do."

Ginny strode out across the yard to the barn and threw equipment into the wagon: planks, claw hammer, saw, a bucket of nails. She hooked up the mule and led it down the track in front of the homestead to the valley bottom and across the fields to the lake. Mist floated up from the water as if it was a scalding-hot bath. The lake was mirror-flat, reflecting the pinks and blues of the early-morning sky.

Ginny swallowed down her sadness. It was a beautiful scene, but the place brought painful memories of her father.

She walked onto the wooden jetty, testing each plank with her foot. She could patch some, but others were too old and needed replacing. She hauled the tools and wood from the back of the wagon and started on the nearest rotten plank, levering it up with the claw hammer, the wood crumbling into the water below. She carefully angled out the nails. They could be used again.

Ginny measured up a plank. Almost the right size. She hammered it in to place, the sound startling a pair of cormorants, who beat their way up from the water. Then she sawed off the hanging edge to use as a patch elsewhere. Stamping on her handiwork to check it was secure, she moved on to the next plank.

The work was slow, but she was patient. The April sun began to warm the air and dragonflies hovered around the water's edge as Ginny worked her way along the jetty.

Her mule stamped and pulled at its harness. Something had disturbed him. Ginny paused and looked up: there was a noise from the path down from the homestead. She stood up fully and put her hand over her eyes to shield them from the sun. A man was leading his horse down the path, over the ruts and rocks. Yet another chancer coming to see how much her farm was worth. Let's hope this one was more serious than the last. Damn it, some people just wanted to have a poke around her home.

The sun was directly behind the man and he was wearing a wide-brimmed hat that shaded his face. But Ginny's stomach dropped as she recognized that relaxed, rhythmical walk. What in God's name was he doing here?

"Mary Lou said I'd find you working here," he called, his

deep voice traveling effortlessly over the field. Ginny did not move.

He tied Arion to a tree, removed his hat and hooked it onto the saddle, then pushed his fingers back through his dark hair. He looked round.

"A nice spot. The view down the valley."

As he came closer, Ginny glared at him.

"Repairs to the jetty?"

Ginny nodded but was at a loss for words.

"Gonna take you a while. By yourself, I mean."

"Got to be done, though." She could hear the croak in her voice.

He stepped onto the jetty and Ginny squared up, the claw hammer still in her hand.

Lex's face broke into a grin. "Here's me, offering to help, and you look ready to swing that thing at me."

A year ago, that same grin had captivated her. She wasn't going to be taken in a second time. No sirree. She held the hammer tighter.

"Just might. I don't know the first thing about you, Lex Carlton."

"Guess that's true. What you want to know?"

Ginny bit her lower lip. She hadn't expected that response. He'd never been willing to share things before. "You an outlaw? You on the run from something?"

Lex roared with laughter. He shrugged off his jacket. "No. No, Miss Snow, I'm not an outlaw."

"Then why did you take off like a scalded cat a year ago. Up and left."

He rolled back the sleeves of his checkered shirt. "Did Amos Sturge not say anything?"

"Nope. Well. Not really."

"Ah. I'm sorry. It's kinda hard to explain. To you, anyway."

"Try, Mr. Carlton. Try darn hard. You made me feel like a fool. I deserve something."

He rubbed his palm over the back of his neck. "Fair enough. You mind if we do these repairs at the same time?"

Ginny had no choice but to step aside. She remembered the last time they had stood close, the way he had gently kissed her. Her fist tightened round the hammer in anger.

He looked at each plank, nodded and raised an eyebrow at her as he tested the ones which were obviously new. He prodded at an older plank, felt round underneath with his hands. "The pilings, they're your real problem."

"I just need to patch it up."

"It'll need doing again in a couple of years."

"I didn't ask for your advice."

"Your call. But in that case, a couple of these struts need strengthening."

He sat down and pulled off his boots, and before Ginny could stop him, he had slipped over the side. The water came to his waist.

"If you wouldn't mind passing me that plank, Miss Snow, and the longest nails you've got. I'd be grateful for not spending too long in the water."

Ginny handed them over, frustrated by the ease with which he was taking control. With only one hammer, there was not much more she could do, so she sat down with her legs hanging over the edge to watch him. There was dark hair on his forearms and the muscles rippled as he moved. She became aware that her mouth was dry.

"So, Miss Snow. What d'you want to know?" he asked, his eyes on the job in hand.

"Let's start with where you're from."

"I've been working all over. Before I came here last year, I'd been out southwest. Cattle drives. But you know that. My family, they're from the East."

"You never mentioned family."

A pulse throbbed in Lex's jaw. "No. Don't reckon I did. There's a twin brother. I'm older by a few minutes and he hasn't forgiven me for that yet. A sister who's kind and gentle, like Mary Lou, but older."

He took a nail from his shirt pocket and continued hammering the plank against the strut.

Now he was finally talking, there was a lot more she wanted to know. "Parents?"

"Mother who would like me to stay closer to home. Father who thinks he's half his age and is in a rage because his body doesn't agree. Truth is, he's been ill this past year. I planned to come back this way sooner, but we thought he was going to slip away."

"I'm sorry to hear it." Was it true? Had Lex really planned to come back?

He glanced over at Ginny and the light reflecting off the water made his eyes shine. Suddenly, she wished she wasn't wearing breeches, that she didn't have tendrils of hair stuck to her neck through the sweat of physical work.

"So why aren't you with them?"

"The old boy rallied. As he always does." Lex started on the next strut. "Guess I'm looking for something of my own. New opportunity. A place of my own."

Ginny watched the precise way he measured up the piece of wood, how he bit his lower lip as he lined up the nails, the explosion of energy as he hammered them home.

"Y'know, I think that's just about done."

He waded back through the brown water to where Ginny was sitting, placed his palms on the jetty and pushed himself out. He turned round so he was sitting next to Ginny, a couple of feet between them, his pants black with water, which ran down his legs into the lake.

They looked down the valley.

She needed to know more, to know the whole story. "The photograph. Is it of your sister?"

He was quiet for a moment.

"No. My fiancée. That's why I had to leave." He pushed back the hair that had fallen over his brow. "There's no way I can say all this without sounding a scoundrel. I went home to break off the engagement. Felt pretty bad as I'd asked her to wait. But after all my traveling, I knew it would never work. I know my heart lies elsewhere."

Ginny's pulse beat harder. She stole a look at his profile; there was a haze of stubble suggesting he hadn't shaved for a while. His eyes were fixed on the trees on the far side of the lake. Suddenly, he leaned back on his arms.

"Turns out, she was thinking the same thing. I'd been away so long, she turned her attention to my brother. Truth is, he was always more suited for her. So, instead of me being berated for being so dishonorable, she's happy, I'm happy, my brother's happy. I would have come straight back to Missouri if my father hadn't taken ill."

He turned to her, his gray eyes fixed on hers. "You know why I wanted to come back, don't you?"

Ginny struggled to control her breathing, desperate not to show any emotion. Not again. She watched the ripples sparkling on the lake's surface.

"I would like... well, to get to know you better. Now I've been released from previous obligations, I thought... er... maybe we could..."

He left the words hanging, unable to find the right phrase.

Ginny stared back at him. "Just so I'm clear, Mr. Carlton. You are asking if you can *court* me?"

Lex shrugged awkwardly. "If that doesn't sound too... um... presumptuous."

Ginny put her head back and laughed. She didn't know

where it came from; it was desperation, rather than humor. She shook her head, trying to control the giggles.

Lex looked at her open-mouthed.

"Has no one in town told you?" she asked.

"I've not been to Brownsville. I came straight here." He narrowed his eyes. "Told me what?"

Ginny pulled up her legs from over the edge of the jetty and turned to face him. She struck a plank with her palm. "The reason I'm patching this, rather than doing proper repairs, is because it's not going to be mine much longer. The bank has called in its loans. The whole place is gonna be auctioned."

This was the first time she had seen Lex wrong-footed. Color drained from his face.

"But... but you *love* this place. It's yours. How can you give it up?"

"I don't have a choice."

He looked around at the fields. "Surely... there must be something—"

"There's nothing. Think I wouldn't have tried?"

Lex ran his hand through his hair. "So... when? When is the auction?"

"Next week."

His mouth opened. "Next *week*?"

Ginny looked out over the pond. "There are some things I'll be happy to give up," she breathed. "I avoid this lake. It's where Papa was found. Bill Mack said it was his heart. It was kind of him. But I knew the truth. I knew he rowed out to the middle of this water, never intending to come back. When the black mood was on him, there was little any of us could do."

Ginny uncurled her legs and got to her feet. She glanced at Lex and wasn't sure if his look of shock was because of her frankness about her father, or the loss of the farm.

"I've had a while to get used to it. Maybe it'll be for the best. A fresh start." Her tone sounded hollow, even to her own ears.

"What will happen to you?"

She picked up his boots and handed them to him. "Find some work somewhere. A teacher, I was thinking. Plenty new schools opened up in the state."

"And Mary Lou?"

"I'll make sure she's safe. Not sure how yet."

Lex pulled on his boots and stood up. He gathered the tools and took them to the wagon. There was a deep line between his brows as they packed in silence for a little while. For once, he seemed lost for words.

"So, Mr. Carlton. A wasted journey. I am flattered by your suggestion of courting me. But your timing is very poor." How she would have welcomed his attention a year before. But she was no longer a homesteader; now she was near penniless. And he was an itinerant worker moving from place to place.

"I... I can see that. If only I'd..." Lex pulled his hat over his eyes and swung himself up onto Arion.

"Although," Ginny continued, with a wry smile, "looked at from your side, in a week's time, you'll consider it a lucky escape."

"I'm not sure I follow you."

She could see his frown despite the shade from his brim. "A man doesn't go courting a woman with nothing to her name."

"I guess... I guess you're right." He stared up at the homestead and the trees on the ridge behind it. "I am so very sorry, Miss Snow. Truly I am. Please, give my best wishes to Mary Lou." He tipped his hat, then wheeled his horse and cantered away, back to the road that would take him down the valley to Brownsville.

Ginny sighed as she watched him go and closed her eyes against the sun. He had come back! After all these months, he had returned. Her response to him was as strong as ever, making her heart race and her breathing shallow. But it wasn't to be, he had made that clear.

As she led the mule up the path back to the farm, anger gathered in her chest. To have high-tailed it so fast, with hardly a farewell. She hadn't thought him quite so shallow. He could at least have tried to make some feeble excuses for withdrawing his suit.

She shook her head and sniffed; she knew him to be a sensible, practical man. She had nothing to bring to a union. It was painful. But it was the way of the world and she'd better get used to it.

TWENTY-EIGHT

Ginny took a final look around the parlor. *If my plan fails, this will be someone else's by tonight. I'll have to clear everything.* She wondered how many possessions they would be able to take with them.

Lex's reappearance the week before had rattled her. She felt angry and wanted the whole place to go to rack and ruin. What did it matter if weeds grew between the rows of beans? Or that mud was left on the blade of the plough? But Mary Lou had pulled Ginny out of her misery, reminding her the Snows still had their standards. So, she had started laying the ground for one last throw of the dice.

Mary Lou had spent the two weeks making the homestead look perfect. She washed bedding, turned mattresses, repaired the small hole in a curtain. She wiped insects from inside the glass shade around the oil lamp. She took out each book to dust before returning it to the shelf, adjusting the spines so they ran in a perfect line.

The room that Ginny's eyes now ranged over was neat, clean and ordered. It smelled of beeswax and lavender.

Mary Lou came down the stairs and into the parlor in her

Sunday best: a pale blue dress topped with a midnight blue cape. She had sewn fresh lace inside the rim of her bonnet.

Ginny looked at her warmly. "You've done us proud. Done the memory of Mama and Papa proud."

Mary Lou responded with a modest smile.

Ginny likewise had dressed with care. She tied the burgundy silk ribbons from her bonnet at her throat, where a ruby brooch was fixed. She wore her dark red jacket over a full skirt of paisley brocade.

They left through the front door to where the buggy was waiting. Ginny pulled the door shut and turned the lock, slipping the key into a small bag at her waist, next to an important letter from her aunt.

Mary Lou climbed up to the bench and pulled on her white gloves. Ginny checked the halter and stepped up beside her, taking care with her boots, delicate with buttons up the outside and a small heel. She glanced at Mary Lou, who gave her a nod. Ginny pulled on her leather gloves, picked up the whip and they started their way to Brownsville.

Ginny wasn't pleased that the auction had to take place in the room at the back of the saloon. It was the largest space in town—other than the church, where the elders would never countenance business being conducted; Jesus had turned the money-lenders out of the temple and the good men knew their bible. But it made everything more sordid. She held Mary Lou's gloved hand as they walked through the bar, knowing all eyes were on them. She glanced at her sister whose stony face showed her discomfort at stepping into a saloon for the first time. Ginny squeezed Mary Lou's hand.

They reached the double doors which stood open to a back-room made entirely of wood except for one stone wall. It was noisy, with people crushed together—this was the most exciting thing to have happened in Brownsville for many months and the townspeople wanted to be entertained.

The hubbub quietened and everyone turned to watch as the Misses Snow entered. Ginny raised her chin and walked in front, her heels clicking on the wooden floor, wishing she could shield her sister from humiliation, but Mary Lou had been adamant they would see this through together. She nodded to Tanner, who sat on the left, his arms folded and mouth downturned. She was surprised to see him in the crowd and not helping to run the auction.

"Here we are, my *mädchen*." Mrs. Hofmann stood up at the front row and indicated the two seats next to her. "I promised to save you proper seats, did I not?"

"We are grateful," Ginny replied, thinking she would prefer hiding at the back. Mrs. Hofmann might not fully approve of the Snow family, but she enjoyed being at the center of any drama.

A few feet in front was a long table with two chairs. Rows of seats faced the table, crushed tightly together so people were wedged as they sat. Men stood around the three sides of the room. The chatter started up again, with predictions of what might happen.

The room was hot under the low ceiling. Ginny untied her bonnet and used it to fan her face. To her right was a sash window and a side door that gave on to the alley running beside the saloon. Someone had pushed the window up and a slight breeze reached her. She glanced across and her stomach tightened.

Lex stood between the window and the door, leaning against the wall. He met her eye and lifted his hat, making a slight bow. The smile that so often played around his mouth was gone, replaced by a firm line. She was mortified to see him and swiftly turned her attention back to Mary Lou, checking she wasn't too uncomfortable, squeezed next to Mrs. Hofmann's generous proportions.

"My, it's hot in here."

"Indeed it is, indeed it is." Mrs. Hofmann continued to fan herself, a musty smell drifting from her clothing.

Ginny leaned closer. "I hadn't thought there would be so many people," she whispered. "Surely they can't all be bidding."

Mrs. Hofmann looked round. "Most people are here to gawk, I'm afraid." She patted Ginny's hand. "But I'm here to support you girls. Some bidders came in on yesterday's train. I had two gentlemen staying with me last night."

Ginny raised her eyebrows. "It's not a large ranch."

"Should raise a good price though."

Ginny bit her lip. This was not what she had been hoping for.

"You look disappointed, dear."

"I thought maybe no one would be interested in such an out-of-the-way place. Then I could make an offer and the bank would have to accept it."

Mrs. Hofmann sat up straight. "How can you afford to bid?"

"I spoke to Amos. The Grange will stand security for part."

"Yah, Mr. Sturge, he is standing at the back."

"And I wrote my aunt in Jefferson City. Begged her to advance me a loan. In memory of my mother."

"And?" Mrs. Hofmann leaned closer.

"She wrote that she would do everything she could. So I'm gambling on her being security for a good amount. Dear Aunt Josephine has been very kind."

Mrs. Hofmann sucked at her teeth. "Well, one must live this life in hope."

Ginny took Aunt Josephine's letter from her bag as if to check it was real. Her Aunt hadn't specified an amount, and Ginny feared so much interest would push the price up.

She glanced around and saw that Lex's attention was still on her. She leaned to Mrs. Hofmann once more to speak quietly.

"And is Mr. Carlton staying with you again? I'm surprised to see him here."

Mrs. Hofmann squinted across to the window. Ginny winced. He must know they were talking about him. "He has been with me a week or so. But he'll be on this afternoon's train. There's a number taking the three o'clock to St. Louis. That's why the auction is scheduled for noon. So business types can get away quickly. *Mein Gott*, I never thought these railroad timetables would be telling us when we can and can't do things."

Even with everything that had happened, Ginny's chest tightened at the thought that he would be gone.

"So, he is definitely leaving?"

Mrs. Hofmann nodded. "It is rather sad. He got a telegram yesterday. Bad news. His father is *very* sick."

Ginny remembered what he had said about his father's ill health. Knowing the pain of losing a parent, she glanced over at him; she wanted to say something to him but knew it was unlikely they would have the chance to speak. The auction of her beloved farm was about to begin.

TWENTY-NINE

With the Snows in their seats, two men walked down the narrow aisle to the table. Ginny recognized the first: Bob Stone, the bank teller, with his distinctive step and thud from his uneven gait. He held a sheaf of papers and was followed by a man Ginny guessed was Mr. Augustus Austin, the auctioneer from the neighboring county, looking still stiff from riding in that morning.

Their wooden chairs scraped the floor as the men sat at the table. Stone spread his paperwork in front of them. He was there to identify local people and alert the auctioneer to serious bidders.

Mr. Austin pushed his spectacles up his prominent nose. He was a wiry man in his fifties with pepper-and-salt hair growing in an upward tuft on his head, giving him a startled appearance. He placed his gavel ready by his right hand, stood and waited for the room to quieten.

"Gentlemen." He made a slight bow to the three women on the front row. "And ladies. I have been suffering from a slight pain in my back which my doctor says is rheumatism. I'd like to get on with this promptly so I can get back home for some rest. So I hope for a nice orderly auction."

He picked up the paper Stone had placed at the top of the pile.

"We only have one lot. Snow Farm, four miles south of Brownsville. Sixty acres of improved land, sixty-six acres of woodland, and fourteen acres of unimproved land, giving us a total, gentlemen, of one hundred and forty acres. You have all had a chance to look at the maps and the schedule of livestock. I don't propose to go through it all now. Likewise, the farm buildings. A two-bedroom homestead, good-size crib barn, plenty of equipment. Anyone who was interested had the opportunity to look at the prospectus or visit the property."

He looked at the room over his spectacles, catching Ginny's eye for a moment. "I daresay few of you are here for the actual bidding. At the moment, the domestic chattels are not up for sale. All depends on whether we can raise enough to clear the debt to Missouri Farmers Bank secured on the land."

He cleared his throat.

"Gentlemen. Will anyone open the bidding at two thousand dollars."

Silence. Ginny held her breath.

"One and a half thousand? One thousand?" Mr. Austin sighed. "Think of my aching back, gentlemen. Is anyone willing to open the bidding?"

She hoped the right moment had come. "Four hundred and eighty-seven dollars." Ginny's voice cut through the room.

Men shuffled their feet and the chattering started again.

Mr. Austin scratched the back of his head. "You're bidding on your own farm?"

"I am."

"And that's a very specific sum you've bid."

"That is the amount I can raise." She stood up, trying to look dignified. "And I guess it's possible no one else will bid.

The bank will have to take my offer, and my sister and me will go back to the farm we've known all our lives."

"But that's not how auctions generally work, young lady," he said, an indulgent look on his face. There was laughter.

Ginny remained on her feet and turned to give a stern look around the room. Some of the men had the decency to study their shoes.

Mr. Austin moved his glasses to the end of his nose and peered at Ginny. "That amount won't pay the debt against the property."

"I know. But I'm confident I can build things up again." She held up the letter for all to see. "And my family have indicated they can help. I just haven't had full confirmation yet."

Ginny's eye briefly fell on Lex, who was staring at her, a line between his brows. She swiftly sat down next to Mary Lou, who slipped her arm through to hold hands.

There was another round of comment from the room. Mr. Austin drew himself to his full height.

"Four hundred and eighty-seven dollars. Do I hear five hundred?" He surveyed the room. There was a reluctance to respond. Ginny prayed no one wanted to be the man who outbid the Snow sisters. Her father might not have been well-liked in the area, but they were local and surely that counted for something.

Mr. Austin eyed the men he considered the serious bidders. He knew how to play the sale. "So, four hundred and eighty-seven dollars, going once—"

"—Five hundred." A voice came from the back.

Mrs. Hofmann looked round and whispered it was a rancher from north of Brownsville, toward Jefferson City. Ginny's heart felt like it was a stone, heavy and cold in her chest. There were murmurs of disapproval and Mrs. Hofmann muttered, "Shameful."

Mr. Austin wiped a sheen of sweat from his forehead. "Six hundred?"

A nod came from Mr. Ellis, the farmer with land directly east of the Snows' land.

"Seven?"

Ginny saw a hand rise on the other side of the room. Another local farmer. Then a bid returned from the man from near Jefferson City. Her shoulders sank a little further with each hand that rose.

The three men battled the price up to just below two thousand when a new voice emerged from the back of the room.

Ginny turned to look: the first of the out-of-towners to show his hand. Mr. Austin raised the price by fifty dollars. The out-of-towner growled, 'Aye,' and two of the local men shook their heads to bow out, leaving just Mr. Ellis to gamble on a few more bids to extend his ranch westwards.

At two thousand five hundred, Mr. Ellis knew he was beat and the room looked expectantly at the out-of-towner.

"Two-six?" Mr. Austin scanned the room, looking like he wanted squeeze a few more bids. Some of the men had not come all this way without serious intent.

"Aye," came a voice from the front.

"That's one of my men from St. Louis. Now the serious bidding, it starts," Mrs. Hofmann hissed to Ginny.

The room quietened in expectation. The two men who had traveled in the night before laddered the price up, a hundred dollars at a time, to three thousand five hundred, and the pace began to slow. Mr. Austin moved to increments of fifty dollars, then twenty-five, and then ten dollars each time. Would he be able to push the price to four thousand?

The two men eyed each other. Ginny knew they would be pondering whether to step over the four-thousand mark, very likely set as the upper ceiling by whoever they were agents for.

"Five thousand."

There was a gasp from the crowd.

Ginny looked over her shoulder and realized the bid had come from Tanner, sitting there in his smart black morning suit, his necktie looped just so. How could someone she trusted be the one to wield the knife?

Mr. Austin stopped, his gavel hanging in the air. Bob Stone whispered something. They conferred further. Bob shuffled the papers and slid one over to Mr. Austin. Ginny leaned forward and could just hear the exchange. Yes, Mr. Tanner had registered his interest as an agent for another party.

"I assure you," Stone said quietly to the auctioneer, "if Mr. Tanner has made a bid, he will be good for his word."

"I am bid five thousand dollars. Are there any other bids in the room?"

The out-of-towners shook their heads, looking angry at their wasted journey. Mr. Austin brought the gavel down on its base. "Sold. To Mr. Tanner's client. Please approach the table to complete the paperwork."

There was a brief round of applause. Ginny glanced at Mary Lou who was biting her lip, her face pale.

Mrs. Hofmann loosened the button at the top of her black dress. "*Mein Gott.* That was the most exciting thing to happen to Brownsville since Fred Bottom and his Players passed through in 1867."

Ginny felt nauseous, embarrassed to have her troubles the source of entertainment.

Tanner threaded his way to the front through chairs and people knotted in groups. Despite this *coup de théâtre,* Tanner's mouth was as unsmiling as before.

Ginny and Mary Lou stood helplessly at the front, Mrs. Hofmann recounting the whole experience as if they had not been there. Ginny wasn't sure what to do. Where do you go when your home has just been sold from under you? She looked over to the side door, but Lex had already disappeared. Had he been discomforted by the spectacle?

"Miss Snow." Tanner stood before them.

Ginny gathered what dignity she could and put out her hand. "No hard feelings. I'm sure you did what was needed for your client."

"Don't leave town just yet."

Ginny frowned. He kept hold of her hand and clasped his other over it. "Please come to my office. I'll be there as soon as this paperwork is over. It's important."

"Who has bought my farm? I'd like to know."

Tanner looked pained. "We will talk further in my office."

"Very well. Mrs. Hofmann, would you be so kind as to look after Mary Lou? Perhaps you could give her something to eat?"

Mrs. Hofmann took charge of Mary Lou. "I have some fresh baking. We can compare apple cake recipes." They disappeared through the throng of people.

Ginny watched her go, brooding on what sort of future lay ahead for her and her sister, now their farm and everything they had ever known had been lost.

THIRTY

Ginny slipped through the side door into the alley, in order to avoid the crowd. She closed her eyes and leaned her brow against the wooden slats. So. That was over. She'd known her plan to bid for the farm was likely to be futile, but she'd thought maybe, just maybe, other bidders would step back. Had they been local. Amos Sturge had let it be known that the Grange was doing what it could to help. She had at least made a stand, cried, "This is mine!" And now? The debts were cleared, but she and Mary Lou had next to nothing. She would sort the house as quickly as possible, selling what she could, then look for lodgings and do any work she could find.

"Miss Snow? Geneviève."

Ginny opened her eyes and turned, dazzled by the sunlight. But she knew that deep voice.

He leaned against the shaded wall opposite, his face hidden by the brim of his hat. He looked like he'd been waiting for her, knowing she would want to avoid walking through the saloon.

"Enjoyed the entertainment before you take the train out of here?" She could not keep the bitter edge from her voice.

Lex took off his hat and stepped out of the shadow.

"You know I'm about to leave?"

"Not much gets past Mrs. Hofmann." She avoided looking at him. There were tears pricking at her eyes and she did not want anyone to see how close to the edge she was. Least of all Lex Carlton.

"I don't know how long I'll be away. I got a telegram from my brother saying Pop has had a stroke."

Ginny looked at the dirt on the ground between them, feeling slightly ashamed. "I'm sorry. Mrs. Hofmann did say. I didn't mean to be cruel. I know how worrying it is to have a father unwell. I hope he is stronger than you fear, and you reach him in time."

Lex studied her intensely. "You've just been through that auction and yet you're thinking of someone else's feelings."

"People are more important than property," she murmured.

There was a burst of voices as a group passed the alley opening on Main Street.

Ginny stepped past Lex. "I need to see the bank manager. We seem to have been here before, Mr. Carlton, but I think this time it really is goodbye."

"No, Ginny. Give me a moment. Please."

She turned back, clutching the edge of her bonnet, hoping he could not see her quickened breathing.

"What I was trying to say at the lake. That I no longer have obligations elsewhere." He struggled with the words. "I have to get on that train. But... but may I write you? Until I return."

"You are still thinking of courting me?" She was taken aback by his words.

"You didn't answer last time I asked."

Ginny put the back of her hand to her mouth but a giggle escaped anyway. She stepped back and studied him, trying to work him out. "You are the strangest man."

The edge of his mouth raised in a smile. "I seem to

remember you laughed last time I made this suggestion too. It's very disconcerting."

"But, Mr. Carlton—"

"Lex."

She gestured toward the door to the saloon room. "Did you not *see* what happened in there? I know you to be a clever man, so it beats me why you are being so stupid."

He folded his arms. "Again, not entirely what I was hoping for."

"Mr. Carlton, I lost the farm. It's all gone." The hysteria of laughter had passed and the awfulness of her situation descended once more. "I'm poor. I'm no longer a good prospect. I'm a *dreadful* prospect, particularly for a man with no obvious source of income himself. I am nothing. *Nothing*."

He stepped forward, the smile gone but replaced by something tender, a softness around the eyes and mouth.

"You are *everything*."

Ginny's heart seemed to stop.

He took her hand. "So, Geneviève. I'd like to write to you. If I may. If that would not... um... offend you."

Inside the saloon, jangling notes thumped from the piano and someone must have said something amusing as there was a roar of laughter. Ginny thought of the small-town gossip if she were seen here with him. She slipped her hand away and pulled on her bonnet, pleased it shielded her face as she was sure her cheeks were on fire.

"Very well. I'm not offended. But mind your letters are *very* diverting. You'll need to send them care of Gibbes Mercantile. I imagine Mary Lou and I will be grateful for some amusement in whatever lodgings we find ourselves."

Before he could respond, she hurried down the alley to Main Street and turned right, toward Mr. Tanner's office and whatever news he was so keen to convey.

THIRTY-ONE

"Thank you for coming so promptly." Tanner coughed nervously and showed Ginny to the back office. He swept papers off the chair in front of the desk and balanced the pile precariously on top of three leather-bound books, each stacked at a jaunty angle. The stub end of a cigar smoldered in a saucer and Ginny wished the windows could be opened to let out the tobacco smoke.

"Bob, bring some iced tea for Miss Snow." He looked at her. "You'll take a glass?"

"Depends on how long I'm gonna be here."

"Unless you'd like something stronger?" He waved toward the bottles on the cabinet in the corner.

Ginny needed to keep her wits about her. "Iced tea will be fine."

Tanner went to the cabinet and fussed with the glasses. "Would you mind if I had something? After all the... excitement."

Ginny nodded but said nothing. The glass chinked as Tanner poured himself a whiskey.

Bob appeared with the iced tea, trying not to catch Ginny's

eye. He muttered an apology as he set it before her and Ginny wondered what exactly he was apologizing for. None of this had been his fault. He'd done the job required of him at the auction.

Tanner sat behind the desk. "Thank you for coming so... Ah, yes, I've already said that."

Memories of sitting in this same chair for the reading of the will flooded back, Tanner's unease as he worked through the sad financial outcome of Elijah Snow's tragic death. Ginny wanted this over quickly. "Mr. Tanner, perhaps it would be best if you just tell me why I'm sitting here again."

"Ah, yes." He coughed again. "Things aren't as desperate as one might think. My client asked me to prepare these documents for you." He handed over two pieces of thick, creamy paper, covered in copperplate script. "If you could read through and sign the second page, then that will conclude our business."

Ginny took the papers and began, scanning at first, and then reading more slowly. She shook her head.

"Pardon me, Mr. Tanner. You seem to have given me the wrong documents."

"You have finished reading them?"

"No. But this document makes me and Mary Lou the owners of Snow Farm."

"Perhaps you could read on." Tanner passed his handkerchief over his brow as Ginny read to the end.

She handed the two pages back across the table. "I'm sorry, Mr. Tanner." She spoke gently. Maybe the heat was affecting the elderly gentleman. "But these *are* the wrong documents. I cannot sign them."

"I'm afraid you must. The person who has bought the farm insists on it being placed back in your hands."

Ginny put her head to one side and frowned. "As tenant? Crop-sharing?"

"No, as owner."

Ginny looked at him in puzzlement. None of this made any sense. "But what about the bank's loans?"

"They have been cleared with the purchase."

"So the farm belongs to the person you were acting for."

"Who now wants to give it to you and your sister."

Ginny sat straight-backed. "Who is this person? Who has bought the farm?"

Tanner pushed a hand through his thick gray hair. "I'm not at liberty to say."

"Oh, come now!"

"I'm sorry, my dear. I'm under strict instructions not to reveal the name." He took another mouthful of the whiskey and pushed the papers back across the desk.

Ginny stood and paced the room, trying to work out what to do. The room had suddenly become very warm.

She leaned both hands on the back of her chair and spoke clearly. "I cannot sign."

Tanner looked up at her, his bushy eyebrows knotted in confusion.

Ginny pointed to the document. "How can I sign when I've no idea who I'm making us obligated to? What if this benefactor changes their mind? What if they want the farm back again in a few years?"

"If you look at clause five, you'll see that is not possible. The farm is yours, to do with as you wish. To keep. To sell."

Ginny flopped down into the chair again.

"No. I can't do it. I can't have Mary Lou and myself beholden to someone we don't know. Obligated."

Tanner fiddled with the pen he had set out for her signature. "This is an unexpected turn of events. I hadn't really considered how this would look from your perspective."

Ginny took a drink of the cool tea. Was she being stubborn? Here was everything she wanted, right in front of her. She should grab hold of it and hang the consequences.

"May I speak frankly?" Tanner asked.

"I hope you will."

"Would I be correct in thinking you are afraid your benefactor could turn out to be some unscrupulous gentleman who, at some point in the future, might make himself known to you. Who might have a claim on you and your sister?"

"That pretty much sums it up. How can I make a decision if I don't know who he is?"

"Or she," interjected Tanner.

"Pardon me?"

"If you don't know who he, *or she*, is."

Ginny leaned forward. "You're saying my benefactor is a woman?"

Tanner sat back quickly. "No, I'm not saying *anything* about your benefactor. As I said, I'm bound to silence. No matter how uncomfortable that is for me. I would much prefer openness, I can assure you, Miss Snow."

Ginny took the paperwork again and began to read. It was a very generous act. From someone of considerable wealth. Someone who cared deeply about Ginny and Mary Lou. It felt like something was being restored to them. Lucille LeRoux's birthright.

"Miss Snow." Tanner cut through Ginny's thoughts. "I hope you trust me."

Ginny nodded.

"If I were to assure you that, in my most earnest opinion, your anonymous benefactor would not ever wish to put you in a vulnerable position, that the person is clear that they have no call on you..."

"Go on."

"Would you be prepared to sign, based on my assurances?"

Ginny looked at the elderly gentleman. Surely he was trying to tell her things he could not put into words. That her dear aunt had found a way to put right a long-past wrong.

She took up the pen and dipped it into the ink. She signed her name in the space and rolled the blotting paper over it.

"My benefactor was very confident of the outcome, given these documents have been prepared in advance."

Tanner cleaned his glasses with relief. "Yes. I daresay the person is used to getting their way."

Ginny smiled at the characterization of her aunt. She sat back and narrowed her eyes at Tanner. "How high were you authorized to bid today?"

Tanner tapped his nose. "Now, my dear, that would be telling. I am very pleased the debts are settled and things are back as they should be. Would you like me to keep the deeds in my stronghold once more?"

Ginny nodded and got up from her chair. She felt a little giddy even though she had refused the whiskey. "I'd better go and tell Mary Lou the good news."

Stepping into the sunlight, Ginny looked up and down the street. Everything seemed different. The colors of the mismatched buildings were sharp and bright; she could hear the happy sounds of children playing in the backstreets. She had a sensation of floating, that a weight had been lifted from her.

She turned to the railroad station at the edge of town, a proud new building with ornate iron columns holding up the roof extending over the platform. She heard the sharp whistle of the three o'clock trans-state, the clanking of metal as bolts strained between carriages and the engine dragged the weight behind. Lex would be on that train. She needed to speak to him. A slow puffing gathered pace as pistons turned and steam billowed from the outsized chimney.

Ginny quickened her step. She had to reach the platform before it left. But with every step, the train's rhythm grew quicker. She arrived at the tracks as the carriages were pulling away. Townspeople who had said their farewells brushed past her, returning to their Saturday afternoon in a small Missouri town.

She watched the train, hoping he might sense she was there, lean out of the window, wave his hat. But nothing happened. The train curved around the wooded hillside and the sound faded.

Ginny turned on her heel and looked back down the Main Street, to exactly the same life she had been living, before the mysterious stranger had been blown at her doorstep by a winter storm a year ago.

But, deep in her heart, she knew life wasn't the same at all.

PART 3

THIRTY-TWO

BROWNSVILLE, MISSOURI—JUNE 1875

Mrs. Gibbes rolled her eyes as her husband swung a sack of seed off his back and onto the nearest space on the floor. "Not there, Levi. Take it through the back."

"When I'm finished," he grunted, going back outside for more of the delivery.

Harriet Gibbes dreamed of a neat store with packets and tins lined up in rows by height on the shelves behind her, of folded bolts of cloth arranged by color on the counter. She fought a daily battle with her husband, who filled whichever space was closest with whatever he had managed to haggle. A tray of eggs balanced on top of a barrel of pickles, a cluster of children's toy drums hung from the ceiling, a pair of ladies' boots rested on top of a bin of nails.

She sighed and turned back to Ginny standing at the counter in front of her.

"Got another parcel for you, Miss Snow."

Ginny wondered if Harriet Gibbes could see the heat rising in her cheeks. The fortnightly visit to Gibbes Mercantile Store had become a source of both anxiety and excitement for Ginny. The store was a social center for townsfolk, particularly men who gathered round the potbellied stove in the middle of the room, chewing tobacco and discussing hog prices. She didn't want her private business observed by half the town.

"And a letter from Jefferson City. Guess that'll be from your aunt."

Ginny was sure there was a regulation somewhere about the postal service being confidential. She ticked off her list as the Gibbeses' boy shouldered the heavier goods out to their flatbed wagon waiting on the street. Oil, soap, candles. Mrs. Gibbes weighed out their coffee beans and fed them through the grinder. The intense smell vied with cured meat, tobacco smoke and leather.

Mary Lou ran her hand over a bolt of tartan fabric. She caught Ginny's eye. Ginny smiled and gave a nod, now she didn't have to chase after every dime. Mary Lou needed a new dress; she was fast growing out of the few at home. And she knew Mary Lou longed for the new fashionable shape she had seen at her cousin's.

Ginny's eye was caught by an emerald-green cotton with tiny yellow flowers. "Mary Lou, would you have time to make something new for me as well?"

"Of course." They had bought a sewing machine the previous month and Mary Lou was swiftly becoming an expert. "But we'll need the right thread. And more needles."

Harriet Gibbes crabbed along between the counter and the shelves behind. She measured out the cloth, stretching it the length of her yardage stick. She matched up bobbins of thread and wrapped them in paper with the needles.

Ginny moved to the only empty space on the counter, ready to pay. Mrs. Gibbes slid over a package wrapped in strong brown paper, a cross of string keeping it in place. Ginny saw her name was written in black ink in clear scrolling letters. She picked it up and hoped Mrs. Gibbes couldn't see the slight tremor in her hand as she put it into her large canvas bag.

"Wider than the last parcel."

Ginny nodded. "How much d'you think that should all come to?"

"But thinner than the last one."

She knew Mrs. Gibbes was fishing. "Yes. It is thinner isn't it."

"And nothing like the one the time before. That one was much lighter. And softer."

"The first one was a shawl," Mary Lou piped up, and Ginny flashed an angry look. Why should Mrs. Gibbes, or anyone else, know what was in these packages?

"A shawl?" said Mrs. Gibbes, leaning forward and handing over the letter. "Looks to me like someone's got an admirer."

"Nonsense. Something I ordered through the Montgomery Ward catalog. Now, how much?"

"Two dollars, I reckon."

"You seem to think I'm made of money. It can't be more than one dollar seventy."

"All that pretty fabric, there. I can let you have it for one dollar, ninety-five."

"But you know I pay cash. I don't need to have it on credit."

Mrs. Gibbes sucked at her teeth and wrote the details in the sales ledger. "One dollar, ninety cents, and that's a steal."

Ginny counted the money out of her pocketbook. She found the fortnightly haggling irksome and had heard of a Quaker-owned business where the prices were fixed for all to see. She wished the Gibbeses might take up the system.

Mrs. Gibbes scooped up the money from the counter and dropped it in the compartmentalized box on the ledge behind. She snorted. "Montgomery Ward indeed. I know what a catalog package looks like. And they didn't look like these ones."

"Good day to you, Mrs. Gibbes." Ginny shooed Mary Lou in front of her, eager to get to the wagon.

. . .

Back at the homestead, Ginny put the parcel to one side while unpacking everything else. Foodstuffs were packed in their places in the kitchen, lamp oil stowed in the storeroom, and the fabric carefully folded on the table in the dining room, next to the sewing machine. They were both eager to find out what news came from Jefferson City. Mary Lou made a pot of coffee and brought out a plate of cookies, while Ginny sat at the kitchen table and started to read through the letter.

"She wants me to go visit them for Independence Day." Ginny read further. "Oh, my good Lord, she asks me to play at the Governor's ball."

Mary Lou settled in beside her. "Tell me exactly what Aunt Josephine says."

Ginny cleared her throat. "*As you may recall, my husband's business partner Mr. Price is very close to the Governor and his family.*"

"Yep, he did mention it. Over and over..." said Mary Lou, rolling her eyes.

Ginny nudged her with her shoulder. When did Mary Lou start speaking with sass?

She continued to read. "*Mrs. Price is on the arrangements committee for the Independence Day Ball. She remembers how beautifully you played last Thanksgiving. The Governor is a great lover of music and Mrs. Price asks that you give a recital as part of the evening's entertainment.*"

Mary Lou's eyes opened wide. "Oh, Ginny. Can you imagine?"

Ginny blew out her cheeks and carried on. "*I should be so proud to see my niece perform in this way. I hope you will make a short holiday of it and stay for a few days.*"

Ginny put the letter down on the table and they sat in silence, taking in the request.

"I can't accept of course," said Ginny. "We can't leave for so long."

"We can do the same as last November. Ask Amos to get someone to run the farm for a few days." Mary Lou's eyes were bright with excitement.

"But we can't be away in July, not when the farm is busy."

Mary Lou picked up the letter and continued to read over the page before putting it down sadly. "Truth is, she doesn't invite me as well. Look, she mentions me keeping an eye on the farm. This is for you."

"Oh, Mary Lou, I wouldn't dream of leaving you."

"But how on earth can you say no to Aunt Josephine?" Mary Lou looked around the kitchen. "She has given us all this. You *have* to go."

Ginny took a bite of a cookie but barely tasted it.

Mary Lou put her arm round Ginny's waist and gave her a hug. "It's a *state ball*, for goodness' sake! I could go and stay with Amos, help out Mrs. Sturge. I'd really like that."

"Mary Lou—"

"—No, I would. It'll be fun to spend some time with a big family."

Ginny lifted the letter to her chest. Mary Lou never failed to amaze her. To pretend it would be as much fun to spend a few days on a farm as go to a ball in Jefferson City. "You think that would work?"

"Write to Aunt Josephine today to say yes. But, mind, I will want to know every last detail when you come back."

THIRTY-THREE

Ginny took her canvas bag upstairs and settled on the bed. Taking her time to unwrap the parcel made the experience all the sweeter.

The first parcel, two months back, had come as a surprise. When she'd unwrapped the paper, she'd found softer tissue paper inside and then a woolen shawl. It was a deep burgundy and she knew instantly it would complement her favorite skirt. The wool was fine, falling in soft folds. A letter had tumbled from the fabric as she'd swept the shawl around her shoulders.

She had picked up the letter. Her name was written in the same strong calligraphy as the address on the parcel. She had not recognized the hand.

Her fingers trembling, she'd unfolded the paper and found one page. Quickly turning to the end, she'd read the signature, the name she had been secretly longing to see.

That first letter was now carefully folded and in her drawer of keepsakes. It hadn't been anything fancy. He said he had heard she was still at the farm and he was pleased. He had described his railroad journey home, listed some of the towns he'd passed through. He had only just gotten home and his father was still with them but in a weakened condition. He had seen the shawl in a shop window; the color made him think of a dress she had worn to chapel one day. He hoped she didn't think it presumptuous of him. He had bought it on the spur of the moment and she might as well have it, whether she was offended by his gift or no. He had signed it Mr. Carlton.

To be honest, she had been hoping for something more in the letter. Something personal. Intimate. But it was a letter. From him. As he had promised, and as she had never quite believed would happen.

Ginny had agonized over her reply. She wanted to say thank you, of course. But the address was vague. It seemed to be a hotel, in a town she'd never heard of. What tone should she adopt? Would it even reach him? She had gone through a shocking amount of paper, writing responses and then discarding them.

She didn't want to be formal. Her heart was too engaged for that. But she had been let down by him before. She did not want to reveal how much he filled her thoughts. So she wrote that she was glad he was there with his father. She wondered who had told him about her good fortune with the farm. She thanked him for the shawl and said how useful it would be, come the fall. She then gently chastised him for his letter, reminding him that the last time they had spoken, she had said she would only accept his letters if they were entertaining. A list of railroad stops didn't really live up to the term "entertainment." Perhaps he could try harder next time?

Ginny had handed the letter over at the post office counter in the store and had then been in agonies for the following weeks. What if he had misunderstood her tone? What if he didn't laugh? If he thought she was genuinely disappointed by his letter?

Ginny had started drafting new letters to follow the first

but realized there was nothing to be done. The moment had passed and she was not going to start begging for correspondence.

Thus it was with not just excitement but some relief that Ginny had collected the second parcel, a month ago. The exchange had not come to a sorry end. This time, the parcel had been heavy, and square, a little larger than her hand.

Sitting in her bedroom, she had cut the string and carefully folded back the brown paper. It was a pair of books. She had opened the cover of the first to look for the title. *Thérèse Raquin* by Émile Zola. She had flicked through the pages: it was in the original French. On the page opposite the flyleaf, there was a short inscription in Lex's distinctive hand. "*Pour passer les soirées.*" Her heart had missed a beat when she realized he had written in French. She remembered when he was first recuperating downstairs: her copy of Flaubert's *Madam Bovary* had been in the pile he had left on the table. She pictured his mischievous smile. He had known all along. He'd said he didn't read French. Why had he lied? To save her blushes, as it was a most unsuitable book for a young woman?

She had turned to the second book: *The Gilded Age: A Tale of Today.* She had opened it but frowned at the unfamiliar names: Mark Twain and Charles Dudley Warner.

A letter lay beneath the second book and this time it was on two pages.

I sincerely apologize for the tedium of my previous letter. For my part, I think it is hard to beat a good list of railroad stops. I fear there is little I can do to give my words the high standard of entertainment that you seek. So I thought it best to send you someone else's writing instead.

I recall from when I was enjoying your hospitality that you read French novels. I find Zola's work a little depressing—what with its downbeat presentation of rural life. But I have only read them in translation; with my elementary French, I have struggled with the inscription.

The second book is a recent publication, so, again, I have not had the chance to read it. I am told one of the authors is from Missouri and I hear his work is amusing.

I'm hoping that a reader's report from you will save me the effort of reading either book. I can then have the air of having read a fashionable novel, dropping references casually into conversation, without needing to take the trouble to read it. Much the best approach, I think.

With all best wishes to Marie-Louise,

I remain your errant correspondent,

Lex Carlton.

Ginny had clutched his letter to her breast as she smiled with joy.

She had read the letter again, glowing. She had picked up the Zola and run her hands over the cover, the spine, the colorful watermark on the flyleaf. She flicked through the pages, stiff and reluctant to part, and breathed in the caramel aroma of the new paper. Her fingers had picked out the title of the second book. She had taken a sharp breath when she realized the circle that enclosed the words *The Gilded Age* was actually a lady's ring.

Don't be so foolish, she'd chided herself, *thinking things significant when most like they are chance.*

The past month, Ginny had measured out her reading time, not wanting to rush ahead and finish both books. While she held the pages in her hands, she felt a mystical connection with the enigmatic man who had sent them.

And now she sat in her bedroom with a third parcel. A

book-like solidity, like the second gift, but much wider and thinner, so it could not be another novel. She plumped up the feather bolster behind her and carefully cut the string.

This time, the brown paper revealed a piano score. The cover was decorated with an intricate swirling design in black and red. In the center was a circle with the name of the composer and the piece: *Frédéric Chopin, Ballade No. 1 in G Minor.*

Once more, she was breathless from his understanding of her. She had played Chopin to him. He had given no indication of recognizing the pieces. Yet here he was, months later, sending a score of her favorite composer. The coincidence with her aunt's letter asking her to perform made her feel that somehow an angel was looking over her, aligning the stars.

She eagerly looked for his letter, wanting to drink in his words.

> *It's possible that the books I sent have absorbed you so much that you have been prevented from practicing the pianoforte. I hope not. As I remember it (though the pain of a near-broken ankle after some days' traveling the hills with no food or water may have affected my recollection), Marie-Louise was quite strict about the importance of daily practice.*
>
> *In case my previous gift has caused you to err, I send you this score. I am told it is fiendishly difficult, so it may require much time to master. I only hope that I am not encouraging you to let the farm fall into rack and ruin.*

There was then a date above the next section, which showed he had picked up his pen some days later.

> *I am sorry to write that my father died three days ago. It was not unexpected and I am glad I was there with him, along*

with my sister. Sadly, my twin did not return from some business in time. My dear mother is bearing it tolerably well.

This will delay my hoped-for return west as there are many matters to be resolved. However, would it be too much to respectfully ask if I may visit you again, once I am able to travel to Missouri? I hope perhaps you could play me the music that accompanies this letter. I would dearly like to hear it.

Lex

Ginny's mouth went dry. She was sorry to hear about his father and wished she could be near to express this in person. Yet she couldn't help but feel a thrill that he would be traveling to Brownsville at some point. He wanted to see her again. This most mysterious of men: someone who traveled alone in winter, moving from state to state, getting agricultural work where he could. But he wrote with such fluidity, nothing like any cowboy she had known. His travels must have taught him about books and music. There was so much she wanted to know about him.

She pulled the ends of the burgundy ribbon she had found to tie together the previous two letters and tucked this third one with them. She knew she would not be able to resist untying them again that evening and reading the letter until she learned every word by heart, just as with the first two.

THIRTY-FOUR

Ginny slapped the reins on the mare's back to urge her onwards after a long day's journey to Jefferson City. She drew the buggy past the stone pillars on either side of the wide drive, black iron gates standing open. The setting sun made the sandy brickwork glow and the windows glint.

The front door burst open and Madeleine rushed down the steps.

"You're here! I was getting worried. It will be dark soon."

Ginny pulled her horse to a halt and jumped down from the driver's bench. The young woman hugged her and laughed.

"Maddie, I'm covering you with dust!" Ginny apologized.

"As if that mattered for one moment."

As before, when Ginny had been here at Thanksgiving, a stableboy took control of the buggy and luggage. Ginny stepped back to pat the horse's nose. "Can you give her extra feed tonight? She's been working since dawn."

Ginny hurried up the steps and savored the warmth of the entrance hall, the smell of polished wood.

"You are looking wonderful as always, Aunt," said Ginny as

Aunt Josephine stepped out of the parlor, wearing a fashionable greige silk dress and her hair perfectly coiffured.

"And you, my dear Geneviève, look as if you have been on dirt roads all day. Which is the truth."

Even though she had been here before, Ginny was awed by the grandeur of the house. Maddie had told her the chandelier had come from Venice, shipped in a thousand little parcels and then threaded together when it reached its new home in the Midwest.

After Ginny had washed and brushed the worst of the dust from her skirt, Maddie led her to the dining room, where a feast of cold cuts awaited her. "Here, let me get you plenty to eat," she whispered conspiratorially, piling food onto Ginny's plate: cold pork slices, pickled black walnuts, a leg of fried chicken.

"I would much appreciate a drink," Ginny said, collapsing into a chair at the table and stretching out her long legs.

A maid poured apple juice into a glass and Ginny relished the cool liquid. Uncle Thomas came in and greeted his niece.

"How is Marie-Louise?" asked Aunt Josephine.

Ginny struggled down a piece of cornbread loaded with butter. She nodded.

"Very well, thank you, Aunt. She's with the Sturge family at the moment. They've been a fine support over the past year."

Maddie pushed forward the pretty Sèvres porcelain plate laden with fancy cakes.

Ginny took one with lemon icing. "And Isiah Boone is looking after the farm with his wife for a few days."

"But you pay him?" asked Uncle Thomas.

"Yes. It's hired help. But it's much easier now that everything is sorted with the farm."

Ginny felt the color rise up her throat and she studied her food. Why had she brought up the farm so soon? Even though Aunt and Uncle had wanted to remain anonymous, she planned to find a quiet moment to thank them privately over the Independence Day period of celebrations.

She was relieved when Maddie jumped in. "So not a thing in the world to worry about. You can have a wonderful little holiday."

When Maddie was satisfied her cousin really couldn't eat any more, she led the way upstairs to her bedroom.

"There's a lovely deep bath waiting. I told Nancy to get it ready for you," she whispered as they reached the door. "And I arranged for the guest bed to be put in my room, just like for Thanksgiving."

Ginny's cases had been brought up and made a neat pile in the middle of the room.

"You don't mind, do you?" Maddie put her hands out to Ginny.

"The mess?"

"No. The sharing."

"Of course not. It's what I look forward to most. Our gossiping into the night."

"It won't be for much longer. Our lives are going to change."

"Oh?" Ginny raised an eyebrow.

"I'll tell you later," Maddie squealed. "Right. That bath."

She pushed open the door to the small dressing room for her exclusive use, where the bathtub stood in the middle with steam rising. Nancy poured in another pail of hot water.

"Good evening, Miss Snow," Nancy bobbed.

"I'm gonna leave you with Nancy and I'll have your things unpacked by the time you're finished."

"I don't need a maid," Ginny whispered close to Maddie's ear.

"I know. But Nancy does *so* like to help." Maddie bounced from the room and left Ginny to enjoy her bath.

Ginny winced as Nancy patted the dust from her jacket, aware of how threadbare and plain her clothes were compared with the fabrics Nancy usually handled.

"I'll get this all clean for you in no time, miss."

"Thank you, Nancy."

Nancy helped Ginny with her underskirt, blouse and cotton shift. She stepped into the warm water and sat back in the tub, closing her eyes to fully experience the water. It swirled around her body, soaking the long day's tension from her limbs, easing the dirt from her hands and neck.

"Shall I help you with your hair?"

Ginny nodded her thanks as Nancy unpinned the tresses and let her brown locks fall into the water. She ducked her head under and, rising, swept strands and water from her face. Nancy rubbed the block of soap into Ginny's hair, releasing a fragrance of lavender. She eased the suds back through the locks and massaged the tension from Ginny's scalp.

Eyes still closed, Ginny reveled in the luxurious sensations. She looked forward to a couple of days experiencing the pampered life of her cousin.

Nancy poured clean water over the tresses to rinse away the soap. The final jug of warm water was fragranced by rose petals to let the smell ease through her hair. Sitting forward, Ginny allowed Nancy to wrap her head in a white linen towel, tucking the ends in securely.

"Would you like some time to yourself, miss?"

"Mmmm," was all Ginny could manage as she closed her eyes and leaned back against a towel balanced over the tub's rolled top.

With the water cooling, Ginny accepted it was time to get out. She pulled herself upright, towel still wrapped around her head like a turban, and let the water run off her body in rivulets. She stepped onto a rug and picked up the soft towel that had been left for her.

Once dry, she looked around. The pile of dirty clothing had been spirited away by Nancy. On the chair was one of Madeleine's dressing robes, thoughtfully left out for her to use. She wrapped the silk around her, the fabric shimmering with the rich colors of the print. Ginny pushed her feet into a pair of slippers.

In the bedroom, the oil lamps were lit and a small fire burned in the grate. Maddie sat in a French-style armchair, cushioned with lilac crushed velvet.

"Feeling better?"

"Never felt so good in my life."

Maddie shook her head. "I do not know how you manage in your little homestead."

Ginny opened her mouth in mock surprise. "And I don't know how you manage in this gilded cage."

"All your things are unpacked." Maddie proudly opened the closet to show the two dresses hanging there.

Ginny raised an eyebrow. "You did that?"

Maddie shrugged. "Well. No. It was Nancy. But I asked her."

They both laughed with the joy of everything being just as it had always been.

Maddie fetched her brush from the dresser, along with a bowl of short ribbons and hair clips. She settled in front of the fire.

"Right. Sit down beside me so I can dry your hair. I want to tell you the most thrilling news about who is coming to the Independence Ball tomorrow night."

THIRTY-FIVE

Ginny let Maddie tease out her waves so they could dry in the warmth of the fire.

"First of all, I want to know why our lives are going to change."

Maddie clapped her hands. "I've been dying to tell you. It's Frederick."

"He's proposed?"

"Not quite. But I think he's gonna. He walks me home from church every Sunday. And he's asked for the first two dances tomorrow night."

Ginny turned to face her cousin and squeezed her hands.

Maddie squealed with delight. "I can't believe it! He's so utterly perfect! I could just sit an' stare at him all day."

"And he's rich. Which always helps."

Maddie gently slapped her cousin. "I'd love him no matter what."

"Definitely love?"

Maddie raised her shoulders and dropped them with a sigh.

Ginny leaned forward and hugged her. "And he feels the same way?"

"Last week, he held my hand when I stumbled and then wouldn't let it go. And when we got to the house, he held me back when everyone went inside." Maddie closed her eyes and a dimpled smile spread from cheek to cheek. "And then he kissed me. Right there on the doorstep of our house. Anyone could've seen."

Ginny pretended to be scandalized. "A proper kiss?"

"On the lips!"

"Well, that's it, then. He's bound to propose. And he'd better do it sooner than later or you'll burst and there'll be nothing left of you."

Maddie broke into giggles.

"To think I've known him a few years and didn't even notice him."

"He seemed rather shy during the Thanksgiving dinner."

"He's been working in the office with father and Mr. Price. Suddenly he became a man."

"I couldn't be more pleased for you."

There was a knock on the door.

"Evening, Miss Madeleine. A glass of warm milk for you young ladies," said Nancy, setting a tray on the occasional table. "And some oat cookies."

Maddie got to her feet. "I can fix things from here."

Nancy quietly closed the door behind her. Maddie set the cookies on the carpet in front of the fire and brought over the drinks. As Ginny pulled her fingers through her drying hair, Maddie brought over the box of ribbons and placed a stool directly behind her.

"All I want now is for you to find someone just as special. And then we can have a double wedding. As if we were sisters, not cousins."

Ginny snorted. "I think you're gonna find that a challenge. I told you last November, there are no nice Fredericks hiding in Brownsville, just waiting to grow up and become eligible."

Maddie picked up a tress and curled it round her finger, threading through one of the ribbons. "But that's my news. I've found the perfect man for you. He'll be at the ball tomorrow and Father has promised to introduce you."

Ginny laughed "You really are the best friend a girl could have. But please don't go getting your hopes up."

"You haven't heard about him yet. Everyone in town is delighted with him. All the girls are dreaming of dancing with him."

"Including you?"

"I don't need to. I got Freddie. So it doesn't matter how rich and handsome he is."

"Rich *and* handsome." Ginny managed to turn her head far enough to raise an eyebrow at Maddie.

"You wouldn't *believe* it. He's from Boston and his family own half the railroads in the United States."

Ginny smiled. She was used to her cousin's exaggeration for effect. "So what's he doing in Missouri?"

"He's been here a week looking at land to buy up."

"For the railroad?"

"I guess so."

Ginny took a sip from her warm milk and pictured more of the iron tracks crisscrossing the land. "Everything is changing so."

Maddie continued with the hair ribbons. "He's called Jacob Alexander Van Bergen."

"That sounds a mouthful." And not the sort of man who would be comfortable in a homestead. Unlike Lex... She shook herself to dislodge her thoughts.

"Tomorrow night you will know him immediately—"

"The one all the women are swooning in front of?"

Maddie tugged at a handful of hair. "I'm warning you, Ginny. He is very charming and enormously handsome."

Ginny could imagine the effect this was having on the ambitious women of Jefferson City. "And so, my dear Madeleine, what would he want with me?"

"That's what I'm coming to. Mother says he has that Harvard education, cultivated an' all. You will be far the most beautiful young woman at the ball." Ginny went to speak, but Maddie pushed on. "No use you trying to deny it. Not your fault you're prettier than the rest. But the important thing is you are so much *cleverer* as well. I heard Mrs. Price tell Mother that it would need a brainy sort of girl to catch his eye. It was like a thunderbolt. I realized you are a *perfect* match."

Ginny broke into a fit of the giggles. "Oh, Maddie. I do so wish we lived closer. You really are the sweetest person."

Maddie shrugged her shoulders. "I just want everyone to be happy as me."

Ginny let her return to tying ribbons in her hair. "But if he's so brainy, he isn't going to marry a girl like me. A girl with no money and no family. What I need is a handsome but *stupid* man, who won't notice."

"But don't you see? He's *so* rich, he doesn't *need* a bride with money."

"*All* men are looking for a bride with money."

Maddie sighed. "Ginny, don't you believe in love?"

It was on the tip of her tongue to tell Maddie all about the feelings she had experienced over the past couple of months, but she bit it back. She wasn't sure Maddie would approve: an itinerant farmhand was never going to measure up.

"And *we're* your family now," Maddie continued. "Mother and Father will always look out for you and Mary Lou."

Ginny turned to look at Maddie and took her hand. "I know," she said quietly. "And I'll be *forever* grateful."

Maddie pursed her lips. "There. That's your ribbons fixed for the night. I'll make them all fancy in the morning."

The young women struggled to their feet and cleared away their evening picnic and the hair things. Ginny put the guard in front of the fire as Maddie turned down the oil lamps and blew them out with a sharp puff. The bitter smell filled the room.

Ginny climbed into the bed tucked near the window and blew out the candle on the table beside her. The room was lit only by the embers of the fire. In the velvety darkness, she couldn't resist sharing her thoughts about Lex any longer.

"I'm sorry, I will have to disappoint you at the ball," Ginny whispered. "But the thing is, Maddie..."

She paused.

"Yes?" a voice came from the large bed. "I'm still awake."

"The thing is... I think my heart has already been taken by someone else."

She heard Maddie sit up in bed. "I knew it! I *knew* you were hiding something! You have to tell me *everything*."

Ginny smiled. "There isn't much to tell."

"I don't believe you. Come on, tell me about him."

"He's that farm worker I mentioned back in November."

Maddie gasped. "The outlaw!"

"He's not an outlaw. At least, I'm pretty sure he isn't."

But Maddie was adamant. "No, no, no. We talked about this. Ginny, he is not the sort of man to make a husband. You said he'd moved on."

Ginny shrugged. "He came back."

"So he's back in Brownsville?"

"Well, no. His father fell ill. He had to leave again."

"There we are then. And can you trust *anything* he says?"

Ginny pushed herself up on to one elbow. "Why would he lie?"

"For a start, he carried a picture of another woman, as I recall."

Ginny couldn't deny that this thought had occurred to her. Was she being naïve? "He says that's over now."

Maddie snorted. She slipped from under her coverlet and padded over to Ginny, the firelight making long shadows across the ceiling. She sat on the edge of the narrow bed. "But you said you knew nothing about him. Where he's from, where he's going."

Ginny sat up and hugged her knees. "I know a little more now. He told me about his family."

"He wasn't there when it looked like you were going to lose the farm. But pops up again now it's secure. How convenient!" She huffed. "Even if not an outlaw, sounds like a schemer to me."

Ginny was about to answer it wasn't quite like that: the last time they spoke was when he and everyone else thought she was penniless. But all she said was: "I can't help how I feel."

"And what *do* you feel?" asked Maddie.

Ginny sighed. She recalled their last meeting in Brownsville.

"When he looks at me... I want him to stop because I think I'm burning. But I want him to carry on because it's like we're holding something. Oh, Maddie, I admit, some of the time I wonder if I'm being a fool and he'll never come back to me. But then something happens and I start thinking about how I will describe it in my next letter. Or I'll see something and wish he was there to tell."

"You've been *corresponding*? For how long?"

"Only a couple of months. And he sends me gifts."

Maddie shook her head seriously. "Oh, Ginny, do be careful of a man who tries to win your heart through gaudy trifles."

"But they're such kind gifts. Things that show he's been thinking about me."

"Such as?"

"A book by a writer I might like. A piece of music."

"And has he been clear about his intentions?"

"Yes. No... I don't know." She fell back on to the pillow.

"Ginny, that is no good. Does he know how you feel?"

"*I'm* not sure how I feel. So he definitely won't."

"Maybe that's for the best. He could *never* be right for you. Cowboys, it's a way of life. They never stay in one place."

"I know. It's idiotic of me."

Maddie patted the quilt before creeping back to her own bed. "Break it off with him, Ginny dear. You really must. Before he breaks your heart."

Ginny turned her face to the wall and pulled the coverlet over her head. What if Maddie was right? Once a man was used to traveling place to place for a living, he might not want to settle. She wasn't sure if she could bear having her hopes raised and then dashed a second time.

THIRTY-SIX

"I hope you girls got some sleep last night," said Aunt Josephine.

Maddie dropped into her chair at the breakfast table and drew her robe around her.

"Of course, Mother. But we had a lot to talk about as well."

Ginny shot her a warning glance and Maddie winked.

"I guess you girls will want to dance past midnight tonight, so make sure you get some rest today."

The maid poured coffee into Ginny's cup as she reached for a bread roll. It was warm, and smelled of fresh yeast. Another servant laid a plateful of food before each of the young women. Ginny eagerly cut through the bacon and fried eggs. Aunt Josephine pursed her lips as Maddie picked her way around the plate.

"What, Mother? We don't all have slim curves like Ginny. I need to fit the new frock from Madame Brevelle."

Uncle Thomas strode in and kissed his daughter on the brow. "Good to see you two girls finally up. I've done half a day's work already."

"And it's a Sunday so you should be at home anyway," scolded his wife.

He poured a coffee and sat at the table. "Geneviève knows what a long day's work entails." They exchanged a conspiratorial look.

Aunt Josephine nodded at Ginny. "And it seems you never wear a bonnet. You're getting freckles across your nose."

"Mother!" Maddie looked horrified on behalf of her cousin, but Aunt Josephine shrugged.

"I need to look out for my niece. My sister would never have allowed something so unladylike."

Ginny caught Uncle Thomas's eye once more, pleading for an end to the conversation. He put down his coffee. "What are your plans for the day?"

"We have a full day, Father. You have no idea how much effort it takes for a lady to be perfect."

They were interrupted by the jingling of the doorbell. Aunt Josephine glanced at the French ormolu clock on the mantelpiece. "That will be the dresses for tonight."

Maddie clapped her hands. "Let's go look at them!" She pushed away the dining chair and rushed into the hall, followed closely by her mother.

Uncle Thomas gave an indulgent smile and then looked at Ginny across the table. "Do please join them." He gestured toward the door.

"I already have a gown, thank you." Ginny felt the need to seize the time alone. "And Uncle, I wondered if I could have a moment of your time."

"Of course."

"I want you to know how very grateful Marie-Louise and I are."

Uncle Thomas sat back in his chair. "We're always happy to help you girls, even more since you lost your father."

"But to have been *so* generous. It means my sister and I have a secure future."

Thomas frowned. "I'm not quite sure what you're alluding to."

"The farm. I mean, buying it at auction and giving it to us. It means everything to us."

Uncle Thomas put down his cup. "Pardon me?"

Ginny colored, now wishing she hadn't said anything. "I know you wanted to keep it secret. And to be fair to Mr. Tanner, he didn't say a word."

"The Brownsville bank manager?"

"About being your agent. That's why I haven't written to thank you. He said it was an anonymous gift. But being here, you must know that I *had* to say something to thank you."

Uncle Thomas narrowed his eyes, making Ginny feel more uncomfortable. He looked toward the door where his wife and daughter had just left and seemed to be choosing his words carefully. "I'm very glad you and Marie-Louise are settled. As you know, I always thought the feud between my wife's parents and your mother was cruel and unreasonable." Uncle Thomas tugged at the bottom of his silk waistcoat to pull it smooth. "I think I need to have a talk with my generous but reckless wife. Not just yet; I don't want ructions to ruin today. But you and I can certainly consider the matter closed."

"Of course, Uncle." Oh goodness, had Ginny just given the game away for her dear aunt?

He glanced up to the ceiling, where footsteps could be heard in Maddie's bedroom above. "And I think you should go see what's making your cousin so excited."

Ginny stood up and went round the table to kiss her uncle on the head before running upstairs to the bedroom to find out what delights the dressmaker had delivered.

Madeleine stood in her corset and underskirts, surrounded by boxes overflowing with silk and tulle. Nancy pulled the laces to tighten the waist and push the breasts higher. She tied the crinolette over Maddie's rear, a series of half hoops on which the bustle would sit. Ginny ran her fingers over the buttercup-yellow fabric and ruffled the silk pleats.

Maddie sighed. "Isn't it beautiful?"

Nancy and Aunt Josephine lifted the billowing material and Maddie stepped into the underskirt. Ginny helped Maddie into the satin bodice, which was all in one with a full-length skirt, and Nancy buttoned it up. The dressmaker Mme. Brevelle knelt to ruche the overskirt into polonaise-style puffed-up swags, the apricot underskirt complementing the yellow top-skirt. Aunt Josephine adjusted the neckline, pulling down the lace of the tiny sleeves to emphasize Maddie's white shoulders.

The women stepped back to admire the effect.

Maddie went up on the balls of her feet. "Well?"

"With a black choker and a pair of white gloves, it will be perfect," replied her mother and turned her daughter to look in the mirror at last.

Maddie cried out with pleasure. "It's *just* what I hoped for."

Ginny stepped forward to lift Maddie's blonde curls into a speculative arrangement. "Freddie will be speechless," she whispered in her cousin's ear.

Maddie flashed shining eyes. "Not completely, I hope. There's a special question I want him to ask me."

Aunt Josephine called over, "What will you be wearing, Geneviève, *chérie*?"

Ginny dropped her eyes. Mary Lou had made a new dress from the emerald material she had bought at the store. It was elegant, but she knew she would look plain next to her cousin. She took it from the closet.

"I know it's simple. But no one will be looking at me."

Aunt Josephine fingered the long sleeves. "It's beautifully made. And a lovely color. But not right for a ball."

Ginny chewed her lip, not wanting to let down her aunt in

public. She caught the glance between Aunt Josephine and Maddie, who pulled a linen sheet off her bed with a flourish to reveal a large dress-box wrapped with a bow.

"So it's lucky we bought this one for you."

Ginny was motionless for a moment, then walked to the bed. She put out her hand to the bow and then snatched it back as if it were scalding hot. She looked at her cousin.

"Really?"

Maddie nodded, grinning with delight at the surprise.

Ginny pulled at the bow and lifted the lid. The dress was white silk, the bodice brocaded with a pattern of flowers and ferns, shimmering as Ginny picked it up. Embroidered cerise roses followed the low neckline.

"We had better check our guess at the fit was right," said Aunt Josephine.

Nancy helped Ginny out of her day dress and into the petticoats needed for the gown. She brought out a second crinolette and carefully pooled the dress for Ginny to step into and drew it up. Mme. Brevelle shook out the confection of layers of ruffles and gathers, as she had for Maddie.

Ginny turned to the mirror and pushed away a tear with the back of her hand. "You are so kind. It's the most beautiful thing I ever saw."

Aunt Josephine sniffed and found her handkerchief. "You look so like your mother. She was such an exquisite woman. She would have been so proud." Josephine gave her niece a hug and stepped back.

Maddie brought out Ginny's dancing shoes. "Check the skirt is the right length at the front."

"Up on to this stool, Miss Snow," said Mme. Brevelle.

Ginny slipped on her shoes and stepped up. Mme. Brevelle kneeled to adjust the hem with pins. She then checked the bodice. "It needs to be taken in a tiny bit here, to make sure it sits just right across the décolletage."

With the fitting complete, Nancy helped Ginny to undress so the dressmaker could whisk away the gown to make sure it would be ready for the evening.

"Let's go for a walk in the garden," suggested Maddie once they were both back in their day dresses. "I could do with some fresh air."

Ginny shook her head. "There's something I must do first: practice my piano recital."

"Oh, of course, my dear. Let's do that now. No one will be in the drawing room."

Ginny gathered the sheet music and they went downstairs to the large room at the front of the house. She propped open the lid of the grand piano and sat at the double stool. One of her great pleasures when visiting her aunt was to sit at this piano, knowing that her mother's fingers had once danced across the keys.

Maddie picked up *Harper's Bazaar* and tucked herself into the sofa. She listened to Ginny begin her practice with scales and arpeggios. Ginny then set out her music in front of her.

"This is what I'll be playing this evening. I hope Mrs. Price approves."

Ginny flexed her arms and gently put her hands in place. Calming her breath, she started to play the music she had fallen in love with over recent weeks. The tune rose and fell, the dancing rhythm twirling beneath her fingers. As it worked up to a crescendo, Maddie laid aside her magazine. The notes spun to a finale and then hung in the air.

Maddie burst into applause. "Dearest. That's the prettiest thing I've ever heard."

"It's a Ballade by Chopin."

"It looks fearsomely difficult."

Ginny grinned. "I've had to practice hard. The score was... It was one of the gifts I mentioned. From—'

Maddie opened her eyes wide. "The outlaw?"

"He's not—"

"The cowboy then. But how would he know...?" She left the words in the air.

Ginny shrugged sheepishly. "He heard me play a number of times." She gathered up the sheet music and folded it into order.

Maddie got up and tucked in next to her on the piano stool. She turned to look at her cousin's profile. "Dearest Ginny. You know how much I care about you, so you must not take this the wrong way. But I would hate to see history repeating itself."

Ginny closed her eyes. "I'm not sure I know what you mean."

"You know I believe in marrying for love. And Mother says that's what Aunt Lucille did when she married your father. But you need your feet on the ground too. Think how you and Mary Lou have struggled.'

Ginny looked sharply at Maddie. "My parents adored each other."

"But that adoration meant your parents had to struggle every day to make that little farm pay, because your mother had been cut off from her family."

"Mama and Papa never regretted their decision."

"It's one thing to make that decision for yourself. It's quite another to force your children to spend each and every day outside, working in the dirt, managing livestock and goodness knows what else."

Ginny turned away in anger at the criticism of her beloved parents. "You really are a terrible snob, Madeleine."

"Please don't let us fall out about this. And it's not about the work. Agriculture is a perfectly honorable way to earn a living. Father still has the hemp plantation. It's about how *hard* you work. Because you have no security." She turned to face Ginny fully. "It's not just *your* future. It's Mary Lou's. And your children's. Go ahead, have this infatuation with the farmhand. But he won't bring you security. And that is what you need."

"It sounds so... mercenary."

"Maybe it is. Or maybe it's simply how it has to be for women. Tonight, at the ball, there will be lots of eligible men."

"I haven't come husband-hunting."

"I didn't say you had. But don't let a fanciful dream stand in the way of other possibilities."

Ginny let her fingers walk down a scale of notes. She knew her cousin was speaking sense, and she regretted her sharp words. But it was so hard when her stomach flipped over every time she thought of the man who had gifted her the music she had just played.

"Very well, Maddie. I promise I will go to the ball tonight with an open mind. Even if I can't quite go with an open heart."

THIRTY-SEVEN

Ginny put out her elbow for Maddie to slip in her arm as the two young women descended the stairs into the Crittens' lobby: Maddie in her buttercup-yellow dress, all ribbons and tulle, Ginny in the shimmering white gown, roses from the garden tucked into her golden-brown hair. Maddie had supervised the pinning and curling of her hair so it shone in a pile of curls above her head and tumbled down her neck. Maddie's fair hair was swept up and kept in place with lace and bows. At her throat, she wore a black choker with a jet pendant. Teardrop earrings emphasized her elegant neck. The ribbons from Maddie's choker were long and fell to the ruffles of her bustle. The young women each had white silk gloves and carried a fan.

"Pretty as a picture," Uncle Thomas said as he put out his hand for his wife and led the way to the carriage waiting at the porch.

The carriage swept up the path to the Governor's mansion, the setting sun making the peachy brickwork glow. The mansion stood in isolation on raised land above the Missouri River.

"There's something stark about it," Ginny said. "I daresay it will look more at ease once trees and shrubs have grown."

"Seventy-five thousand dollars," whispered Aunt Josephine. "And built in less than a year."

"It certainly is very fine," said Ginny, her eyes drawn upward past the sash windows to the top floor, which contrasted with the lower levels. This floor was faced with slate fish-scale tiles, white-edged dormer windows standing proud. The top of the building was crowned by spiked metalwork. She preferred this plainer French style to the elaborate embellishments of Bellevue, though she would never say so out loud.

The Crittens' coach waited in line to move in front of the grand entrance, the horses stamping the earth.

Maddie strained to gaze into the brightly lit rooms. "What if they start the first dance before we get there? That would be a *disaster*."

"Maybe another time you will be ready a little earlier?" her father responded drily.

"Don't be such a tease." Aunt Josephine tapped her husband's arm with her fan.

"I'm surprised we took the carriage at all," said Ginny. "It's so close, we could easily have walked."

"The point is to arrive *à la mode*—in style," said her aunt.

A servant opened the door of the carriage and they climbed down. Ginny and Maddie shook out the trains of their skirts. They followed their elders up the steps to the double doors.

Ginny's breath was swept away with the elegance of the room. The walls were papered in pale primrose; the wooden floor was made of complex herringbone patterns and shone like ice on a winter pond. The room glowed from the chandelier of globe oil lights which took the eye up to the decorative ceiling high above.

They were met by the Governor and First Lady. Mr. and Mrs. Price hovered nearby to make the introductions.

The Governor smiled on the two young ladies. "We have cleared this hall of furniture to make plenty of space for dancing. I look forward to seeing you taking a turn very soon."

Maddie and Ginny made low curtsies in reply.

Ginny couldn't remember being in a room with so many people. The women dazzled in a riot of peacock colors, whilst the men were in sober black and white, like penguins who had wandered into the wrong place. There was an occasional flash of the blue and yellow of military uniform. Ginny thought the chattering was like a flock of birds at nesting season, loud and varying in pitch but exact words hard to make out.

Mrs. Price greeted each of them. "It is *so* lovely to see you, Miss Snow. I look forward to hearing you play again."

"Perhaps I could put this music score with the piano?" Ginny asked.

"Of course."

Ginny followed her to the deep bay to the left of the hall, where a staircase seemed to float from the wall.

"Isn't it beautiful?" said Mrs. Price. "Made of walnut. Only one of its kind in the state. They call this area the Nook."

Ginny felt the name inappropriate for such a fine space. Even the grand piano standing partway below the staircase looked small. She returned to her relatives, who were still admiring the grand hall.

A young man parted the throng to meet Maddie and Ginny recognized Freddie. He grinned sheepishly and took Maddie's hand.

"I thought you were going to miss the first dance you promised me."

"Well, I'm here now," said Maddie. "And you remember my cousin Miss Geneviève Snow?"

"Yes, of course. From Thanksgiving Day."

Ginny gave a curtsy. "Mr. Price, it's lovely to see you again."

Frederick bowed his greeting. "Freddie, please. May I take you two ladies through for some refreshment?"

Freddie put Maddie on his left arm and Ginny on his right and made his way through the double doors at the end of the hall, to the sumptuous dining room beyond.

Ginny gazed around at her surroundings; the turquoise walls were decorated in gold motifs, below the dado was deep red wallpaper. The biggest table Ginny had ever seen ran down the middle of the room. Candles reflected the silverware and the crystal glasses scattered rainbows on the walls. The table was laden with sliced watermelon, early grapes tumbling from fruit bowls, pickled walnuts, platters of cold cut beef and terrines of layered vegetables.

Freddie led the way to the ornate sideboard and a golden bowl full of raspberry-colored punch. A maid ladled the drink into three glasses.

"To a magical evening," said Freddie.

Ginny lifted her glass.

Freddie glanced at Maddie as she hid her giggles behind a gloved hand.

"We'd better find Mother," Maddie said.

They made their way through a wide opening into the double parlor, an elegant room with a curved bay matching the Nook on the other side of the hall, but this time with tall sash windows with views through trees to the Missouri River. The mirror over the marble fireplace was surrounded with gilt and reflected the light from the chandelier.

Aunt Josephine was by the window, in the center of a small group of fashionably dressed women. Their attention was held by the tall gentleman in front of her. Aunt Josephine caught Maddie's eye over the man's shoulder and motioned for the cousins to join them.

Maddie grabbed Ginny's hand to lead the way. "That's him," she hissed. "The man everyone's so excited about."

Aunt Josephine moved to allow Maddie to step into the group. "You have already met my daughter, Miss Madeleine."

The man bowed. "Charmed, once again."

"But you won't have met my niece."

He turned to Ginny as she joined them and she looked up at the dark gray eyes she had dreamed about so often.

For a moment, they both stood motionless, as Ginny saw reflected there the shock and surprise she felt.

"Miss Geneviève Snow," Aunt Josephine continued. "My dear sister's daughter."

His hair was shorter than she remembered, and tidied away from his face. He was clean-shaven and without the dark bristles that so often spread across his jaw when he had been in Brownsville. He bowed slowly.

"This is Mr. Jacob Alexander Van Bergen."

Ginny failed to curtsy. "Lex," she whispered below her breath, and felt the blood draining from her face.

"You might be familiar with the name?" Aunt Josephine said, trying a lighthearted laugh. "Van Bergen. From the railroads, and so many other ventures."

Lex recovered first. "But as you can see, Mrs. Critten, we *have* met before."

"Indeed?"

Ginny nodded.

Lex straightened his shoulders. "But it was some years ago. As I recall. In St. Louis. You were visiting. Or perhaps on business. With your father."

Aunt Josephine stared at Ginny. "An extraordinary coincidence. Isn't it, Geneviève?'

Ginny's throat was dry. "Yes. It is. Extraordinary."

"Miss Snow, given how long it is since we met, would you allow me the first dance of the evening?" His voice was as honey-smooth as ever.

Ginny darted a glance over to Maddie, whose eyes were wide in amazement.

"Of course she will," Maddie chimed in.

A quartet of musicians began to tune their instruments in the corner of the great hall, and before Ginny could say any more, the Governor positioned himself on the curved staircase. Everyone moved closer to hear the official welcome.

Ginny slipped back to the window so she would be out of anyone's eyeline. Her gaze was drawn to the stiff back and broad shoulders in front of her in an immaculately fitted black jacket. She struggled to keep her breathing under control.

During the Governor's rambling speech, Maddie crept closer to Ginny and they shared a glance. Maddie whispered into her ear, "I've never seen a man so thunderstruck."

Ginny slowly shook her head. "Madeleine, you have no idea."

"I can't wait to hear. Not only is he rich and handsome, there's a touch of mystery too." She nudged Ginny's shoulder and Ginny attempted a smile. But it was no use. She sniffed away the tears that were threatening, and Maddie saw the emotion and grasped her hand, giving it a squeeze.

"I'm fine. I'm completely fine," she whispered as the speeches came to an end. A memory of studying him chopping wood came unbidden to her mind, those muscles as they flexed to swing the ax high. Ginny's cheeks grew hot. What was he thinking of, calmly standing there in front of her? She was close enough to reach out to touch his shoulder.

He turned round and those gray eyes met hers once more. His jaw twitched as he put out his hand.

"Shall we?"

Ginny silently put her gloved hand in his as he led her to the dance floor.

THIRTY-EIGHT

Lex led Ginny to the middle of the waltzing couples, trying to maintain a veneer of calm when inside his heart was racing. He placed his palm in the small of her back without letting go of her gloved hand. He had never seen her in fashionable evening dress and she was as bewitching as ever.

Ginny reached up to lay her left hand on his shoulder. Her smell was blissfully familiar: lavender with undertones of mint.

He led with small steps so that he could hold her close as they began to dance. Leaning down so his mouth was near to her ear, he spoke softly.

"I had no idea you would be here."

Ginny refused to look at him. "Obviously."

A wisp of her hair tickled his cheek. He swallowed hard.

"I met the Crittens a few days ago. They seem pleasant people."

As Ginny's mouth remained resolutely shut, he tried again.

"She is your aunt? Your mother's sister?"

Ginny turned her head to him, her eyes blazing. "Are you trying to make small talk?" she hissed.

"It's the usual currency at a ball."

"How dare you. How *dare* you!"

Lex spun her to a quieter part of the room, where they continued to dance.

Ginny bit her lip, he hoped to prevent herself from speaking loudly. A vein in her neck was pulsing. "I don't want to embarrass my family by creating a scene. But how dare you laugh at the situation?"

"What else can I do?"

Ginny stood on her toes to make sure her mouth was close to his ear so only Lex could hear. "Either *you* tell them, or I will. And not just my family. *Everyone*."

"You'll tell them what, exactly?"

"That you're nothing but a cheap con man." She spat out the words.

Lex raised an eyebrow. "That's a little harsh."

She looked up at him again, her dark eyes glittering. "Everyone here has swallowed your outrageous story about being a Van Bergen. But remember, *I* know the truth, Mr. Carlton. Oh yes, you might play the part of a wealthy industrialist with great flare. But a well-cut jacket won't cover up the truth."

Lex considered her words for a moment. "Ah. Yes. I see now."

"Or were you just pretending to be a jobbing farmhand for hire as well? Were you planning to cheat the townspeople of Brownsville in some way? You never did quite fit in as a cowboy."

Another couple threatened to knock into them and Lex expertly spun Ginny away. He glanced around the room. While some eyes were on them, no one seemed to notice the furious words she whispered into his ear.

Ginny shook her head. "To think that I fell for you. How could I have been so *blind*?"

His chest tightened and he studied her face intently. "You—?"

But words flowed on from Ginny. "What was your plan here? To ensnare some rich young heiress like my cousin?"

"I assure you nothing could be further from my mind."

The strains of the waltz were coming to an end.

She looked him straight in the eye. "So. Do you have the courage to tell everyone you're a charlatan? Because I will, if you don't."

"May I... Would you honor me with a few minutes of your time. To explain?"

The music stopped and Lex tucked Ginny's arm firmly under his. Before she could protest, he had guided her through the dining room, out of the French doors and onto the narrow terrace.

The sun had set, leaving the air cool and refreshing. The first stars were appearing, Venus low on the horizon, brighter than all the others. The sound of revelers bubbled onto the terrace and mixed with the chirping of insects.

Ginny stood by the low balustrade. There was nothing to see in the dark beyond the terrace, and he knew she only pretended to study it to avoid looking at him. Lex stood beside her. He could hear her uneven breathing and his gaze slid over the soft skin of her shoulders.

"I'm sorry you found out this way." His throat was dry and he wished he'd brought a drink out with him. "I wanted to tell you the truth. But at the right time. You see, I haven't been deceiving your family, nor the people of Jefferson City. And in many ways, I was not deceiving the people of Brownsville. But I am deeply sorry that it seems, of everyone, I *have* deceived you."

She closed her eyes, the lashes brushing her cheek. "Lex, please don't speak to me in riddles."

He took a breath. "For the past two years, I have been—as you rightly pointed out—a migrant worker. A cowboy for hire. I traveled widely, from state to state, ranch to ranch. I did not lie to you about that."

He turned and leaned his hips against the balustrade, arms folded, looking at her profile. She glanced at him; her full lips formed a line.

"But I am also Jacob Alexander Van Bergen. My family have always used my middle name, Alexander—Lex—I suppose to distinguish between me and my father. Carlton is my mother's maiden name. It seemed easier for the past two years to not use a name that is so recognizable from the railroad. Now my father has died, the time has come for me to make some hard decisions. And my business here in Jefferson City needs my full name. With all the expectations that brings with it."

They stood in silence.

Ginny leaned on the balcony wall for support. Lex put his hand on her arm and she sharply pulled it away.

"If this is true, then you are cruel. As well as a deceiver."

Lex frowned. "How so?"

She looked up at the sky and groaned. "All those letters, Lex. The gifts. How could you do that? How could you raise my hopes when you knew we would *never* be together? That your destiny and mine could not be more different?" Ginny pushed a tear from her cheek and stepped away. "I never want to speak to you again! I never want to see you. I will burn those letters. The honorable thing would be for you to destroy mine too."

Lex took a step closer. "Ginny—"

Both her hands flew up to hold him back. "And I will send each gift back to you. It will be as if we never met."

This time, he held her hand and didn't let go. "Ginny. You know as well as I do. Our lives can never be as if we never met."

She glanced at his face and the air between them thickened like before a storm. He fought the desire to pull her to him, to kiss the beautiful skin of her shoulders, thread his fingers through the dark-gold hair.

She may have felt it too, but she lifted her skirts and ran back into the mansion, into the swirl of happy dancing couples.

THIRTY-NINE

"Ginny!"

Her hand was grabbed by Maddie, who carved her way through the throng, throwing a smile one way, a quick "good ev'ning" and curtsy the other, until they came to the library on the far side. The room was set with chairs in pairs and trios, ready for dancers with tired feet or older revelers who had difficulty hearing conversations over the sound of the fiddles. A line of matrons had already settled into the long, green couch opposite the fireplace.

Maddie spotted a pair of upholstered chairs behind the door and pulled Ginny toward them.

"I do declare, I've never been so surprised in all my life. Why didn't you say you knew Mr. Van Bergen?'

"I didn't know I did."

Maddie shook her head. "Whenever you met in St. Louis, you must have made an enormous impression on each other. But were you not properly introduced? Is that why you didn't know him?"

Ginny closed her eyes. The whole thing was so utterly confusing. "I'd rather not talk about it quite yet."

"Oh goodness." Maddie shook out her fan and spoke behind it. "Nothing untoward happened, did it?"

"Of course not!" Ginny snapped. "What do you take me for?"

"I'm sorry. That was plain stupid of me. But there seemed such a... connection. Between you. And when you were dancing: you had a lot to talk about."

Ginny's head jerked up. "You heard us?"

"I wouldn't eavesdrop on you. But I couldn't help watching you both. He is such a fine dancer. My, you made a handsome couple."

Ginny didn't know what to believe. She sat back in her chair and gazed at the ceiling. The corner was painted with fat little cherubs, playing among fluffy clouds. They seemed to be laughing at her.

Freddie popped his head round the door. "There you are, Maddie. I was hoping for your hand for the mazurka."

"I'm afraid I'll be sitting out this dance. Would you be a darling and get a glass of sarsaparilla for Ginny?"

"Is she unwell?"

"Just the heat of the room. She'll be right as rain in a moment."

Freddie hurried off to the dining room.

"Maddie, are you sure?" Ginny spoke so quietly that her cousin had to lean forward. "Are you *sure* he's Jacob Van Bergen?"

A line appeared between Maddie's brows. "What do you mean?"

"How do we know?"

"You've met him before. You must know."

"But you are right—we were never properly introduced. How do we actually know he is who he says he is?"

Maddie laughed nervously. "How do we know *anyone* is who they say they are?"

Ginny grasped Maddie's hand. "But that's my point."

Freddie returned with the sarsaparilla, which she took with a shaking hand. Maddie nodded to Freddie to indicate he should leave, and waited for Ginny to put down the glass on the occasional table beside them.

"I'm not clever enough to answer your question deeply," Maddie said. "You need a clergyman for that. Or perhaps a philosopher. But I can tell you that Mr. Van Bergen arrived in town about a week ago. He's staying in the city's finest hotel and dresses as a man of means."

Ginny snorted. "Has he paid his bills yet?"

"Ginny, I really don't know what's got into you. Mr. Price knows him from the East. I'm sure of that because I heard Father talk about it to Mother. Mr. Price is involved in the sale of Rosemount Ranch, north of the river."

Ginny pursed her lips.

Maddie continued. "That's why Mr. Van Bergen is here. He's looking at land to buy." She paused. "Do you want to tell me what has *really* happened?"

Ginny shook her head. It was all so humiliating. "I think it might be best if I went home now."

Maddie widened her eyes. "But everyone is looking forward to your piano recital."

"I don't think I can play." Ginny took the glass again and finished the sarsaparilla.

"Nonsense. You were note-perfect this afternoon. Now, I don't know what has happened here this evening. But I know you. You need to face up to things. Otherwise, you'll be cross with yourself and think you've let everyone down. And Mother won't want you to set tongues wagging throughout the town, wondering why you left early."

Maddie took the empty glass and stood up just as Freddie returned.

"Perfect timing. Freddie, my dear, would you take Ginny

and partner her for the next dance? Do not take no for an answer." She pulled Ginny to her feet and took her face in both palms. "You might be cross with me now. But you'll thank me in the morning. Now, off you go."

Freddie looked surprised but held out the crook of his arm. "Better do as she says."

Ginny slipped her hand through it and, for a second time that evening, reluctantly allowed herself to be led to the dance floor.

Ginny threw a cautious glance around the room and her gaze was drawn like a magnet to where Lex stood on the edge of the dancers. He was part of a knot of people, mostly men, and seemed to be concentrating hard on what was being said to him. He nodded and contributed to the conversation, his relaxed stance exuding confidence. How could he remain so calm when she had been thrown into confusion?

Freddie spun Ginny away to the other side of the hall. Maddie was right. It was good to have something else to think about. At the end of the mazurka, he delivered Ginny to Maddie and Aunt Josephine, who were standing near the staircase. Freddie put out his hand to Maddie to claim his reward for being helpful earlier. It was an old-fashioned eight-person reel and Maddie tripped off happily.

There was the usual struggle to find the right number of partners for each set. "Another lady needed here," a middle-aged woman cried from the set nearest to Ginny, and a young man stepped forward to invite her to join them. The three other pairs looked at her expectantly.

Ginny ran her eyes over Lex's side of the hall once more. He was still part of his group. There was no danger he might join the dance and Ginny find herself face to face with him again. She nodded to her partner and took her place.

Ginny had often been amused that people found country dances so difficult. It was just a pattern of moves, repeated over and over. How did people forget them? But tonight she was the one who turned the wrong way to cast off the line of dancers, or forgot to move forward into a wheel until someone pressed the small of her back. Her partner laughed and took it in good spirit. The confusion was part of the fun of the traditional dances. But Ginny had the disconcerting feeling that her mind was decoupled from her body, and everything she did was two seconds too slow.

At the end of the reel, Ginny curtsied low to her partner, who took her back to her aunt.

"You all looked like you were having a swell time!" Aunt Josephine beamed.

Ginny smiled weakly, realizing that her aunt's eyes would have been mostly on Maddie who cut a buttercup-colored dash among the dancers.

The Governor took a few steps up the staircase and announced a pause to the dancing while the musicians rested and the grand piano was moved closer to the hall. He suggested people fetched another drink while the recital was set up.

A knot twisted deep in her stomach as Ginny realized there was no way out of playing. And that the score she had brought, the piece she had been practicing for so many weeks, was the gift from Lex.

FORTY

The score was already on the stand above the keys. Ginny grasped Maddie's hand and slipped into an antechamber.

"This dress," she whispered. "It's too tight. My arms are restricted for playing. See?"

Maddie turned her round and quickly unhooked some fastenings down the back of the bodice. She tutted. "The things I have to put right." She loosened the boning and adjusted the sleeve so it sat on the curve of Ginny's shoulder. "And the corset?" Maddie asked.

"No. That's fine. I never lace it tight."

"You're lucky you don't need to. You are so slender."

"Maybe I should recommend long days in the fields as a way of developing a fashionable figure."

Maddie giggled. "Now, how's that? Better?"

Ginny nodded and Maddie spun her round.

"It's a touch looser, so I need to check we won't have a disaster with you spilling out. My, that way *no one* in this town would *ever* forget you."

Ginny finally laughed and once the laughter started, it was hard to stop. She really was taking herself far too seriously. She wasn't the first girl to get her heart badly bruised by a charming man who was not what he seemed. And she wouldn't be the last. *Chin up and show him you're made of stronger stuff.*

The Governor knocked on the door. "People are mostly back in the hall now, Miss Snow. Let's not keep them waiting."

She followed him to the Nook where the piano had been wheeled into place. A variety of chairs and couches had been moved into the hall and were occupied by ladies and the elderly men. Everyone else stood behind the chairs.

Ginny tried to ignore the audience as she settled on the stool.

"Ladies and gentlemen. I am delighted to introduce Miss Geneviève Snow, who will entertain us at the pianoforte." The Governor leaned in. "What are you going to play?"

Ginny opened the score and found her voice. "Chopin's Ballade No. 1 in G minor."

He turned to the audience. "Chopin's ballad number...?"

"One."

"In gee..."

"G minor."

"Precisely."

There was polite applause as the Governor took a seat with the First Lady on the front row.

Ginny sat up straight and placed her fingers on the keyboard. She took a deep breath, breathed out slowly and began.

The opening chords were dramatic, grabbing the attention of the audience members who had begun to chatter. Then a lyrical passage introduced the melancholy main theme. Soon, Ginny was completely absorbed in the music. Her fingers tripped over the notes and her foot sustained the reverberations at moments of intensity. Her sensitive phrasing conveyed the poetic song of love. The romantic harmonies wrapped themselves around her as her fingers tumbled over the keys. She swayed her body in time with the flowing rhythm. She moved to the most dramatic part of the piece, playing at a feverish speed. Some of the chords seemed discordant, but the music resolved itself, moving into the final crescendo as both her left and right hands moved across the keys to meet in the middle and then onwards. With a final waterfall of notes, she played the closing chords.

Her hands rested on the keys for a moment whilst the notes hung in the air. The ten minutes had passed in a blink of the eye and yet seemed to have lasted for ever.

There was a burst of applause and the spell was broken. Ginny got up and stood by the piano to make a curtsy, smiling shyly, feeling she had revealed something intimate.

And there Lex was, his head to one side, his mouth a line. Was it the beginning of an ironic smile? Or anger at her earlier outburst? He held a wine glass and was the only person not applauding. Their eyes locked for a moment. He lifted his glass to her and drank a mock toast. Was it mock, or was it true? She couldn't tell anything anymore.

A hand tapped her elbow and Ginny realized the Governor had been saying her name. Her back prickled as she gathered her score and made her way to the antechamber, hoping to take some deep breaths to settle the blood pumping through her body. In a few swift strides, Lex reached the room before her and stretched out to open the door for her.

"I've never heard that piece played more beautifully."

His voice caressed her, and she shivered as if he had stroked the bare skin of her shoulders.

Ginny flicked her eyes up to his and pulled the score closer to her chest to conceal how hard her heart was beating. "You flatter me. If you've heard it before, you'll have noticed how many notes I hedged. I was relying on it being an unknown piece in order to get away with all the difficult parts I skated over."

Maddie arrived with Ginny's gloves. Lex took the score so Ginny could pull the white silk over her fingers and past her wrists, his presence making her more aware than usual of the scar on her arm. Maddie's enthusiastic comments flowed past.

Lex inclined his head toward her and whispered, "Now, you don't *really* want to hand this gift back to me, do you?"

Ginny stared at him defiantly and saw that familiar smile playing at the side of this mouth. How could he be so teasing when her mind was in turmoil?

He pressed the book back into Ginny's hands and strode away.

Ginny turned to Maddie and implored her. "Truly, I'm feeling unwell. I know it's a bothersome thing to ask, but could Uncle have his carriage brought round for me?"

Maddie was staring after Lex. "If you insist. I'll go speak to Father now."

"But you must stay and enjoy the rest of the evening with Freddie. I beg of you. I'll send the driver straight back once he's taken me to Bellevue."

"I can't leave you if you're unwell."

"To be candid, I would prefer a little time alone." Ginny smiled weakly. "And I'll get Nancy to make a fuss of me. Hot milk and sweet cookies."

Within minutes, Ginny had slipped out from the hall and was waiting in the cool evening air for her uncle's carriage.

Climbing in, she looked back at Maddie's anxious face. "Please don't say anything to anyone about me leaving. I'll feel better once I've had some sleep. I promise."

The coachman geed the horses onwards and Ginny settled into the corner of the carriage in relief. Her humiliation was over and she would not have to face him again.

FORTY-ONE

Ginny sat in front of the gilt-edged mirror. The morning light meant there was no hiding the puffiness of her eyelids. She had spent half the night trying to work out what had happened the evening before. Lex being a Van Bergen seemed scarcely believable. Even in Brownsville, she had heard of those industrial families on the East Coast, forging a new country in the wake of the War and becoming fabulously wealthy in the process. But if it were true, what on God's earth was he doing in the Midwest, traveling from place to place, enduring hardship and potentially danger?

And what did he want with her? He had asked to court her and those letters suggested serious intent. But that was impossible. Dear Cousin Maddie might have romantic notions of a man like him being free to choose, but Ginny knew that was a fiction. Their new United States might not have the hidebound rules of Old Europe, but money married money. How could he have been so cruel to allow her to care for him when their lives were so different?

Lex had been kind and thoughtful after the attack by Trike. She remembered him leaping on his horse and chasing down that errant steer. That was the man she had fallen for. She had no idea who this new man was, with his perfectly tailored suit, his manicured hands, his combed hair.

Maddie pulled up a chair behind and worked her way through the knots in Ginny's hair. "The curling an' ribbons make it look pretty, but, my, we pay for it the next day."

Ginny traced her fingers over one of Maddie's pomanders. She sniffed it and puffed a spray into the air.

"Were you really fast asleep when we got back?" Maddie asked, and she caught Ginny's eye. "No, I didn't think so."

"I'm a terrible guest." Ginny knew she had to put on a brave face. "But to make up for it, you can tell me every detail after I left. Most importantly, did Freddie propose?"

Ginny looked at Maddie in the mirror and a smile burst on her cousin's face, making her dimples deeper than ever.

"Yes, yes, yes, yes, yes!"

"Oh, Maddie. I'm so happy for you. How did it happen?"

"I don't know really. It had happened before I noticed."

Ginny frowned.

"What I mean is... we were outside on the terrace and Freddie said about whether the ball would be held every year forever, because it was magical and wouldn't it be grand to bring our own children to it. An' I said, yes, but he would need to make sure any men interested in our daughters were honorable. An' he said they would be the prettiest girls in the county. But we'll have sons as well. An' I said, yes, lots. And we looked at each other, and held hands, and started to laugh."

Maddie stopped combing Ginny's hair. "And then he said, in that case he'd better ask my father. An' I said... well, I'm not sure what I said because I was laughing so much."

Ginny swiveled on the stool. "I'm so very pleased for you. You are *perfect* for each other."

"He's coming here today. This morning. Oh!" Maddie's

hand shot to her mouth. "I forgot to say. There's a big trip arranged. You *have* to come."

Ginny raised a brow. "What have you got planned?"

"We're all boarding the ferry over the river and then driving out for a picnic."

"That sounds fun. I've never taken a steamboat."

"It's so Mr. Van Bergen can view Rosemount Ranch."

Ginny handed the brush back to Maddie and turned to the mirror, noticing that her face looked pale. "Mr. Van Bergen?"

"It's the ranch he's thinking of buying. Mr. Van Bergen made a point of inviting you."

Ginny bit her lower lip. "That's very kind, but I don't think I'll be able to join you."

"Why ever not?"

"I must get back to Mary Lou."

"But you're leaving tomorrow. That's what we all agreed."

"I want to get back sooner. I feel uneasy being away from the farm so long."

Maddie brushed Ginny's hair with more force. "I know *exactly* why you don't want to come and it's *killing* me trying not to ask for details. It's been killing me all night and all morning, to be honest."

Ginny considered taking Maddie into her confidence, but it would all sound so unbelievable. She looked at her reflection. "You've untangled every knot. Come on—time to fix your hair."

She stood up and they swapped places. Ginny began with the tangles at the bottom of Maddie's blonde locks.

"However, I was a good friend, as promised," said Maddie, "and asked some discreet questions about him—Mr. Van Bergen. Just to end your crazy notion that he isn't, after all, one of the richest men in the States."

Ginny frowned as she braided Maddie's hair.

"I found out his father died very recently. There's a twin brother who got married last year. Mr. Price says he's the one running the main business now. From Boston, where the family lives. And there's a sister. Mr. Price thought she was a bit younger but couldn't remember the name."

At least that matched what he had told her by the lake at home, although none of that mattered, now she knew he'd been lying to her.

Ginny tossed her head. "I don't know why you're telling me this. I'm not in the slightest bit interested."

But Maddie continued: "Freddie says the Rosemount Ranch is just a side interest. He must be here for something bigger. It'll be to do with the railroad, maybe making a big... *bridgehead* was the word Freddie used. Like Sedalia further west."

Ginny twisted the braid into a spiral and clipped it in place.

Maddie patted it to check it was firm. "All secure, thank you. If we don't get downstairs soon, we'll miss breakfast."

As Ginny returned up the stairs to Maddie's room after breakfast, her legs felt heavier than railroad sleepers. Aunt Josephine had made it very clear she expected Ginny to join the day's outing and did not want any offense to be given to their important visitor. As Ginny owed her whole well-being to her aunt and uncle's generosity, she could not disappoint them.

She was relieved that the bedroom was empty and paced back and forth. At breakfast, Uncle Thomas was clearly interested in finding out more about Jacob Alexander Van Bergen and the many companies he owned. Aunt Josephine had chattered about the ladies who had danced with him later that evening, speculating that he might have an eye on the Governor's daughter. Despite herself, she had felt a pang of envy but immediately chided herself.

The simple truth was Lex wasn't the man she thought he was; the skilled farmhand at ease in the open air was an act.

They were not an alliance of equals. She had pictured herself as an independent woman, choosing her partner, much as her mother had done, even though it was an elopement. That picture was now in pieces. She was furious with him for not being honest with her. Perhaps he hadn't because, deep down, he knew there was no future for them.

So why continue with gifts and letters? What on earth did he want with her?

She slowed down her steps and thought of the book at the bottom of her trunk: his gift of Zola's *Thérèse Raquin*. It was no more suitable as reading material for a young woman than... well, than *Madam Bovary*, the book he had pulled from the bookcase at the farm. What would a rich young buck want of a penniless woman such as her, other than—oh goodness—to be his mistress?

Ginny sat down heavily on the bed. No. Surely not? She could not believe that of him. Lex had always been kind and respectful.

The door burst open and Maddie entered, a hat in each hand.

"Mother might be happy in an old-fashioned bonnet, but *we* need to be wearing hats."

She pulled Ginny to the dressing table and firmly fixed a black one to Ginny's hair at a jaunty angle. There were rather more feathers and bows than Ginny would have chosen, but she was surprised how elegant it looked.

The doorbell rang and Maddie rushed to the window.

"It's Freddie!" She stood on tiptoes to see as much of him as possible and then grabbed her parasol and flew out of the room.

Ginny followed to the top of the stairs, but the sound of a deep voice stopped her in her tracks. Her heart drummed at his warm tone.

Ginny crept round the balustrade and peeked through the painted spindles.

His dark hair was swept back and from this high vantage point his shoulders looked even broader. Uncle Thomas was shaking his hand.

"Mr. Van Bergen, so kind of you to invite us on this surveying trip."

"I thought the ladies might enjoy the excitement of a steamboat across the river."

Maddie clapped her hands with delight. Uncle Thomas showed Freddie and Lex into the morning room and the voices drifted away.

Ginny rested her head against the balustrade, her eyes fixed to the spot where he had stood in the entrance lobby. He was as handsome and infuriating as ever. He had not been honest with her and that hurt. He was as much a stranger now as that first night when Mary Lou had brought him to their home.

She closed her eyes. Stranger or not, she wasn't sure if her heart could bear another day of being close to him.

FORTY-TWO

Lex watched Ginny come down the stairs, slowly, step by step. His chest tightened at the sight of her. At the bottom, she nodded and murmured, "Mr. Van Bergen," but swept through the door to the carriages.

How had he let everything become such a mess? He must put it right today.

Outside, two large carriages waited, each with four horses. The Critten carriage was driven by a servant. Maddie and Ginny climbed in the back with Freddie and Aunt Josephine. Mrs. Price waited in the other carriage, her husband standing by.

"I hear you're quite a horseman," said Mr. Price to Lex. "Would you like to take the reins?"

Truth was, he'd much rather be riding with Ginny, despite her evident fury with him, but he could see his only option was to take up Mr. Price's suggestion. Maybe it was for the best; he needed to find a chance to speak to her alone.

. . .

They were soon at the riverside. The hot July air felt clammy with the residue left by the steam trains and boats. Men worked like ants, loading and unloading the railroad cars, or taking things from the ferries and onto the waiting wagons. Tracks spread out like the branches of a silver birch, separate but parallel. Bolts clanked between carriages as they shunted down the multiplicity of tracks. Men yelled at each other over the sound of a steamboat releasing its horn.

At the ferry pier, Lex adjusted his hat and followed Ginny along the wooden boards.

"You ever been on a steamboat before?" Lex asked.

She shook her head.

"It won't take long. There's no need to be afraid."

For the first time, she turned to him, a gleam in her eyes like the darkness of a ruby.

"Who said I was afraid?"

He bit his lip at this flash of the fierce Ginny he had known back in Brownsville. Damn, he really had bridges to build.

The steamboat moved close, its wide hull skimming the river. The flag at the stern was tattered at the seam but flapped out proud. The steamboat had two levels and the large paddle at the rear. The funnel midway belched smoke, like an old man with a pipe.

Lex watched Ginny take a boatman's hand as she stepped from solid pier onto the floating boat, gentle as a cat testing a branch to see if it would take her weight. She walked with a sway to counter the movement of the deck, her parasol ready to act as a walking stick. Mr. Price and the two older women retreated to an ornate bench in the shade. Ginny followed Maddie and Freddie to the bow.

The boatmen called out as the mooring lines were unhooked from the bollards on the pier and tossed onto the deck. The wheel at the back started to turn, a whooshing noise as the river water churned across the paddles. The boat lurched forward and Ginny grasped the metal guard in front of her. Lex took a step nearer. Freddie had passed an arm round Maddie's waist and had drawn her close. Lex ached to do the same with Ginny, to pull her to him. From Ginny's frosty behavior that morning, he was pretty sure he would receive a slap on the cheek if he tried. Instead, he kept his attention on her, knowing his eyes were hidden by the shade of his hat.

Black smoke billowed from the funnel as the boat gathered speed and drove a path slightly upstream to take account of the current. The wind picked up.

Ginny held her hat with one hand. She called to Maddie: "I'm taking your lovely hat off, rather than risk it being blown into the Missouri."

She untied the ribbon and held the rim tight in one hand, the other still curled around the railing. Locks of her hair had come free and were being blown back from her face. As the boat pitched and rose on the waves, a smile spread across Ginny's face. She closed her eyes and let out a whoop. Maddie laughed and leaned back into Freddie.

Lex folded his arms to tamp down the tingling sensations in his chest.

The boat slowed as it approached the shore and the pilot expertly drew it against the jetty. Lex fell in behind Ginny as they made their way to the gangplank.

"I remember you once saying you enjoyed the train to St. Louis. It looked like you were pleased by your first steamboat ride as well."

"Maybe I take delight from traveling faster than is good for me," Ginny replied.

Mr. Price had arranged for two carriages and a chaise to be available on the northern side of the Missouri. Freddie and Maddie hastily climbed into the chaise. Aunt Josephine and Mrs. Price exchanged a look; they were engaged now, so what else could you expect of young people in love? Mr. Price would drive one carriage and Lex the other. Ginny climbed in behind Mr. Price before anyone could suggest anything different, Aunt Josephine getting in beside her. This left Lex to assist Mrs. Price into the remaining carriage. His eyes slid across to the other carriage, but Ginny was hidden by the hood.

The sun was directly above them. Sweat crept down Lex's neck. He wished he could shrug off his tailored jacket and drive in his shirtsleeves, as he would if still a laborer at Snow farm. Lex kept his buggy close behind Mr. Price's as the road undulated over low hills. Hemp plantations extended on either side, mile on mile of tall, spiky crops, emerald green under the penetrating heat. Some were being harvested by hand, bundles laid on the ground. The fresh smell pricked Lex's nostrils as they hurried past. The fields were full of Black workers. A woman stretched out her back, a man shaded his eyes to see if he recognized the carriages. A foreman yelled and the workers returned their attention to the crop.

"You're in proper Little Dixie now, Mr. Van Bergen," said Mrs. Price, noticing his gaze.

He felt uncomfortable and suspected this view hadn't changed much in the past thirty years, despite the Civil War.

Lex followed the chaise and Mr. Price's carriage up a track until they reached a mansion overlooking the fields.

"Rosemount Ranch," announced Mr. Price as soon as they had all climbed down, with as much pride as if the property had been his own. "It's empty now, but it would be a fine house to bring back to life."

Lex studied the house. It was symmetrically balanced, a white door in the center, two windows on either side. The white surrounds and green shutters contrasted with the small rose-colored bricks of the walls. The porch was generous and provided a balcony for the rooms above.

"Come inside," called Mr. Price, leading the way.

Lex's feet echoed on the floorboards and motes of dust floated in shafts of sunlight.

"Would need a fair bit spent to make it as it once was." Mr. Price winked at Lex. "Doubt that would be a problem for you, though."

Lex turned into a side room to hide his annoyance at the comment, but Mr. Price followed him.

"What happened? Why was it abandoned?" Lex asked.

Mr. Price waved a hand. "The War. Many plantation owners found it a difficult time. Threw in their lot with the wrong side, as things turned out."

Footsteps pattered in the room above and there was the sound of laughter. Maddie and Freddie were investigating the house. Lex returned to the hall, where Ginny stood waiting, running her hand over the wooden banister.

"Are you not going to explore as well?"

She shook her head.

He stepped closer. "What do you think of it?"

"Truthfully?"

"Of course."

Ginny traced her finger in a pattern through the dust. "Even though it's a hot day, there's something cold about this house. Something cruel."

Lex was surprised. But looking around, he understood what she meant.

"I arranged for a meal to be provided," said Mr. Price, joining them. "Out on the veranda."

They returned outside and sat at the table that had been set up in the shade. Maddie and Freddie arrived last, sharing a private joke. A Black woman laid the table with fried chicken, potatoes, boiled eggs, corn bread. A child hid in her skirts, large-eyed, skinny-legged and bare-footed.

"I noticed a lot of Black workers in the fields," Lex said.

"You'll find plenty of good workers nearby," replied Mr. Price.

"Do they own any of the land?"

Mr. Price smiled in a way that made Lex feel he was being treated like a child. "No. But we've built them plenty of schools. Their own churches, where they can go every Sunday. Don't think they've got much to complain about."

Mrs. Price piled her plate with more fried chicken. "It's a handsome house. Mrs. Critten, I daresay it reminds you of your childhood in the South?"

"It is handsome," said Aunt Josephine. "But it's a dollhouse compared with Green Oaks."

Lex turned to her, his interest captured. "The plantation where you grew up?"

"There was a colonnade of pillars all around, so thick Lucille and I would try to reach round to each other and touch hands." She inclined her head toward him. "Lucille was Geneviève's mother."

Lex glanced at Ginny, but her face was turned away and she appeared to be studying the fields beyond.

"A balcony ran the whole of the second floor and a pair of curved staircases swept down the front to the lawn. Lucille and I would practice walking down those staircases, imagining we were arriving at a ball." She took her fan from a pocket hanging from her waist. "My, it's hot today."

"What did you grow?" Lex asked.

"Sugar. Ours was a sugar plantation. But we didn't just grow it. That was where Papa was so clever. We had a refinery as well. That was where the real LeRoux money was made."

Everyone had eaten their fill, except for Ginny who had pushed the food around on her plate.

"Can I show you more of the estate?" said Mr. Price, rising to his feet.

Lex nodded and they all rose, the ladies opening their parasols as they stepped out into the intense sunshine. The Black woman cleared the plates. Lex noticed Ginny holding back and surreptitiously wrapping a piece of chicken in her handkerchief. He was about to ask what she was doing when she slipped it into the hands of the child, who took it and ran back inside the house.

FORTY-THREE

As Ginny joined the party, Lex fell back to walk beside her. He glanced across, but her parasol hid her face from him. He shook off his jacket and folded it over his arm but was still hot in his fitted vest.

"You're the only one here who really knows about agriculture. What do you think?" he asked.

"Hemp is a lucrative crop. Lots you can do with it. Ropes, fabric. The seeds are edible, makes a good oil."

He smiled at her characteristically well-informed response. "How do you know all this?"

"I read, Mr. Van Bergen. As well you know." She arched an eyebrow. "I think Aunt Josephine is right—the best thing would be to manufacture it into something else before it leaves the plantation."

"Like your grandfather did."

"Indeed."

They walked in silence for a while.

"But what do you think of it? Rosemount Ranch, I mean. You seemed unhappy in the house."

She stopped for a moment and surveyed the land. "Truly? I feel uncomfortable here. It's like stepping into the past."

"Because of your aunt's memories?"

"No, it's not that." She breathed in through her nose before speaking again. "The War was fought to end slavery, but it doesn't feel like much has changed here. You remember Isiah Boone?"

"Sure. The Black man from cattle branding last year."

"He was from Little Dixie. He said he would be afeared to return."

Ginny walked onwards, leaving her chilling statement in the air.

When it was time to return to Jefferson City, Maddie and Freddie commandeered the chaise again and bolted off ahead of the other two carriages. Josephine insisted she and Mrs. Price travel together, with Mr. Price driving. Lex was pleased that it left the final carriage to Ginny and him, although he noticed Ginny beginning to protest with her aunt.

"I have something important to discuss with Mrs. Price," said Aunt Josephine. "Run along and be a good girl. I'm sure no harm will come to you with Mr. Van Bergen."

Ginny snapped her parasol together and turned to the carriage where Lex was waiting. She leaned on his hand to step up to the seat but refused to make eye contact.

Lex had been looking all day for the chance to speak to Ginny privately, but now the opportunity came, he was nervous. Her words at last night's ball were still with him. Yes, she was angry, no doubt because he had kept things hidden from her, but she had said she had fallen for him. That gave him hope and now he had to persuade her to trust him again.

"I haven't had a chance to ask about Marie-Louise. Is she well?"

"Perfectly, thank you. She is staying with Amos Sturge at the moment."

They rode on unspeaking, the squeak and grind of the wheels seeming to get louder. He decided to dive right in.

"Last night, you said you had fallen for me."

Her mouth became a thin line. "Did I?"

"In between lots of other things."

"It's possible I was falling for Lex Carlton. But I have no idea who Jacob Alexander Van Bergen is."

"May I explain things to you?"

Finally, she looked at him. "You mean, explain why you lied to me? For months?"

"Why I kept things concealed."

"Amounts to pretty much the same thing, from where I'm sitting."

Lex took a long breath. "Think about what it's like for you with Snow Farm. I know farming is hard, but it's a good amount of land, well tended. A well-built homestead. One of the first things I learned when I reached Brownsville was that you're considered a catch."

Ginny batted away a copper-colored moth that had found its way under the carriage hood. "Don't be absurd."

"You know it, Ginny. You know why farmhands line up with Mr. Sturge to work there."

"Are you suggesting—"

"There's no point denying. It's the way of the world. But how does it *feel*?"

Ginny turned to him, frowning. "Feel?"

"How does it feel to never know why people behave the way they do. Is it *you* they are interested in? Or the farm? Am I right?"

A color came to Ginny's cheek, but she did not answer.

"Multiply that by a hundred," Lex said. "My whole life. Every friendship. Every person I meet. You've seen it here today. They laugh at my jokes. They listen to my opinions, purely because my father was one of the richest men in the States." He pulled at the horses to slow down as the road became rutted. "My life was mapped out in front of me. Extending in lines to the horizon, just like our railroad tracks. Everyone assumed I'd go into the business. My parents fought me tooth and nail about joining the Union forces instead of staying at college. Perhaps they were right."

Ginny turned to him, just for a moment.

"It was only a few months, right at the end," Lex continued. "But... well, being in the thick of a battle, it changes a man. Afterwards, I wasn't comfortable living in the city on the East Coast. I've always had a longing for the open skies and I thought maybe it would restore my spirit. My brother spent a couple of years in England and Germany, looking at manufacturing ideas. So I persuaded my father to let me do the same, but traveling westwards."

"He allowed that?"

"I said it was to find new business opportunities. But, Ginny, the freedom! I can't tell you how liberated I felt. I dropped the well-known name and used my mother's maiden name. And it was true, people responded to me differently. If I got things wrong, I'd get bawled out for it. When I got things right—it felt wonderful because I knew it was *me*. I was making a difference."

When he glanced over, her face seemed softer than before, her jaw no longer fixed.

"By the time I stumbled across your farm, living as Lex Carlton had become natural for me. It was my truer self. That's why it didn't feel like I was deceiving anyone."

They could see the Missouri River stretching out as the road sloped downwards to the ferry terminal.

Ginny picked at the frills on the parasol across her lap.

"Thank you for explaining everything so clearly. It does at least help me to understand some of what happened."

Lex was frustrated that the reins of two horses kept his attention when he longed to reach out and take her hand. "So, perhaps we might continue...?"

She turned to him, eyes flashing. "Continue what, Mr. Van Bergen? Corresponding? For what end?"

Lex frowned. "What end?"

"You are a Van Bergen, I'm a small-town homesteader. We live in different worlds."

"But what if—"

"I'm not prepared to let my heart be hurt again, when you... when you inevitably come to your senses."

"But, Ginny—"

"And perhaps... perhaps your intentions are not honorable anyway."

Lex's jaw tightened. "I'm not sure what you mean."

"You are a rich man used to getting what you want. As there is no likelihood of marriage between us, there seems to be only one other thing that you could want with a poor woman with no family to speak of."

Lex snorted in response, unable to form his words. "You think... you have that low an opinion of me?"

Her eyes narrowed as she glared at him and there was a slight pinkness to her cheeks. "I haven't forgotten that you encouraged an attachment despite being promised to someone else."

He gripped the reins so hard, the leather bit into his palm. "That's not... I didn't mean for that to happen."

She put up her hand as a barrier. "I don't think I've ever asked anything of you, Mr. Van Bergen, but I do so now." She seemed to be struggling to keep an even tone. "We have to be in each other's company today for perhaps an hour more. I ask you to not address me in that time. And afterwards, you will never make any attempt to contact me again. No letters. No gifts."

They had reached the cluster of buildings at the riverside.

"Geneviève..."

"Will you at least treat me with some respect? I know I am powerless, but please honor my wishes. Promise to never make contact."

He sat for a moment, calming his breath, anger welling up inside. Damn it, he'd done his best to explain, even revealed things about himself that he kept cloistered in his heart. And did she really think his intentions might not be honorable? God knows he'd tried to be honest with her today, but it had made not the slightest difference. Well, he had his pride and was not going to beg.

"Of course, Miss Snow. I promise, you will *never* hear from me again."

FORTY-FOUR

Ginny knew she should have packed the night before. But she had been so weary, she just couldn't face it. So here she was, before breakfast, rushing to get everything done. She kneeled in front of the trunk and placed the piano score and *Thérèse Raquin* at the bottom. Last night, she had considered a grand gesture of maintaining her independence by presenting them back to Lex. But that would embarrass everyone, her most of all.

Maddie tried to help by piling things on the bed. "Good job that trunk was half empty when you arrived. You'll need this crinolette to make sure the dress falls properly."

Ginny's hand rested on the white gown. "I couldn't take this."

"But it was a gift." Maddie folded the skirt.

"When would I ever wear it again? It's far too grand for Brownsville."

"Maybe you'll need it should you ever meet Mr. Van Bergen again?"

Ginny paused with her hands on the edge of the trunk and closed her eyes. "I promise you. That's never going to happen.

Maddie came and knelt next to her. "I've been trying not to ask about it."

"I know, and I'm grateful."

"But it's got me tied up in knots, trying to keep my mouth buttoned. Is there truly no hope?"

"Maddie, you want everyone to be happy. But you must know: a Van Bergen will marry someone from his own background. Someone from Boston or New York. Someone with money."

"It doesn't have to be like that."

"Yes. It does. I learned this from my own mother. Look at how impossible it was for her to marry outside the Southern society she was brought up in."

"But Mr. Van Bergen seemed attached to you."

"I'm from a small town, but I've read enough novels to know things don't work out well for poor women." Ginny slipped the other novel into the trunk—*The Gilded Age.*

"Nevertheless. I insist you keep the dress. And you'll need this crinolette. It will make all your dresses look fashionable." Maddie went to her closet. "And the hat you wore yesterday. It looked so elegant on you. Far more than when I wear it."

It went into the trunk, which Ginny struggled to stop Maddie filling with gloves and scarves.

"If you don't like them, I'm sure Mary Lou will."

Ginny couldn't deny that was true, and she wanted her sister to share in the treats she'd experienced thanks to her cousin's generosity. She closed the trunk's curved lid and buckled the straps.

"You'll find happiness somewhere, I'm sure of it." Maddie's dimples got deeper. "There's always the outlaw. The one who sends you gifts. Let's pray you are right and he's a farmhand and not a train robber."

A wave of relief came over Ginny that she had not told

Maddie that the farmhand and Mr. Van Bergen were one and the same. How would she have ever explained that?

At breakfast, Aunt Josephine was unusually distant with Ginny. Maybe it was because breakfast was earlier than usual as Ginny needed to make an early start. Aunt Josephine was not an early riser. But Ginny feared she had let her down with her behavior the previous day.

"Uncle Thomas wants a word," said Aunt Josephine, spearing a cherry tomato. "As soon as you have eaten."

Ginny knocked on the door of the study and was invited in. Uncle Thomas indicated for her to sit in the chair by the fireplace and he took the seat opposite. The grate was empty as the house was already beginning to warm from the summer heat. She folded her hands on her lap, not sure what to expect but feeling unease in the air.

"My wife and I have a happy marriage, built on trust," Uncle Thomas began. "That is why I was so disturbed by our conversation on our first evening."

Ginny settled back a little. So, it was about her thanking him for the gift of the farm.

"I thought my wife must have found money for you, but I had no idea how. I must say, it concerned me and led to a long conversation with her early this morning. We, your aunt and I, agree that I should tell you the whole of our financial position, painful though this is."

"Uncle Thomas, I had no intention to cause distress—"

He waved his hand for her to stop. "This house looks opulent, but it's mortgaged to the future, to a promise of a growing business. One needs certain appearances." He crossed his legs and plucked at the trouser fabric to straighten the pleat. "Your grandfather, Gabriel LeRoux, died in 1856 and everything from Green Oaks Plantation came to my wife. If things had been different, half would have gone to your mother. But we know that story."

Uncle Thomas took a breath and Ginny could see this was difficult for him to relate. What might be coming next?

"Right at the beginning of the War, still 1861, we were involved in what I think can only be termed a fraud. A banking fraud. The men running the Missouri State Bank supported the Southern cause and came to families such as ours for help. At Josephine's insistence, the whole of her money was made available to the South. There were assurances that it would be paid back in full once the Confederacy prevailed. Obviously, that day never came. All was lost. We were not alone; many wealthy people from this part of Missouri suffered the same fate."

Ginny felt an uncomfortable prickling around her neck. She wondered if her parents had known that Josephine so strongly supported the South. Or that all the inheritance was lost. "I am so sorry to hear this, Uncle. It must have been a hard time for you."

"Everything you see here comes from my family, and my hard graft. I'm afraid the LeRoux money has gone. Much as we would have liked to provide money for Snow Farm—and maybe morally some of the inheritance was yours—we were not in a position to help. And, to be honest, if we had, we would have done so openly."

Ginny found herself on her feet. She paced to the window so her uncle could not see the distress on her face. Her mind was spinning, searching for answers. "But where else can the money have come from?" She turned back to him, rubbing a thumb into her palm as she tried to regain control. "Who else could afford to be so generous?"

Uncle Thomas looked at her with concern. "I don't know. It's very mysterious. But I promise you, it wasn't me, nor my wife."

. . .

Having hugged Maddie and waved goodbyes, Ginny geed her horse to begin the journey home. She was not looking forward to the long road with only her tangled thoughts for company. Ever since the discussion with her uncle, Ginny's heart had been racing like a cattle stampede.

She knew one person with enough money to buy her farm with ease. And what better way to have control over her? He knew she would do anything to keep Mary Lou safe, a roof over her head. But he hadn't mentioned it, not even when she was suggesting he was behaving dishonorably. Why make the purchase anonymously, hand it back to her, but when he had the opportunity, say nothing? Her head spun as she thought what it all meant.

One thing she was sure of: she would never find out the truth from Lex. Because she had been very clear that she never wanted to see him again. That bridge was well and truly burned.

FORTY-FIVE

"And Tabitha's cat had kittens. She's trying to persuade Amos to let her keep one. As a pet, I mean. It was black with a little white smudge on its nose. The sweetest thing." Mary Lou lifted the stew pan to the kitchen table and looked at her sister. "Ginny, you haven't heard a word, have you?"

"I'm sorry, my sweet. I was miles away. What were you saying?"

"Nothing really. Just Tabitha and her cat." She spooned out the evening meal.

Ginny pushed the vegetables around her plate and took a small mouthful. Since the conversation with her uncle yesterday morning, she had lost all interest in food.

"Tell me, how's Cousin Maddie?"

"Maddie? Oh, she has wonderful news. She is going to marry Frederick Price. D'you remember? The man we met at Thanksgiving."

"Hallelujah! And can we go to the wedding?"

"I hope so. When I know the date, I'll ask Amos to arrange someone to look after the farm for a few days. It seems to have worked out well the last few days." Ginny thought again how much easier their lives were without the debts on the farm which had made every decision a struggle.

Mary Lou broke into a wide grin. "I can't wait." She glanced at her sister again. "But why aren't you happier? You're not jealous?"

Ginny playfully tapped her arm. "No, I'm not jealous. Or maybe just a bit. I'm... feeling out of sorts. It's a long drive in the pony trap. I'm still a little tired."

"You can't go to bed yet. You've said nothing of the Independence Day Ball."

Ginny took another mouthful and forced herself to swallow. She then told Mary Lou about the rooms, the fashionable dresses, the smart gentlemen. She spoke of candelabra shining bright, of food spread out on cloud-white tablecloths, of drinks served in cut-glass goblets.

"And did you dance?"

There was a stray lock of hair at her neck which Ginny spun around her finger. "A little. I danced with Maddie's fiancé."

"And?" Mary Lou leaned in closer across the kitchen table.

"And what?"

"And who else? I can tell you're hiding something."

"And I danced with another gentleman. He led very well, and I suppose I should have enjoyed it." Ginny felt a shiver as she remembered the feeling of Lex's hand on her back. "But I'm afraid my mind was on other things. By the end, I'm pretty sure he didn't want to dance with me again."

Mary Lou rolled her eyes. "Sister, you're not very good at this are you?"

"At what?"

"Flirting."

Ginny burst out laughing at the seriousness of her sister's

tone. "Not you as well! I have enough of this from Madeleine. Telling me I have to try harder."

"Madeleine is right. And your recital? Surely that was a success."

"I got through it without too many mistakes."

"You practiced so hard. I bet it was wonderful."

"There was a lot of applause, which was pleasing." Ginny stopped, her mind snagged on the memory of Lex standing near the back, watching her intently but not clapping. Would everything remind her of him? She wished she could share the truth of what had happened with her sister, but it was too painful, too confusing. She wouldn't know where to start.

Mary Lou brought a bowl of fruit from the shelf. "Look. Plums from the orchard. We're gonna have a good crop this year."

Ginny took one and cut it in half with her knife. Her teeth pushed through the skin to the sweet flesh, which turned acidic on her tongue.

Mary Lou scowled at Ginny's dinner plate before taking it away but thought better of complaining about the wasted food. "Why don't you play something on the piano while I clear up. I would love to hear some music."

Ginny hesitated, uncertain if she could face opening the keyboard, but she went through to the parlor and was soon glad of Mary Lou's urging. Although the sound was poor compared to the grand piano at the Governor's mansion, Ginny loved her piano's homely feel. The notes were like old friends, the ivory on some worn to a yellow shade, whilst the rarely played ones remained the color of milk.

She pulled a Chopin Prelude from the stack of music and the luscious notes filled the small homestead.

Mary Lou came through with some mending and sat by the window to catch the evening light. "Come now, sister. I want something brighter than that."

Ginny played on to the end, the music so familiar she didn't have to look at the score. She sighed. Mary Lou was right. There was no point feeding her melancholy. She was harming no one but herself. It had been her and Mary Lou against the world for more than three years. That wasn't going to change any time soon, so she might as well saddle up and face things.

"You're right." Ginny rifled through the scores. "A tarantella."

As she lay in bed listening to birds singing in the very earliest light, Ginny realized getting on with life was more difficult than deciding to change the music she played. A week had passed since her return from Jefferson City. Despite throwing herself into hard work on the farm, Ginny slept fitfully. She watched the light creeping round the edge of the curtains, but her mind ran on one thing: Had Lex saved Snow Farm?

Frustrated by being unable to control her thoughts, Ginny got up and shrugged on her dressing gown. In the kitchen, she nudged the embers into flame and got a pot of coffee brewing. She carved a thick slice of Mary Lou's bread and spread it with soft cheese curds. She slid onto the bench at the scrubbed table and watched the flames dance under the coffeepot.

He'd sat here, many times, his long legs pushed out across the kitchen floor. Making jokes with Mary Lou. Ginny would overhear them when she'd been recuperating and, deep down, she had liked it; having Lex in the house felt safe in a way she hadn't experienced since both her parents were alive.

"You're up early." Mary Lou broke into Ginny's musings.

"I didn't think I'd fall back to sleep. So I might as well get up. Coffee?"

"Lovely."

Ginny poured both of them a mug. They sat together at the table in sisterly silence.

"So. Could I have a kitten?"

"We've plenty of cats. They work hard keeping the mice down."

"As a pet. In the house."

Ginny swilled the coffee in her mug. "I'm not sure how that would work out."

"I'd look after her in the house."

"But she couldn't stay inside all the time."

"And then I'd let her out. To go hunting."

Ginny lifted an eyebrow. "So halfway between a house cat and a barn cat?"

"That's it."

"I'm not sure the kitten would like it. Being pulled between two homes."

"But if I fussed her enough, she'd be fine."

Ginny shrugged. "Maybe."

"Maybe? Can we try it with the next litter? Could I choose one?"

Mary Lou had not stopped coaxing Ginny about the cat for a week now. Ginny finally gave in. "As long as you care for it very carefully."

Mary Lou jumped up and kissed her sister on the forehead. "Time I made a proper breakfast."

She busied herself with the frying pan. Ginny watched and felt that sensation of melancholy sweep over her again. It was no good. She must do something about it.

"I'll need a good breakfast to keep me going all morning. I've decided to go to town."

"Oh?"

"I need to see Mr. Tanner."

Mary Lou spun round, an egg nestled in her hand. "I thought everything was sorted with the bank now." Her voice was tight and eyes wide open.

"It is. There's nothing to fear." Ginny bit her lower lip. "But there's something important I need to ask him about." Ginny could not go another day, not knowing for sure, one way or the other.

FORTY-SIX

The heat beat down as Ginny rode into Brownsville. The sun had pushed most people indoors. Shutters latched shut in an attempt to keep the interiors cool gave Main Street a look of having its eyes closed. Swallows dipped and swooped, feasting on the flies which bred in the warmth.

She had practiced what to say, trying it out in her head. She'd even spoken it out loud as she rode alone along the country road, working through one approach and then the next. And she had come up with her plan. It meant a little subterfuge, but then Tanner was the one who had insisted on hiding things. So it was hardly her fault.

Ginny pulled up her horse in front of the bank and slipped down from the saddle to the sidewalk. She smoothed her light summer skirt, untied her straw bonnet and pushed open the door.

A farmer was at the counter, so Ginny held back. Bob Stone was attentive as the man seemed to discuss the well-being of every member of his family. Eventually, he left and Ginny stepped forward to the cashier's opening in the ornate grille.

"Miss Snow. It's very good to see you."

"And you, Mr. Stone. I'd like to speak to Mr. Tanner. If I may."

"I'm afraid he's with someone at the moment."

"Oh." Ginny bit her lip. This wasn't what she had prepared for in her head.

"Would you like to call back?" asked Bob Stone.

Ginny turned to the door but knew she was being a coward. "I'll wait. If you don't mind." She took a seat by a small table piled high with newspapers. She took a closer look. *The Clarion.*

"It's mighty hot today," said Bob. "May I get you some water?"

"Thank you."

Bob opened the half door in the counter and placed a glass on the table.

Ginny's foot tapped and she pulled her shoe under her skirt. "Do you think he'll be long?"

Bob pulled a face. "Impossible to tell with Mr. Tanner." He returned to his work behind the counter.

She sat, flipping through pages, reading articles but with no idea what they said. Eventually, the door at the back of the bank swung open and she heard Tanner's voice reassuring a client. A man Ginny did not recognize came through to the public area, shook hands with Tanner and left.

Ginny was shocked by how Tanner looked. His face had always been thin, but now it was cadaverous. His once bushy white hair had thinned. He saw Ginny waiting and a flash of something passed over his face. Nervousness? Embarrassment?

"Miss Snow? How are you?"

"Very well, thank you, Mr. Tanner."

"Forgive me, I must have forgotten we were meeting today."

"Oh, no. I haven't made an appointment."

Tanner fiddled with the length of black silk tied elaborately at his neck. "Nothing wrong, I hope."

Ginny put the newspaper squarely back on the pile. "That depends. Perhaps we could talk in private?"

He stood aside and as Ginny entered the familiar office, she caught her breath as the memory of her last visit swept over her. The room was no different: the same smell of parchment and the sour whiff of cigar. She sat in the same chair opposite the large desk still covered with papers.

Tanner swept up a letter and shoved it in a drawer.

"Would you care for a drink?" he asked.

"I'm fine. Mr. Stone already brought me water. You might need one, though."

Tanner raised an eyebrow and poured a whiskey. He sat in his upholstered chair and leaned back, his eyes still on Ginny.

"Doctor Mack tells me I shouldn't drink. It will hasten my demise. I tell him if I don't have long, I certainly won't spend it denying myself things that bring me pleasure."

"You're unwell?"

Tanner waved his hand. "I apologize, Geneviève. That was maudlin of me. Let's forget I said anything."

She took a breath and sat up straighter. Seeing Tanner so ill had unnerved her, but she needed to know the truth. She would creep up on this sideways.

"I went to stay with my aunt last week. For the Governor's Independence Day Ball."

"My. That sounds very grand."

"The last time I sat in this room, you implied she was my benefactor. That she had bought the farm."

Tanner ran a finger around his collar, loosening it so some air might cool his neck. "Did I? As I explained, I'm sworn to secrecy on that matter."

"You made sure I considered the benefactor could be female. *Was* female."

"I'm not sure that's *exactly* what I said—"

"I think you know I believed my aunt and uncle had made

the gift. So, I thanked them for being so generous. But—as I'm sure you can guess—they were mystified by my words."

"As your benefactor wants to remain anonymous, I would expect him, or her, to deny knowledge."

"Yes, that's what I thought at first. But, Mr. Tanner, this is just the preamble to the heart of the story."

Tanner looked at her steadily.

"At the Governor's Ball, I was introduced to Mr. Jacob Alexander Van Bergen."

This prompted a coughing fit that Tanner had difficulty bringing under control. He covered his mouth with his handkerchief and Ginny thought she could see spots of blood.

"I see you know the gentleman," Ginny murmured.

She waited for Tanner to fold away the handkerchief before she continued.

"There was a striking resemblance to Lex Carlton, once resident of our town. This led to a conversation during which the full extent of his influence on my life was revealed."

Tanner sat forward on his chair. "The *full* extent?"

Ginny felt uncomfortable causing Tanner distress. She tried a smile. "So, you see, I am the bearer of good news. You must be the keeper of many secrets in this town, but I sense that knowledge of my benefactor was a burden to you. Perhaps one duplicity too many. Now we both know to whom I owe my good fortune, you need no longer keep it secret."

Tanner took a handkerchief from a different pocket and dabbed the seeds of sweat gathered on his brow. "You are right, my dear girl. I am much relieved. It didn't sit well with me. I'm at a stage of life where I want to slough off cares and secrets. Although you must understand, it was the only way I could see of the farm being secured for you and Mary Lou."

Ginny sat back in her chair and whistled out a long breath. She closed her eyes. At last, she knew. What she had suspected for the past week was confirmed.

She stared again at Tanner, her fingers nervously tapping on the wood of her chair. Now she craved to understand every detail. What exactly had happened? And why?

"How did it come about?" Her voice was husky.

Tanner gulped his whiskey. "First time Lex told me who he was, I didn't believe him. I daresay you had difficulty reconciling the two."

She snorted at the memory. "Indeed I did."

"I mean, even now I'm not sure how to refer to him. Lex Carlton or Mr. Van Bergen."

"But how did he get you to act for him? As agent."

"He was very persuasive."

Ginny smiled ruefully. "I remember you saying my benefactor is used to getting their own way."

Tanner puffed out his cheeks. "Now you see what I mean. Jacob Alexander Van Bergen. Goodness me. Who'd have thought it? I did lots of checks, of course. Made sure the money transfers were legal tender. My, the telegram wires blazed hot for a couple of days."

Ginny frowned. "And why be so secretive?"

"Many reasons. For one thing, if word had gotten out that a Van Bergen was bidding for the land, it would have pushed the price sky-high. Business folk wondering what he knew. Maybe guess a new railroad was planned."

"But... but he paid far more than the farm was worth anyway."

"Property is worth what someone is willing to pay for it. No more. No less. And Mr. Van Bergen wanted to secure the property. Between you and me—and I know this rather detracts from the generosity of his act—I don't think it seemed such a huge amount of money. From his point of view."

Ginny thought of the tract of land they had visited in Little Dixie. Her farm would have been swallowed up in such a large plantation.

"But why keep it secret from me?" This was what was puzzling Ginny. She had accused him of being dishonorable as they had returned to the steamboat. She remembered his angry response. The obvious thing would have been to tell her then about the purchase.

Tanner sighed and thought about this question. "I think you touched upon the issue yourself in this very room. You didn't want to be obligated to someone in the future. To owe someone something. That's why at first you didn't want to sign for the freehold. I think he understood that about you. Your need for independence. He wanted to keep it hidden so you would never feel beholden to him."

A thumping began in Ginny's chest, like when the air had rushed past her on that train ride, all those years before. She had got him all wrong. Keeping it secret was his way of being honorable.

"Which makes me wonder why he told you the truth about the purchase," Tanner mused. "After he'd bound me to secrecy."

Ginny bit her lip. "He didn't exactly tell me. It was more that I worked it out."

"But... you said he had told you."

"I have been learning from you, Mr. Tanner. I may have implied things that weren't strictly true."

Tanner allowed a smile to creep over his cheeks. "I have confirmed something Mr. Van Bergen hadn't actually said?"

Ginny put her fingertips to her temples. She was feeling slightly nauseous and having difficulty putting the different pieces together. "But if Lex—Mr. Van Bergen—never wanted me to know he had made the purchase, why did he buy the farm at all?"

Tanner leaned forward and the skin around his eyes softened. "Isn't it obvious, my dear?"

"Not to me."

"He cares for you. Deeply."

Ginny hoped Tanner wouldn't notice the heat rising in her chest and up her neck.

"He said that?"

"He didn't need to," said Tanner softly.

They sat in silence for a while.

"I'm wondering perhaps whether the feelings are reciprocated?" asked Tanner, a twinkle in his eye.

Ginny let out a groan. "Even if they were, there's no point any more. When I first saw him at the Governor's mansion, it was like... being thrown off a horse. I was winded. I accused him of being a confidence trickster."

"Oh." Tanner nodded and steepled his fingers.

"An' then I got very angry with him. I said I would send his gifts back."

"Gifts?"

Ginny nodded.

"But surely Lex didn't give up so easily?"

"He didn't. He invited me on a trip to visit a plantation the next day. When we parted, I told him I never wanted to see him again." Ginny's eyes filled with tears. "After all, even if his intentions *were* honorable, I could never fit into his world. We're too different. It wouldn't take long for him to realize that. He accepted my demands and promised never to contact me again."

"Ah. This explains the letter I received a few days ago. I had wondered." Tanner opened the draw and pulled out a letter. Ginny recognized the handwriting. "It's from Mr. Van Bergen as I'm sure you've guessed. He says he's finished his business in Missouri and has returned to Boston. He asks me to keep an eye on your well-being because he won't be returning West."

Ginny's mouth went dry. Of course he had left. She had asked him and he had promised. "Maybe I could do with that whiskey you offered earlier."

Tanner struggled to his feet, poured her a glass and refilled his own. Ginny breathed in the unfamiliar fumes and felt lightheaded.

Instead of returning behind the desk, Tanner pulled out a ladder-back chair and sat close to Ginny. "I'm gonna tell you something I haven't spoken about for thirty years. When I was a young man, I fell in love. Crazy about her. Thought of her night and day. She was an Osage girl. Long, straight black hair, eyes which looked into my soul. And she loved me back. Said she was willing to leave her people for me. But I was a coward. I was afraid of what people might say. I told myself it was to protect her. My folks wouldn't treat her with respect. Truth was, I worried about myself, that it was me they wouldn't respect.

"So I left her. Moved on. Pretended I'd forgotten about her. But there's not a day I don't regret that decision. I wake up alone. I eat alone."

Tanner's eyes seemed to focus on something far behind Ginny. "I went back to the same place ten years after. Her people had been moved on by then, of course. But I asked after her and an old timer remembered and showed me her grave."

Tanner took a slug of whiskey. "When Bill Mack told me I was dying, a weight went from my shoulders. Finally I'll get to be with her again."

Tanner leaned forward and took Ginny's hands.

"My point is this, Geneviève. The man who sat in this room and insisted I buy Snow Farm loved you. Loved you with the fire I remembered having for my Osage girl. But if you've got him to promise never to see you again, he's gonna stick with that. He's that sort of man. So it's down to you. If you love him—and I think you do—I'm begging, don't make the mistake I made. Don't let the differences between you keep you apart."

Ginny sniffed and slid a tear away from below her eye with her forefinger. "I could... I could try writing to him?"

Tanner shook his head. "He might allow himself to think he's protecting you from the gilded cage of life as a Van Bergen."

"So what can I do?"

"Do you love him?"

Ginny nodded. She had told Maddie that she wasn't sure how she felt about him. But this past week, knowing she would never see him again, it was the torture of having loved and lost.

"Then there's only one thing you can do. Go to Boston, find him and tell him."

PART 4

FORTY-SEVEN

ST. LOUIS, MISSOURI—AUGUST 1875

A Black porter opened the door to the ladies' car. Ginny took a breath in surprise: the train was as well appointed as a hotel lobby, with ornate oil lamps hanging from the high ceiling and carved wooden panels on the walls.

"I've put your trunk in the luggage car, ma'am," said the porter.

"Thank you, er—"

"George. Call me George."

Ginny hoped she was not stepping dirt into the carpet as she made her way down the aisle to an upholstered seat midway down the carriage. It was a far cry from the bone-shaking train journey from Brownsville the day before, where there was no separate provision for ladies. There, her shoe had crunched on nut shells as she'd edged into a window seat, trying not to make eye contact with any of the men, glad she had her father's Smith & Wesson in her pocketbook. The car had filled with tobacco smoke. When a man had peeled an orange and offered her a piece, she had politely refused; he had dropped the skin onto the wooden floor.

Although this was called the ladies' car, there were a good

number of men accompanying wives or mothers. Ginny was relieved to see some women traveling alone. A matronly woman in her sixties sat on the other side of the aisle; a husband and wife settled in the seat opposite Ginny and introduced themselves. The train pulled out of St. Louis at twenty minutes past seven in the morning, crossing the wide Mississippi on the Eads Bridge.

Ginny had spent the previous night in a boarding house owned by a relative of Bertha Hofmann. Mrs. Hofmann had also written down the name of a respectable hotel in Boston. There seemed to be a network of German hoteliers across the country. Ginny had been surprised when Mrs. Hofmann had helped with the recommendation. She had not told anyone other than Mary Lou about the trip. Apparently, Tanner had been uncharacteristically indiscreet. Ginny had thanked Bertha profusely.

"We were always willing to help you, *Schätzchen*," said Bertha. "You just seemed to push the town away. Now, you go snaffle up that handsome young man."

In no time at all, it seemed the whole of Brownsville knew that the farmhand who had been with them over the past year was a Van Bergen. Bertha had declared in Gibbes Mercantile that she had suspected all along, something met with a skeptical raised eyebrow by her friend Harriet Gibbes.

Ginny had told Mary Lou the story—or as much of it as she felt able. Lex Carlton had gifted them the farm and she really *had* to travel to Boston to thank him. Mary Lou had replied that she was not stupid: a letter or even a telegram might do the job. This was an affair of the heart. She set to thinking how to make sure Ginny would not feel the need to hurry back, should things progress as they all secretly hoped.

It was Amos Sturge who came up with the solution for the management of the farm. Isiah Boone's wife had recently had their first child. They were looking for steady work, something where his wife could be nearby. Amos suggested Isiah and his family move into Snow Farm for as long as was needed, along with Mary Lou. He knew Ginny and Mary Lou did not have the color prejudices still found in pockets in the area. The Boones would get a cut of the profits for the year, rather than being paid by the day, with board and lodging. Mary Lou was happy with the proposal, particularly as she kept her kitchen and bedroom, and once Isiah had been assured this was not a sharecropping arrangement, he agreed.

Mary Lou had helped Ginny pack. It was hard to decide how much to take and what to prepare for. The journey to Boston would take three days, but Ginny had no idea how long she would stay. If things went badly, she might be on the first train back. Women's clothing was such that traveling light was impossible at the best of times. Mary Lou had insisted on packing the white ball gown. "They're rich," she had said, "you might need this dress so you look the part."

Ginny stared out of the window, mesmerized by the landscape passing so fast. Colors changed as the sun rose and moved across the sky. She was thrilled by the sensation of speed. The constant movement had been disconcerting to begin with, but as she got used to it, she was soothed by the rocking.

The husband and wife opposite were friendly and happy to talk.

"Your first time on a train?" the lady asked.

"I've been to St. Louis before. But this is my first time further east. And my first on a Pullman."

"Wonderful, isn't it? Smarter than a hotel. My husband works for the railroad."

"How interesting." Ginny thought of Lex and the Van Bergen business and hoped it might be useful to learn what she could.

The man was pleased to have an opening to talk about his work. "I'm an engineer. Bridges mostly."

He explained the processes used in the newly completed Eads Bridge. He then moved on to the benefits of the line they were using.

"They have re-laid almost the entire track and made it thoroughly ballasted. Means there's none of them clouds of dust you usually get."

"Dear, she's only been on a train once before." The woman laid her hand on his arm.

The gentleman was in full flow now. "Lots of lines, you get a sort of seasickness from the carriage moving around. Not on these, though."

"Why's that?"

"It's the wheels. Other carriages have compromise wheels to accommodate narrow or wide tracks. This line means we have wheels that don't slide around."

The car jerked its way over some points and they all ignored the evidence which seemed to be disproving the man's information.

"And they're made of paper."

"Oh, come now. You are teasing me, sir," Ginny said with a smile.

The man grinned. "There's lots of pieces of paper crushed together and that goes in the center of the wheel. Makes everything much smoother and quieter."

Eventually, the woman could see that her husband was wearying Ginny.

"Would you accompany me to the powder room at the end of the car?" Ginny's new friend whispered. Her face must have conveyed surprise because the lady leaned closer. "They don't have locks on the door. If you stand guard for me, I'll return the favor."

. . .

The couple invited Ginny to join them in the dining car. The bill of fare had a wide range of dishes. Ginny ordered a lamb chop and tomato sauce.

"That will be seventy-five cents," said the waiter.

Tanner had insisted Ginny had plenty of cash. Enough for the ticket to Boston, of course—and the ticket back in case the gamble didn't come off. Then cash for food, a hotel. Tanner had an inkling she might need extra for new clothes.

Ginny handed over a dollar bill and put the change in her pocketbook. She would need to keep track of things.

The couple ordered their food.

"And, George, bring the wine list," said the husband.

Ginny whispered to the woman, "I don't think that waiter is George."

The woman smiled condescendingly. "All the porters and waiters are Black. And they're all called George. I guess it's simpler that way."

They returned to the ladies' car for the afternoon and pulled the blinds halfway down to keep the sun out. The view seemed unchanged from when they had left to take lunch.

"How fast are we traveling?" Ginny asked the gentleman.

"My, by now we must be covering thirty miles every hour. A wonder, is it not?"

Ginny watched the horizon, which seemed to be a fixed object held at arm's length, while the fields and trees nearby rolled past.

When they returned from their evening meal, the car had been transformed. The pairs of seats were pulled together to make a bed. Above, the ornate wooden panels had been released from the ceiling and swung down to make a second bunk above. Each bed had fresh linen and white pillows.

Ginny found that the night was surprisingly comfortable. The train stopped occasionally, each time jolting Ginny back awake, but that was the worst of it. The motion soothed her, and the rhythmical beat of the wheels covered the snores and snorts of her fellow passengers.

Her friends left the train at Leavittsburg, but by then Ginny felt like a seasoned traveler. She scanned through newspapers left behind on seats, watched the landscape slowly change, and dozed.

Around four o'clock on the third day, the buildings began to alter. Villages grew into towns. Long factory buildings hugged close to the tracks, belching smoke. Ginny caught her first glimpse of the ocean: pewter, flat and melting into the sky. It was not blue as she had imagined from reading books.

The train crossed the river and into the heart of Boston. Passengers who had been luxuriating in the Pullman car burst into a flurry of activity as they gathered their belongings. Ginny held back, now wishing her friends from the journey were still here to show her what to do.

Stepping down from the car, Ginny looked around her; she had never been in such a large space. The roof was high but filled with smoke. All was noise: wheels squealing on iron tracks, the metallic chink as cars joined each other, men shouting instructions, a long high-pitched whistle. Families greeted each other after long times apart, porters wove between passengers, pushing trolleys loaded with luggage.

Everyone was leaving the platform, so Ginny followed the crowd to the entrance area. The building was pretending to be a baronial hall: tall windows with gothic arches, a roof made of wooden spans and buttresses. Sounds echoed around her as people dashed to and fro. Ginny's excitement had disappeared and was replaced by anxiety that she was deeply out of place.

A porter appeared with her trunk on a trolley. She followed him outside, hurrying to keep up, fearful of losing him and her luggage in the mêlée. He waved the next cab forward. Ginny told the driver the name of her hotel and the porter helped Ginny inside. She slipped a coin into his hand and the horse jolted forwards before she was properly settled.

Boston was different from everything she had imagined. The buildings were much taller than in St. Louis, the streets narrower. She wondered how on earth she would find Lex among this multitude.

What if this had been one big mistake? Now that Lex was back in the world where he had grown up, maybe he'd seen the folly of marrying a country girl. Maybe she should buy a ticket for the next train back.

The cab soon pulled up. "Muhlenberg Guest House," the driver called out.

Ginny looked up at a terrace of tall houses. The sign at the bottom of a steep stoop made it clear this establishment was for ladies only. The inside window shutters were closed, making the building seem cloistered from the outside world.

Ginny persuaded the driver to take her trunk to the top step before he dashed off for his next fare. She reached up to the large knocker in the middle of the wooden door. She looked at the rough skin on her fingers and the traces of mud wedged under her nails no matter how hard she scrubbed. There was no mistaking she was from a farm. Ginny pulled her gloves back on; at least she could hide the truth for a while.

FORTY-EIGHT

By the next morning, Ginny had gathered up her courage. She thought of Tanner's words, his urging of her to take a chance. She thought of Bertha Hofmann providing unexpected help, of Amos Sturge, of the Boones looking after Mary Lou. She thought most of her sister, so honest and true. Ginny had come all this way; she had nothing to lose but her pride. And pride would be cold comfort if she lived the rest of her life regretting that she had not found Lex and told him the truth about her feelings.

Ginny breakfasted in the front room of the guest house, where a number of lone women were staying. It was run by a large, dowdy woman who could have been a sister of Bertha Hofmann.

"I wonder if you might help me," Ginny asked as a plate of eggs was laid in front of her. "I'm looking for Mr. Van Bergen."

The landlady raised an eyebrow. "Van Bergen?"

"Have you heard of him?"

The woman chuckled. "Hard to miss."

"Do you know where I might find him?"

"The Van Bergens have lots of businesses here. Do you

want one of the warehouses? Their office? Perhaps the new Van Bergen Women's Hospital?"

"I... I don't know. I hadn't realized there would be different places. Perhaps I should start at the office. Is it far?"

"Less than a mile. I can send a boy to find you a cab."

"Please, don't trouble yourself. A mile will take no time at all to walk."

The landlady pursed her lips. "I'll draw you a map."

In less than an hour, Ginny was on the streets in central Boston, the piece of paper gripped in her gloved hand. Mary Lou had adapted her favorite burgundy skirt into a fashionable shape, over which she buttoned her fitted jacket with a long peplum spread over the bustle. Around her shoulders, she pulled the shawl Lex had sent her, as if a shield from the uncertainty ahead. She tried to keep her unruly hair in place under the black hat that Madeleine had gifted her.

The only indication that it was a port city was the smell of salt on the morning air. The buildings were so tall, Ginny felt she could barely see the sky. Everything looked new-built: stone and brick edifices stood four or five stories high, casting shade across one half of the road. The buildings matched each other, windows in a row from block to block, unlike the structures of any shape and size thrown up in Brownsville.

The sidewalk was firm underfoot, but the streets were strewn with horse dung, the earthy smell released as carriage wheels rushed through the mess. Ginny wondered how the carriages managed to avoid each other as so many hurtled down the streets. A road to the left opened up and she could see the mast and booms of a sailing ship in harbor. She stopped to stare and a man nearly walked into her. Apologizing, she turned her attention to weaving her way down the sidewalk. Men walked as quickly as they could, heads down and purposeful.

She navigated her way from church spire to spire, each white and needle-like, declaring their ability to withstand the changes of time. With each landmark, her chest tightened, knowing she must be coming closer to her destination. She came to an area where the streets opened up, some even had trees planted at intervals along the center. Seagulls squawked overhead.

Ginny reached the building the hotel owner had described: an imposing structure in gray stone with colonnades leading the eye up to the mansard roof. It was so substantial, it took her breath away. There was a frieze the width of the building above the first floor, with the words VAN BERGEN carved into the stone so they would last for a hundred years.

She had tried to practice in her head what she would say, but nothing seemed right. For the past four days, she had hoped words would come to her. But here she was, still not sure how she would express her thoughts and feelings.

Taking a deep breath, Ginny went up the steps and into the lobby. The space was cool and gleamed with dark wood. She approached a man behind a desk.

"I'm looking for Mr. Van Bergen."

The man narrowed his eyes. "Which one?"

Of course. There were twin brothers. "Alexander. Mr. Jacob Alexander Van Bergen."

The man slid his eyes down her body. Ginny tried to smooth the fabric of her skirt.

"You have an appointment?"

"No."

"What is this in relation to?"

Ginny cleared her throat. "A private matter."

Now a sneer appeared on the man's face and Ginny's skin began to prickle.

"This is a place of business. I suggest you take private matters elsewhere."

Ginny felt small and embarrassed. She turned toward the door, at a loss for what to try next. But she had come all this way. She was not going to let an officious little man stand in her way. She turned back to him.

"I see there is a seat over there. I am gonna sit in it and stay put until you tell Mr. Van Bergen I am here."

Without waiting for a reply, she sat in the chair.

The man bristled but went into the office behind. He re-emerged with an older man who stood in the doorway. She watched them whisper and felt both men's eyes upon her. Clearly they were weighing up whether she would create a scene, and if that would be worse than alerting their employer.

The older man came forward and made a slight bow. "Your name?"

"Miss Snow."

"Follow me upstairs."

Ginny's heels clicked on the marble steps. They reached a second lobby, which was divided from the main part of the floor by a wooden wall to waist height with glazing above. Through the glass, she could see a large hall, far plainer than the entrance foyer below. The steady hum from so many men was like the sound when she took the top off her beehive. Some were on high stools, hunched over desks, others stood, gathered around tables.

"Stay here," the man instructed Ginny, and he opened the door into the main area. The hum grew louder.

Ginny was drawn to the glass and watched the man walk to a group around a table at the far end. Her stomach clenched as she recognized Lex's dark hair as he leaned over a large piece of paper on the table. He wore a beige vest over a white shirt, his sleeves rolled up in that way she remembered. He pointed to something and spoke to the man to his left. Pushing back his hair, she recognized it as a movement he made when frustrated with something.

The older man had reached the table and stood behind Lex, leaning close to whisper in his ear. Lex frowned and seemed to be checking something with the man. The older man nodded toward the lobby. Lex stood completely still for a moment. He threw a comment to the men at the table and motioned with his hand for the older man to remain. Then he strode across the room, his jaw locked firm and his mouth a straight line.

Ginny's heart sank. Oh God, why had she come? Seeing him so at ease in this setting, why did she ever think he would want her? And now he was angry, perhaps exasperated. Why had she been so stupid to open this heartache again? She moved to the other side of the lobby, wondering if it was too late to flee back down the stairs.

Lex stood in the doorway and stared at her. His eyes blazed as they moved over her face and body, but he did not speak.

Ginny swallowed. "I..." No words came. Her mouth was dry.

She turned to the stairs, but in two strides Lex was beside her, catching her arm to draw her back.

"I'm sorry," she whispered. "I should never have come." She looked up at him, locked in place by his slate-gray eyes. And then, suddenly, he was kissing her.

She gasped and moved her head away, mortified that his employees might see them. But he pulled her to him and she found she was kissing him back, her fingers tracing the slight stubble on his jaw. He drew her closer, and her body melted against his, remembering the smell of his cologne and sweat.

He stopped and leaned his back against the wall, his hands on her hips, pulling her to him. She rested her hands on his chest and he leaned his forehead against hers.

"I thought I'd never see you again," he murmured. "You being here... Is something wrong? Mary Lou? The farm?"

Ginny shook her head. "No. Nothing's wrong. I just... I needed to say some things to you."

"You came all the way to Boston—to say something?" He half smiled and she heard the teasing laughter in his voice.

"Well, it's pretty important. At least, it is to me."

Footsteps grew louder coming up the stairs. Ginny stepped away from him, looking down at the floor. Lex pushed himself upright and put a suitable distance between them.

"Let's find somewhere more private to talk. Wait here a moment."

He returned to the hall, rolling down his sleeves and grabbing his coat and hat. He threw some words at the men around the table, who looked mystified.

The older man returned to the lobby and coughed.

Ginny felt her cheeks burning, but before she could think about what had just happened, Lex was with her, guiding her down the stairs and out onto the street.

He tucked her arm into the crook of his elbow and, without speaking, walked briskly down the sidewalk, then across the street, dodging the horse-drawn cabs, down a couple more blocks.

Ginny stopped dead. There was a field of rubble and stone. A chimney breast stood tall with part of its original wall, scarred black. The front of a building tottered, unsupported by side walls, light shining through the empty spaces where once there were windows.

Lex finally spoke. "The fire."

"I had no idea it was so devastating."

"Boston's done a good job. Nearly all rebuilt in just a few years. You get used to these remaining pockets. Sorry, I shouldn't have brought you this way."

He turned back, past a church and over a wide road into a park.

"This is where I wanted to bring you. Boston Common. What folks round here think of as open countryside. But we know different."

She looked up and caught his wink. The grass was neat and paths straight, with couples promenading, parasols protecting the ladies from the increasing heat. Ginny stared at the golden dome soaring above the State House.

"Sure is something, isn't it?" Lex said, before leading Ginny to a wooded area away from the crowds. He found a bench below an oak tree and Ginny sat. She peeled off her gloves and unpinned the hat and placed them carefully on the bench.

"Now," said Lex softly. "What was so important that you spent three days on a train to come here and tell me?"

FORTY-NINE

Lex resisted the urge to sit even closer to her. It was strange seeing her in city clothes, in the noise and bustle of Boston. Her eyes seemed bigger than before, and she reminded him of a deer finding itself alone in a forest.

When his office manager had whispered "Miss Snow" into his ear, he had thought it was a slippage between an imaginary world and the real one. When he had realized she truly was standing in the lobby, different emotions had fought inside him. Anger. She had made him promise never to contact her again. He had kept his word, no matter how much pain it had caused him since saying goodbye in Jefferson City. Would he have to go through all that anguish again? Then a wave of fear. What could be so wrong that she had traveled here and tracked him down?

Seeing her standing at the top of the stairs, a different emotion had hit, one he was not particularly proud of: an intense desire. She was the most beautiful woman he had ever known. Her skin glowed from her active life, a world away from the drawing rooms of Boston, where ladies avoided the elements. Kissing her had been a visceral reaction.

But, sitting here now, under this tree, he knew he must be gentle, give her time. Wisps of her dark-gold hair had loosened when she removed her hat and caressed her neck. Her response to his ardent kiss made him hopeful, but he had taken missteps with her in the past. He sat sideways, his left shoulder leaning against the back of the bench so he could drink her in, his left leg tucked up on the bench. She sat like she was in church, her hands together, her eyes fixed on the earth in front.

"I'd like to apologize." Her voice was tentative.

"Whatever for?" An apology wasn't what he expected.

"Being so rude in Jefferson City. Not just the ball. Afterwards as well."

"It was my fault, I should have had the courage to say something earlier. When I was writing—"

She put up her hand. "No, please, I need to say all this, no matter how hard. My head back then was so mixed up. I'd become attached to Lex Carlton. You know that, I'm sure. I believed you had serious intentions. But I couldn't for the life of me think of a reason why Jacob Alexander Van Bergen would be interested. I didn't know who you were. You know, inside."

He moved a fraction closer. "What changed?"

"Finding out that it was you who bought the farm."

"Oh." Lex was wrong-footed. "I thought my instructions to Mr. Tanner were clear on that."

"Don't blame Tanner. I kinda worked it out for myself. But the point is—you didn't mention it in Jefferson City. My independence is important to me, you know that. You could have made me feel, well, obligated. But you said nothing. Tanner convinced me your feelings were true." She sighed. "But by then it was too late. I'd said I never wanted to see you again. And chasing after you would make me look like a forty-niner on a rumor of gold."

Lex grinned. "But you *are* here. So something must have happened."

"Tanner encouraged me to roll the dice. And I know this is likely too late. That you are settled in Boston, maybe even found someone new. Lord knows there were enough mothers parading their daughters in front of you at the Governor's Ball. Daresay it's much the same for you here."

Lex laughed, but again Ginny moved her hand to indicated she wouldn't be interrupted.

"But I had to say it, to your face. And if it's all too late, I can travel on home, but at least know I'd had the guts to try."

"Say what?"

Ginny hesitated so Lex took her hand and spoke.

"Because I'm happy to say it first. That I loved you under those Missouri skies and I love you still."

She looked straight at him, her eyes bright. "You are the first thing I think of when I wake, the last thing at night. I love you, Lex."

Lex leaned in and his lips brushed hers, more gently than before. He closed his eyes and absorbed the smell of her, the taste of her. He ached to be with her as she laid her head in the dip below his shoulder. He held her close and watched the sun making patterns through the oak leaves.

"How would you feel about a wedding very soon? Since coming back to Boston, I've been sleepwalking. I want to wake up and start living again."

She threaded her fingers through his. "I'd wed you tomorrow if it were legal."

He laughed. "Where are you staying?"

"Muhlenberg Guest House near the station."

"I'll get your things collected and brought to the house."

Ginny sat up and looked at him, a line between her brows.

"You'll be staying at my home from now on," Lex said. "Suddenly introducing you as my fiancée to my mother isn't going to be easy. I admit that. But Phoebe will help smooth things over. My sister."

Ginny bit her lip. "Maybe it would be best if I stayed elsewhere until your mother is used to the idea."

"Best get things over with, when it comes to my mother," he said, getting up.

She stared at him, her eyes wide. "What, *now*?"

He pulled her to her feet. "'Fraid so. You happy to walk?"

He put her arm back into his elbow, pulling her closer this time and strolling at a leisurely pace. They turned toward the State House and walked up Beacon Hill to his home.

FIFTY

They reached a tree-lined elongated square with a patch of grass corralled behind metal railings. On either side was a run of tall houses made of burnt-sienna brick. Lex stopped at the house at the end of the row. Ginny looked up at it: a wide door with an elegant fanlight above. The house was only three windows wide, but the two windows to the right were part of a graceful curve which extended the whole five stories.

"It's so *tall*," Ginny said.

"Land is Boston's most precious resource. Have to build up because we can't build out."

"It's simpler than I expected." She glanced at Lex, worried he would be insulted. "After Aunt Josephine's house in Jefferson City, I mean."

"Bostonians think it's bad taste to be too showy." He all but danced up the steps. Pausing at the door, he whispered, "And it's not our *only* house."

She looked up at him and caught his wink and that half-smile she loved. It gave her courage to face whatever was inside this imposing Boston building.

A manservant met them in the hall and took Lex's hat.

"Where's Mother, Crouch?"

"About to take tea in the garden room, sir. Miss Van Bergen is there too."

He took Ginny's hand. "That will make things easier. Now, Mother knows nothing of you and this is not gonna be easy, but it's better if we just face it head-on. Like branding a wayward steer."

Ginny didn't quite suppress a laugh. "I'm not sure you should be speaking of your mother that way."

Ginny followed him past a curving staircase and down the corridor to the back of the house. Another giggle escaped from her. Lex looked back and raised an eyebrow.

"I just realized. I'm about to join a Boston tea party."

"That's the spirit." He grinned and pushed open the door.

Ginny was surprised by how airy the garden room was, with light refracting from gilt mirrors. The teal wallpaper was painted with intertwined vines.

An older woman sat near the French window, beyond which was the garden. She was dressed in black silk.

"Mother." Lex crossed to her and kissed her on both cheeks.

"Alexander. What brings you home so early?"

As he straightened up, her eyes fell on Ginny standing near the door.

"And Phoebe." Lex went to the davenport desk on the other side of the room and kissed the top of his sister's head. He returned to Ginny. "Mother, I'd like to introduce Miss Geneviève Snow. My fiancée."

Ginny felt all the air had been sucked out of the room. She took a few steps forward and put out her hand to the stern-looking woman. "I am so pleased to meet you, Mrs. Van Bergen."

The lady stared at Ginny blankly, ignoring the outstretched hand, before returning her steely gaze to Lex. "Alexander? What on God's good earth are you talking about?"

Lex turned to his sister who had risen from her chair. "And this is my favorite sister—"

"Only sister—"

"—Phoebe."

She was a feminine version of Lex: dark hair, a warm smile. She wore a Prussian blue gown with a square neck and her throat was milky white. "Did you say Miss Snow? I've heard so much about you."

"You have?" Ginny's tone betrayed her surprise.

"Alexander was always talking about you." Phoebe came forward and shook Ginny's hand. "Until suddenly he stopped, the last time he returned from the Midwest."

Ginny felt blood rising to her cheeks. She doubted Lex had anything good to say about her.

"But he didn't say that you were his fiancée now."

Mrs. Van Bergen thumped the arm of her chair. "*I* haven't heard a word about you."

Phoebe turned on a sweet smile. "Well, Mother, why don't you invite her to sit and have tea with us? Then you can find out all about her."

Mrs. Van Bergen grunted. "Alexander, go tell Smith to bring extra things. And you, sit there by the window so I can get a good look at you."

Lex and Ginny each did as they were told. Ginny felt like a steer at Brownsville cattle market and it was not pleasant at all.

"Snow, you say? I don't recognize the name."

"My father, Elijah Snow, died some years back. He was a farmer. In Missouri."

Mrs. Van Bergen looked like she was sucking a lemon. "Missouri? Not Boston?"

"No, ma'am."

"And your mother?"

"Also dead."

"How unfortunate. But *she* was from Boston." Mrs. Van

Bergen made a statement rather than a question, as if it were impossible for there to be no Boston connection.

"No. She grew up in Louisiana. Her father was Gabriel LeRoux. A sugar plantation owner."

"Louisiana?" The tone suggested Ginny had come from the moon. She wished she could escape into the small garden where the flowers and shrubs beyond the glass bobbed seductively in the light breeze. Or, at the very least, open the French window to get some air.

Lex returned to the room and his mother fixed her cold eyes on him.

"We have *never* had Southern folk in our family."

"I'm not sure you can call Missouri the south... " said Lex.

"Nor Westerners neither," said Mrs. Van Bergen, patting her gray hair.

"What can I say, Mother?" Lex shrugged. "It's a new and exciting world."

Phoebe laughed, but Ginny was feeling uncomfortable under his mother's scrutiny.

"When did you arrive?" asked Phoebe.

"Yesterday."

"But, Alexander, why didn't you tell us she was coming? I would have loved to go to the station to meet her."

He sat in a chair near his sister, and glanced over to Ginny, uncertain how to answer. "Things weren't entirely fixed."

Mrs. Van Bergen's voice rang out. "And how long have you known each other?"

"We first met last year," said Lex, "in February."

"But I know nothing of her. Nothing!"

"Which is why I have invited Ginny to stay here, rather than at a hotel. I'll arrange for her things to be brought."

"How wonderful!" said Phoebe. "We can talk books. I hear you are a great reader. And perhaps you could play the piano for us."

Ginny's mouth fell open slightly. Lex really had spoken about her. She glanced over at him and he smiled in that way he did when he was slightly embarrassed, chewing one side of his lip.

A maid entered with the tea things.

"Right," said Phoebe, taking charge while her mother sulked. "Let's get you something to drink."

"The Rose Room." Phoebe opened the door to the guest room on the fourth floor. The windows in the bow looked out over the small park. "I guess your things will be delivered soon from your hotel. But if you only arrived in Boston yesterday, you might still be tired from the journey? Perhaps you'd like a rest. Take a nap."

Ginny was about to explain that she was used to working long hours and three days sitting on a train was a luxury. But she did not want to rebuff Phoebe's considerate gesture and agreed to the idea.

"I'll come back up and fetch you in an hour."

Ginny wandered over to the bow. Beacon Hill was the highest part of the city and she looked out over the roofs. The houses seemed tucked together.

She went back to the bed and sat on the edge. The mattress was soft and the bed wider than any she had experienced. She might as well give this a go, she thought, untying her boots. She lay back on the bed and sleep swept over her.

Woken by the knocking, Ginny rolled over to see Phoebe's head popped round the door.

"Ah, you're awake. At last," said Phoebe.

"What time is it?"

"Almost time for dinner."

Ginny swung her legs over the side of the bed and sat up. "I'm so sorry. I had no idea—"

"Don't worry. It gave Alexander a chance to calm Mother down."

Not the best of starts—to have her future mother-in-law need to recover from the shock of meeting her. This visit to Boston was not at all how she had imagined it; but then she hadn't known what to expect. There had been every chance she would have been on the first train home. And now, here she was, staying in Lex's home.

She glanced in the mirror. Her hair looked as if she'd spent the day on a horse. She unpinned and brushed it and then twisted the full length to curl and fix it back on to the top of her head.

Phoebe handed her the hair grips. "The good thing is he's had a chance to speak to Thaddeus and Florence. They always have their evening meal here."

Ginny rubbed her temple. "Thaddeus..."

"Our brother and his wife." Phoebe looked at Ginny's reflection. "Better get going. Mother hates people to be late for dinner."

FIFTY-ONE

The family was already gathered in the dining room as Ginny entered. It was a large room at the back of the house with two sets of French windows looking out over the walled garden.

"This is my brother, Thaddeus," said Lex.

Although Lex's twin, the dark hair was the only similarity between the brothers. Thaddeus' face was fleshier, his lips fuller. He put out a hand with an air of expecting it to be kissed, like a supplicant kissing the ring on a royal finger.

"My wife, Florence."

So this was the woman Lex had been engaged to, the woman who had moved her affections from Lex to Thaddeus. It was a shock to see a figure from a photograph the year before come to life. Ginny immediately recognized a lady of fashion. Florence's hair was the color of champagne and carefully coiffured on top of her head, held in place by a jeweled flower. A black choker matched with pendant earrings emphasized her ivory neck. Her dress was navy blue and Ginny realized the family must still be in mourning for Lex's father.

Florence put out her hand and made the slightest of handshakes. Ginny was startled by the green eyes fixed firmly on her own. Florence's mouth was a thin line and Ginny could detect no emotion.

"Delighted to—" Ginny began, but Florence had already turned to her place at the dining table. Was this a deliberate snub?

"Let's not wait any longer," said Mrs. Van Bergen, sitting at the head of the table.

Ginny hurried to sit next to Lex and found herself opposite Thaddeus. The chair at the other end of the table remained empty.

As the first course of soup was served, Thaddeus reported on his day's work. "And everything is in place for the Minister of Public Works' dinner, Mother?"

"Of course."

"We must secure the Canadian contract for the future of the Van Bergen business. There are plenty of other companies courting him."

"Do stop going on about it, Thaddeus. This may be our first social event since your father died, but remember I have been hosting dinners since I was a young woman."

"Of course, Mother." Ginny noticed the briefest of looks heavenward.

"And I will be here to make sure everything goes smoothly," said Florence, smiling at her husband.

It wasn't until the main course of ham and vegetables that Thaddeus turned his attention to Ginny.

"My brother says you own a ranch."

"Yes. More of a farm."

"How big?"

"One hundred and forty acres."

"Small, then."

Ginny looked Thaddeus in the eye. "Adequate to our needs."

"You said your father is dead," said Mrs. Van Bergen. "Who manages the farm?"

"I manage it myself, along with my sister."

Florence smirked as she helped herself to another piece of ham. "How unconventional."

"Tell us about your sister," said Phoebe.

"Marie-Louise is fifteen."

"What are her interests?"

"I suppose you could call it homemaking. She is an excellent cook."

Florence spoke under her breath but loud enough for Ginny to hear. "Perhaps she could share some recipes with our housekeeper."

"You both have French names," said Mrs. Van Bergen. "Perhaps an affectation of Mrs. Snow."

"Mother," growled Lex in a warning tone.

Ginny pretended to ignore the slight to her mother. She breathed in through her nose. "As I said, my grandfather was Gabriel LeRoux. *His* father was from Grenoble in France."

"France? What faith were they?"

"Faith?" asked Ginny.

"Religion."

"Oh. My mother's family were Roman Catholic."

Mrs. Van Bergen put her knife and fork down on the table and narrowed her eyes at Ginny. "Roman Catholic!"

"Geneviève plays the organ in her Lutheran chapel," said Lex, as if this secured her Protestant credentials.

"My father's family were Presbyterian," Ginny added, hoping that would meet with approval.

"Well, that's something, I suppose," grumbled Mrs. Van Bergen.

Lex gave Ginny's hand a squeeze.

With the next course, attention turned away from Ginny, to her relief. Lex had warned her about his mother and this was a small price to pay for his love. But, my, it made the ladies of Jefferson City look positively benevolent.

At the end of the meal, Mrs. Van Bergen stood to lead the way upstairs to the drawing room.

Phoebe slipped in beside Ginny. "Would you do me a great favor in the morning?"

"If I can."

"I need new clothes for a trip next month. I'm going to Jordon Marsh. It's a department store with everything together —dressmakers, milliners, cobblers. Might you come with me?"

"Yes, of course. If you like." Thank goodness there was *one* member of Lex's family who was being kind to her.

"It will be a chance to get to know you better." She turned to Lex. "Are you happy for me to steal your fiancée away for the morning?"

He laughed. "I doubt I have much say in the matter."

"That's settled, then," said Phoebe with a smile. "And the day after, we are all going to the regatta."

As they walked to the hall, Lex caught Ginny around the waist. "I need to say goodnight now, darling."

Ginny's hand went to her chest. "You're going?"

"I'll be sleeping at my club. Mother would never countenance us sleeping under the same roof before we're married."

Ginny swallowed, trying to hide her disappointment that he was leaving. "No. Of course not. I hadn't thought."

"Some of my family haven't been very kind, have they? I can be here for breakfast if you like. The Union club isn't far."

"No, I'll be fine with Phoebe, I'm sure."

He pulled her into an alcove by the stairs and kissed her lips, pressing his hands in the small of her back. She melted into him, feeling the firm muscles beneath his starched shirt, wishing he was wearing the soft check cotton of his country clothes.

"This is why we need to be wed *very* soon," he whispered.

. . .

Phoebe took Ginny into the drawing room. The windows were shuttered and the swagged curtains drawn. The furniture was elegant, upholstered in shot silk. There was a piano at the far end of the room and a writing table nearby.

"Come and join us here," said Mrs. Van Bergen sitting at a card table.

"I've never been much good at cards."

"Nonsense, surely. A clever girl like you? I'm partnering Florence, so Thaddeus needs you."

"You needn't worry," said Florence. "We don't play for money."

Ginny peeped at Phoebe for support.

"Oh, no use looking at her," said Mrs. Van Bergen, waving a hand. "Neither Alexander nor Phoebe can abide cards. And Phoebe always has letters to write in the evening."

"Sadly, it's true," said Phoebe. "I have correspondence about the women's hospital that I must complete."

Ginny took her place. "I'm afraid you will need to run through the rules."

Florence explained the procedure.

"Let's have a game to practice."

During the round, Florence explained each move Ginny should take, why each card had been laid.

"Right. Now for real." Florence dealt the cards expertly.

Ginny's hand was poor, but her communication with Thaddeus poorer. They lost the first hand.

"And what do you think of Boston?" asked Florence, shuffling the cards.

"It's very different to anything I've experienced before."

"Have you traveled much?"

"I have never been outside Missouri before."

Florence stared at Ginny as if she were an exhibit at the zoo. "And yet you traveled here by yourself. How extraordinary."

"There were many single women on the train," Ginny

replied. "You railroad owners have made it a wonderfully safe way to travel."

Florence dealt the next hand.

"Perhaps we'll have better luck this time," Thaddeus grunted.

Florence continued her commentary. "Most strange that you run the farm yourself. That will explain your complexion of course."

"My complexion?"

"Your skin." Florence put down a card. "Why your face is so dark. One might call it ecru?"

Ginny wasn't sure what that meant but knew it was an insult. Her neck was hot with embarrassment.

"And your hands," said Mrs. Van Bergen, following suit.

Ginny instinctively hid her hand of cards down below the table.

"Come along now," said Florence. "Your turn."

Although Ginny began to understand the game, Thaddeus sighed or griped each time she laid the wrong card. She became less confident and began to make worse decisions.

"No! There's no point laying that heart when you know they are likely to still have spades," Thaddeus spat as the game progressed.

By the final round, Ginny had all but given up. They lost heavily and Thaddeus threw the remaining cards into the center of the table.

"Good job we *weren't* playing for money," he said, pushing back his chair and pouring himself a whiskey.

"Time we retired," said Mrs. Van Bergen, rising to her feet.

Ginny had never been so relieved. She returned upstairs to the guest bedroom, her legs heavy. This was her fault for arriving unannounced in Boston. But, surely, now they had met her, the worst of it was over.

FIFTY-TWO

Ginny woke with a start as a maid threw back the heavy drapes and a shaft of sunlight shot across the room. She remembered last night and groaned before swinging her feet onto the Persian rug. She would not be defeated. Lex had seen something in her to fall in love with. She was not going to let him down.

The dining room was empty when she entered, so she fetched herself coffee from a silver pot on the sideboard. She wondered if she were late. Perhaps Boston folk rose early and were doing whatever occupied their days by now. In answer, Mrs. Van Bergen swept in; she winced at the sight of Ginny, as if hoping she would have disappeared overnight.

"Good morning, Mrs. Van Bergen."

"Miss Snow."

Mrs. Van Bergen indicated to the maid to start serving the food.

Ginny attempted a conversation. Had Mrs. Van Bergen slept well? Did she have a busy day ahead? But responses were brief and they fell to silence. Ginny's cheeks reddened and she worried that her manners were gauche.

. . .

By ten o'clock, Phoebe and Ginny were in the carriage.

"I promise we'll have fun this morning. And then it's lunch with my darling brother."

The carriage drew up at the junction of two streets, outside a large modern building, six or more stories high.

"Jordon Marsh," said Phoebe. "Everything in the same store."

As Ginny followed Phoebe indoors, she thought of Harriet Gibbes's pride that she also supplied anything a person could need.

The store was busy, yet there was a hushed tone. Phoebe sailed past counters with leather gloves, an area with hats displayed like stuffed birds, a wall with shawls hung like an oil painting. She made her way to a tall, thin lady with bouffant silver hair and glasses on a chain.

"Miss Van Bergen, delightful to see you."

"This is Miss Snow, just arrived all the way from Missouri. Soon to be my sister-in-law."

This caused an immediate response. "Jacob Alexander is to be married?" The older woman placed her spectacles on her nose and looked closely. "I'm dyin' to hear how you captured him. Although with such a beautiful face, it's not a surprise."

Ginny flushed. "I'm not sure *captured* is the right word—"

"Ensnared? Lassoed?" The woman led the way into a room.

Phoebe followed. "Mrs. Clunberry is the best dressmaker in Boston. We're in her kingdom now."

The room was full of rails of dresses, bolts of fabrics and bobbins of tassels. There was a table along one side and two full-length mirrors.

"Your dresses are here ready for you, Miss Van Bergen. But would I be right in guessing you are really here for a trousseau?"

Phoebe clapped. "Exactly! The whole thing, top to bottom."

"Oh, Phoebe!" said Ginny. "Nobody said you were engaged. Congratulations."

"Not me, silly. *You*."

Mrs. Clunberry nodded to her assistant to remove Ginny's shawl.

She stepped away, vexed to have been wrong-footed, and feeling a little like a cornered animal. "No, I'm fine. I really don't need anything."

Mrs. Clunberry looked her up and down. "I beg to differ. Come along. Susan needs your measurements."

Ginny could see she was outnumbered. She gave a silent prayer of thanks to Tanner for insisting she brought extra money. "Maybe just one dress. But it will need to be practical."

Mrs. Clunberry put on her spectacles. "Practical doesn't really say *trousseau*, now, does it? I'll be working from your foundation garments up. We need to think of day wear, evening wear. And, as you will be a married woman, suitable nightwear."

Ginny grasped Phoebe's hand and whispered, "I have enough money for one dress and that is all."

Phoebe laughed. "Alexander will pay for it."

Ginny's eyes widened. "He knows about this?"

"Of course not. Men don't think about such things."

"Then I can't buy all this without him knowing." She folded her arms and would not let Susan continue with her tape measure. The flurry of activity came to a halt.

Mrs. Clunberry sniffed and took a long breath. Her eyes softened for the first time. She led Ginny to a chair and sat close.

"Miss Snow. When I arrived in Boston, I was a scared girl, just off the boat from Ireland. All I had was my skill with a needle and thread. It was tough for a few years. I often went to bed hungry.

"I wondered why the rich women were buying from other seamstresses when I knew my work was better. And one day I caught myself in the mirror: I still looked like a poor Irish immigrant. So the next frock I made was in the most fashionable design. And it was for me. I changed my hair, changed my shoes. I even changed my name and called myself 'Mrs.' as if I were a widow. And, suddenly, all those Boston Brahmin women were coming to me."

She gently took Ginny's chin in the palm of her hand. "My dear. You are marrying into one of the wealthiest families in the United States. These aren't dresses. They are a uniform. They are a disguise. And without them, Boston society will eat you alive."

She stood up. "So. Shall we continue?"

Ginny nodded. The tape measure was extended once more.

Phoebe conducted the proceedings from thereon. "We need a couple of dresses for immediate use. Is that possible?"

"I have a ready-to-wear day dress in Miss Snow's size. It's a beautiful dove-gray with midnight-blue edgings. Susan can make a couple of adjustments and it will be with you any minute."

"Anything for evening wear?"

Mrs. Clunberry brought out a scarlet-and-black silk dress. "This is my sample frock. It has this lovely deep neckline. A very sophisticated style and so dramatic. Miss Snow has the figure to carry it off."

Ginny ran her fingers over the satin and wondered what Mary Lou would make of all these dresses.

"I could have this ready for tomorrow," Mrs. Clunberry continued.

"Perfect. We have an important dinner tomorrow night."

Ginny raised her eyebrows. "Lex didn't say anything."

Phoebe toyed with a piece of ribbon. "With the Canadian Minister of Public Works and his wife. Thaddeus mentioned it last night. He's been like a bear with a sore head about it."

Mrs. Clunberry gave the dress to Susan. "And who is designing your wedding dress?"

"I'm taking Ginny to Monsieur Demarque this afternoon."

"You are?" asked Ginny.

"Excellent choice." Mrs. Clunberry nodded her approval.

"But I thought we were meeting Lex," said Ginny.

Phoebe picked up a feather and tucked it into her hair, looking in the mirror to see the effect. "Yes, for lunch. I sent a message to his club this morning saying I'd need you this afternoon as well."

A maître d' settled Phoebe and Ginny at a table by the window at a fashionable restaurant opposite the Old State House.

Phoebe took charge of the situation: "Some water please. We're waiting for my brother."

Ginny felt the other diners' eyes on them and was unsure why. She was wearing the dove-gray dress that Mrs. Clunberry had recommended and was feeling uncomfortable in the stiff fabric. Gazing out at the milling people on the street, she saw Lex pick his way between the carriages, his hat in hand. Her stomach turned over, as it did most every time she looked at him. He was so different in this city environment, his suit cut to emphasize his broad shoulders, his pants tighter than the ones he wore to work on the farm.

He entered the restaurant and spotted them at the table. His broad smile showed he was the same Lex as ever. He strode over and planted a gentle kiss on Ginny's cheek.

"Been having fun?" he asked.

"I'm not really one for dress shopping, but Phoebe has been wonderfully kind."

"I can imagine," he said with a glance at Phoebe.

"Dearest brother, we had a *ball*. I am adoring being seen taking luncheon with the most beautiful woman in Boston. What do you think of the new dress?"

Lex grinned. "Ginny always looks bewitching. I can't say I particularly notice the dress."

"Men. They have no idea." Phoebe began to order food for all of them.

"What do you have planned for this afternoon?" Lex asked his sister.

"Something very important. But beyond that, my lips are sealed."

"What are *you* doing?" asked Ginny

"Back to the office with Thaddeus. More planning for the Canadian proposal."

They said goodbye at the doorway of the restaurant.

"Will I see you tonight?" Ginny asked, trying to keep the neediness out of her voice.

"Yes, of course," Lex said, giving Ginny a kiss on the forehead and squeeze of the hand.

Phoebe led the way through the busy streets to Monsieur Demarque's shop. Ginny knew she should be excited to be choosing her wedding dress, but she wondered if this would be another experience where she felt out of place.

FIFTY-THREE

Monsieur Demarque's establishment was tucked between two heavy stone buildings. It felt like walking into a private house. The ladies were ushered into the front room as a small, barrel-shaped man swept in. Phoebe made the introductions.

"This is Miss Geneviève Snow, who is to marry my brother."

"*Enchanté,* Mademoiselle Geneviève." Monsieur Demarque bowed over Ginny's hand and kissed it.

"*Merci. Tout le plaisir est pour moi.*"

Demarque snapped upright, his eyes bright. "*Vous êtes française?*"

"*Non, ma mère était originaire du sud. Louisiana. Mes grands-parents étaient français.*"

Demarque clapped his hands. "Near enough for me. Now, we must speak English for the benefit of the heathens in the room." He indicated Phoebe and the assistant, with a flourish of his hand. "But share our true thoughts in secret, *bien*?" He clicked his fingers. "Let us begin by looking at some pattern books."

The assistant brought forward a large publication, each page with an illustration of a wedding dress.

Demarque fired questions. "The color? Hmmm. White might not be right for your complexion. The contrast will bring attention to your skin tone."

"Miss Snow owns a ranch," Phoebe said by way of explanation.

"I seem to spend more time outdoors than the ladies of Boston think acceptable," Ginny muttered. She leaned to Demarque. "I was wondering, what's 'ecru'?"

"It is a grayish yellow. Like the color of unbleached linen. No, not the color for you at all. Ivory, that's what we need. Now, the style. You have lovely curves. A straight back. Ideal for the fitted styles coming out of France. *Mais*, they can look a little... regulated. So, I propose a long veil to soften the whole effect."

And so they continued. Fabrics, textures, gloves and shoes were each discussed.

"And your hair. Will it be up?"

Ginny hadn't thought about any of this.

"What do you think?" she asked Phoebe.

Phoebe smiled. "Whatever you prefer."

"Up then."

Phoebe handled the details. As they were leaving, Ginny put her arm through hers.

"Thank you. I could not have done this without you. You have thought of everything."

"I've been planning my own wedding since I was six," replied Phoebe. "Like most women."

Ginny smiled at the memory of Mary Lou doing something similar but realized that, until meeting Lex, she had been happy with the idea of independence.

. . .

The carriage took them home in time for a rest before dressing for dinner. Ginny considered her options: the white gown she had worn to the dance in Jefferson City or the new dove-gray dress she was wearing. Bothered by Monsieur Demarque's comments about the effect of white on her complexion, she decided to remain in the day dress.

As soon as she entered the dining room, she knew it was a mistake. Mrs. Van Bergen, Florence and Phoebe were all in evening dress and jewels. Florence glanced at her and put a hand to her mouth to cover a smile.

Mrs. Van Bergen's voice cut through the room. "I excused you for not changing for dinner last night as I assumed your things had not been brought. But I thought Phoebe was sorting some appropriate clothes today."

"Yes, she kindly took me to Jordon Marsh this morning," Ginny said.

"Such a shame Mrs. Clunberry didn't have anything in stock that you could wear immediately."

Ginny fiddled with the lace at the neck of her dress. "But this is—"

Mrs. Van Bergen had already turned away. "And neither of the men back from the office yet. Their father never neglected the home. But I'm not prepared to wait any longer."

The main course was being served by the time Lex and Thaddeus made their apologies and sat down. Ginny sensed a tension between them. The conversation was mostly about what was needed to win the Canadian contract. Tomorrow's regatta might be a chance to lay the groundwork as most of Boston society would be there. Ginny could contribute nothing to the conversation.

As with the previous night, Lex said goodbye soon after the meal.

"I feel I've hardly seen you today," Ginny said, aware that she sounded as if she were complaining.

"In between all Thaddeus' demands, I'm making arrangements for us to be married as soon as possible." He kissed the top of her head. "And it's good for my family to get to know you. Phoebe adores you already."

"I'm not sure about the others, though."

"I know it's hard, but give them time."

With Lex gone, Ginny went up to the drawing room, as she had the night before. Florence was already seated at the card table.

"I'm playing solitaire as Miss Snow does not approve of cards."

"It is not that I disapprove," she replied. "More that I am unfamiliar."

Florence laid out the opening pattern. "And how do you occupy yourself in the evenings at home?"

"There's usually something useful to do, such as darning stockings."

Florence's sly smile indicated that Ginny had said the wrong thing.

"Or I read. Or play the piano."

"The piano? Mother," Florence called out. "Shall we hear Miss Snow on the piano. She says she plays."

Mrs. Van Bergen glowered. "I don't want someone banging about on my pianoforte at this time of night. You know I prefer quiet in the evening."

"Ginny, could play you something soothing," Phoebe said. "Alexander told me she is very good."

Florence made a tight-lipped smile. "How sweet of Alexander to be so supportive of his fiancée. But I think what passes for 'very good' in the Midwest will be different to the standards of Boston."

Ginny bit her lip to hold herself back from defending her people. Instead she looked around for a book but found only magazines, so she settled with *Harper's Weekly* in a quiet corner of the room. She was exhausted by being judged all day long and could feel a headache gathering around her temples.

"Mrs. Van Bergen, would you mind if I had an early night?"

She was dismissed with the wave of a hand.

Sleep did not come. She was so uncomfortable in this house, in this city. Yet it was the house where Lex had grown up, the city where he had received his education. He was at ease here. Could she leave Missouri behind and live here?

She rose and opened the sash window. The hot August air slinking into the room made things worse. She swung a dressing gown over her shoulders, shrugging her arms into the generous sleeves, pushed her toes into slippers and crept downstairs to the garden room. She eased open the French window to the backyard and breathed in the scent of wisteria. It was not yet dark and only the brightest planets were visible. She sat on a stone bench next to the carp pond and listened to the crickets.

Squares of yellow light spread across the paving as someone lit the gaslights in the dining room. With the heat, windows were still open and she could hear voices. She thought of slipping back into the garden room but feared her movement might draw attention.

"Don't ask me, Mother. I never understood him. Even before he joined the army." Thaddeus's voice. Ginny heard the clink of a glass. "Can I get you one as well?"

"Bourbon with soda." Florence's voice floated through the air.

"Whatever made him propose to her? I thought I'd brought him up to know how important our family is in Boston."

Ginny went cold as she realized they were talking about her.

"The reason is obvious, surely," said Florence. "I don't like to be indelicate. But a young woman making a desperate journey halfway across the States?"

"My God! You think she's *with child*?" asked Mrs. Van Bergen.

"Why else would Alexander be rushing this wedding?"

"My brother can be so stupid. If that's the problem, money can easily fix it. Only he would think he had to marry the girl."

"Thaddeus, you'll have to speak to him."

"I'll try, Mother, but I don't think he'll listen to me." A chair scraped the floor. "And it doesn't solve the problem of tomorrow night."

"I don't understand why you are so worried about it," said Florence.

Thaddeus sighed. "I hadn't wanted to say anything. Truth is, the business is on a knife-edge. If we get the Canada contract, all will be peachy, and for a long time. But if we don't, then things could start unravelling. The minister is the linchpin to this deal. I've done my research. We need to woo him. He likes to think of himself as cultured and sophisticated. He reveres the idea of family life. We can't risk a hick from the Midwest saying something vulgar at the wrong moment."

Ginny listened with tears building. She struggled to control her breathing, terrified they might see her there, listening to every word.

"Florence and I can keep her out of the minister's way tomorrow," said Mrs. Van Bergen. "I have every confidence that you will secure this deal. You have your father's blood running in your veins. And that's what troubles me so with Alexander. He has his father's spirit as well, even if he tries to deny it. I know my son. He'll never be happy with that girl."

The voices faded, but not before Ginny heard Mrs. Van Bergen's final words.

"They are from two different worlds. It's like a horse mating with a donkey. They only produce mules."

The rectangles of yellow light disappeared as someone turned down the gaslight. Ginny remained seated, her heart beating so hard, she could hear whooshing in her ears. The words spun round her head. How dare they be so insulting to her and to Lex?

But as the evening air cooled, part of her feared much of what they said was true. She didn't fit in here. She was going to cause a rift in the family. Maybe one just as bad as her own mother's from her LeRoux grandparents. She slipped inside through the French window and crept upstairs to her room, where she paced, desperately trying to decide what to do for the best.

FIFTY-FOUR

By the time the maid opened the curtains the next morning, Ginny knew what she had to do. She asked the maid to tell Mrs. Van Bergen that she was unwell and would not be down for breakfast. Then she sat at the dressing table to write a letter to Lex.

Soon, there was a tap on the door. "It's Phoebe."

Ginny climbed back into bed and held a handkerchief to her face. "Come in."

Phoebe poked her head round the door. "Oh goodness, you don't look well. Shall I send for the doctor?"

Ginny's eyes were puffy from lack of sleep and her nose was pink from crying. "It's just a head cold. I don't want a fuss"

Phoebe came over and put her hand to Ginny's face. "No fever. That's something."

"I'm so sorry, but I won't be able to join you all at the regatta today."

"Oh, my sweet, that is such a shame. But I'll stay here and look after you. I've had a lifetime of watching boats in the harbor."

"No, I insist you go as planned. I would hate to keep you from the family. A day's rest will do me good."

Phoebe narrowed her eyes, trying to study the detail of Ginny's face. "Well, if you're certain?"

"I am."

Phoebe left the room, but a maid appeared soon afterwards, the full range of breakfast items on a wide tray with short legs so Ginny could eat in bed. She forced herself to swallow what she could, being uncertain of when she would next eat.

Ginny listened to the comings and goings as the Van Bergens prepared to leave, feet running up and down stairs, calls for parasols and gloves. The front door slammed and the clamor moved outside until Ginny could hear horse hooves and a carriage creaking as it pulled away from the house.

Ginny tiptoed out of bed and dressed in her burgundy suit. It fitted like a familiar glove. She hauled out her travel chest and folded her clothing into it, leaving the new frock in the closet. Looking through her pocketbook, she checked exactly how many dollars she had. She hesitated for a moment about whether to put the Smith & Wesson in the trunk but decided to slip it into her pocketbook.

Ginny padded down the stairs of the empty house, right to the basement level. A maid started in surprise to see her appear there but took her to the housekeeper's room.

"I thought you were unwell," said Mrs. O'Harvey, equally astonished.

"I'm feeling much better now. I've decided to send all my purchases ahead of me, back to Missouri." Ginny aimed for a confident tone of voice.

The housekeeper looked Ginny in the eye.

"So..." Ginny cleared her throat and spoke more loudly. "So

I'd like you to arrange for the carriage to take my trunk to the railroad station."

"When, Miss Snow?"

"Now. As soon as it can be arranged."

"The carriage is with the Van Bergens."

Ginny bit her lip. Of course it was. "Don't you have another carriage? A wagon?"

The housekeeper nodded and seemed to be weighing up the situation. "I'll tell the stable-hand. It'll be ready in quarter of an hour."

"And could someone bring my trunk down from the guest room?"

The trunk was loaded onto the wagon and Ginny waited outside in her traveling coat.

"There's no need for you to go to the station, ma'am. We'll see to everything," said Mrs. O'Harvey.

"I'd prefer to make sure it's done myself. And I could do with some air."

Mrs. O'Harvey made a slight bow. "As you wish. Farewell, Miss Snow."

Ginny climbed up next to the driver, who cracked his whip for the two horses to move on. She glanced up at the house and felt her gut clench. This was Lex's home and she was turning her back on it.

At the station, the driver waved down a porter and Ginny climbed to the sidewalk.

"You go back to the Square," said Ginny.

The driver frowned. "I can't leave you here. I've been told to make sure this trunk gets on the St. Louis train. And how would you get back to the house?"

"I can manage the luggage. And I'm used to walking every day. I'm looking forward to the exercise."

"But you don't know the way back."

"Nonsense, man. Beacon Hill. And if I get lost, the gilded dome of the Massachusetts State House couldn't be easier to find. I'll have no trouble."

The driver persisted. "The Van Bergens would say I'm not doing my job if I leave you."

"You are not my guard. And I am not the prisoner of the Van Bergens. If I want to see to my own affairs with my luggage and then take a walk, then that's what I shall do."

The driver shook his head and muttered words Ginny could not hear. He slapped the reins on the horse and the wagon lunged away.

The porter put the trunk on a trolley and led the way inside. Ginny found the ticket agent: the next train was in three hours and there were seats available. She could only afford an ordinary car, not a sleeping car, and that near cleared her out. She had a couple of dollars spare for meals on the way.

Ginny settled down on the bench to wait until the train was ready. Going home might look like a defeat, but she had to do it, for the sake of the man she loved.

Around two o'clock, the porter approached Ginny. "The train is being prepared. Shall I take your trunk?"

"Thank you. But might I trouble you to ensure this letter is delivered?" Ginny held out an envelope. "It's for Mr. Van Bergen. I'd guess you'd get a tip for your trouble."

She needed Lex to understand her actions, so maybe one day he would forgive her. She refused to make him chose between her and his family. The last awful days had shown she would never fit into the Boston Brahmin way of life, so marrying her would cause a rift with his family. Her heart ached at the idea of being the source of such a fissure with his mother and home.

The porter put the letter in his pocket and Ginny followed him down the platform. There was so much smoke and steam, Ginny could hear but not see the enormous engine being prepared by the drivers. Railway stock rumbled into place and workers shouted to each other as they rolled wagons of coal ready for the journey.

Ginny grasped the brass rail to steady herself as she climbed the steps to the car. But then, through the noise, she heard her name being shouted. She turned and her mouth went dry.

Lex strode toward her, his jaw set and eyes dark.

FIFTY-FIVE

Lex's heart was pounding both from the rush to the station and the fear he would arrive too late. He put one foot on the bottom step, frowning up at Ginny, who looked as startled as a white-tailed faun.

"I don't understand. You're... you're *leaving* me?" Lex was unable to control the anger in his voice.

Ginny wet her lips. "It's best like this." There was a rasp to her voice, quite unlike her usual clear tone.

"Best for whom?"

"For you. For everyone."

Lex ran both hands through his hair. "I don't see how you getting on this train can be best for me."

A woman in a green hat with an enormous feather tutted as Ginny blocked access to the car. Lex glanced round at the woman and then back up at Ginny.

"Can you at least come back onto the platform to discuss this?" He put out his hand for her to climb down. Feeling her fingers in his palm and standing so close he could smell her perfume, his anger melted.

"Something's happened to make you feel differently about

me," he said.

"I... I guess that's true. Seeing you here in Boston."

An emptiness opened deep inside him. "You don't love me anymore."

She looked up at him, her chin wobbling as she struggled to speak. "I love you as much as ever."

Lex folded his arms. "As much as ever. But not enough to be my wife."

Ginny closed her eyes and shook her head slightly. "Marriage isn't just about the husband and wife. It's about family. Your family will never accept me. They want you to marry someone suitable."

The muscles in Lex's jaw throbbed. Damn his interfering family. "This is my mother, isn't it? She's told you this."

"Your mother has not spoken to me." Her eyes drifted to one side and he got the sense she was hiding things.

"Thaddeus?"

Lex noticed Ginny flinch at the name. By God, this was down to his brother.

"Jeez, when I get my hands on him—"

"But, Lex, it's true! I could say something stupid tonight and bust the whole deal with Canada."

"Geneviève. You can*not* leave me simply because my brother is a complete idiot."

"But they will force you to choose. And if you choose me, it will cause a chasm. You will be divided from your family."

Lex frowned as he tried to understand why she would think this. Hadn't she seen how different he was from his family? He cupped his hands around her chin and studied her brown eyes, the dark lashes, the pinkness of her full lips.

"This isn't about my family," he said in a low voice. "It's about yours. It's about your mother being cut off from her childhood home. It's about your grandmother and grandfather dying before they forgave her."

Ginny blinked back the tears pricking at her eyes, looking as if years of hurt would burst from the dam if she gave into the feelings.

"Lex, I couldn't bear your life to be like hers." Ginny rummaged in her pocketbook, trying to find her handkerchief. Lex pulled one from his breast pocket. "Yes, she loved my father, but she married out of her society, just like we're doing. I think she always wondered what might have been."

The conductor hurried along different knots of people embracing on the platform. "Passengers must embark," he ordered.

Lex pushed away a tear from her cheek. It was the softest of movements. He'd always had difficulty talking about his feelings, but concealing things from Ginny had hurt her back in Missouri and the same thing was happening again.

"I've never belonged here in Boston," he said, stepping back. "Growing up, I built dens in the tiny scrap of grass in front of the house. I would have lived outside if my father hadn't dragged me back in the evening. Strangely, I found satisfaction in that part of army life: being under canvas, feeling all weathers on my skin. I came back to Harvard and felt completely at odds with my friends."

He pushed his hands into his pockets. "Yes, the reading, and poetry, and music, they soothed my soul, but I'd escape off on long rides whenever I could. Thaddeus was embarrassed by me and told my father it was a phase. They weren't sure what to do with me. I wasn't interested in politics, the law, business. And when I first traveled West, it was like..." He searched for the right words. "It was like I'd come home. The wide spaces where you could ride all day and not see anyone else. The forests, even the deserts. I was finally happy."

He smiled at the memory and then looked into Ginny's eyes. "And when I first came across you it was as if God was playing a joke on me. To have found the few things I missed about Boston—books, music—deep in the heart of the country—it was so strange, I didn't trust it at first."

The conductor reached Lex and Ginny; time was running short.

"You need to know," said Lex, "I don't belong here and will be leaving Boston sometime soon. I'd like it to be for Missouri. I want it to be with you."

She was staring at him intently.

"The train is ready to depart," said the conductor.

Lex took her hand. "Will it be with you?"

The world fell silent; his eyes did not leave Ginny's face.

"Yes," she whispered.

The whistle sounded. "Sir, I must insist—"

A warmth spread across his chest as Lex smiled down at her. He felt like sweeping her up and carrying her away from the station. "Let's get this fixed," he murmured conspiratorially.

Lex pulled a card from his vest pocket and gave it to the conductor, who read the name and coughed.

"There's a trunk in the luggage car that needs to be disembarked," said Lex. "Arrange for it to be delivered to the address on that card."

The conductor touched the peak of his hat in half salute and hurried off to find the porter who had helped Ginny earlier.

"I admit, sometimes life is easier when you own the train," he said with a grin, threading Ginny's arm through his as they strolled back down the platform to the entrance hall.

Back on the sidewalk, Lex took Ginny to where his horse was waiting.

"No!" she cried. "It can't be. Arion?"

"Of course I still have Arion. He's my best friend. And the quickest way to get to the station. But I'll flag us a carriage and tie him behind."

Ginny patted Arion's velvety muzzle.

"Unless..." Lex laughed, a mischievous thought bubbling up. "Unless we both ride home on him."

"Now, that *would* set the Boston ladies' tongues wagging."

"Well, I certainly hope so." Lex lifted Ginny up and swung onto the saddle behind her. "It's not very comfortable, but the journey won't take long."

"I think I could put up with any discomfort, to have you near like this."

He held her so close to his chest, he could feel her breathing and her hair tickled his cheek. He could stay like this forever.

As the street began to steepen at the base of Beacon Hill, Ginny asked a question. "How did you know I was there? At the station?"

Lex paused as he remembered the last few hours. "The only word I can find is instinct. Deep inside, I knew something was wrong when you didn't come to the regatta. Phoebe tried to reassure me you just needed a rest. But there was something about my mother when I asked after you. A look in her eye."

A slight pressure from Lex's knee told Arion to turn onto a narrower street. "So I came home early. I asked where you'd gone and the housekeeper said the station. I've never saddled Arion so quick. I was terrified I would miss you."

Ginny leaned into Lex. "I'm sorry to have caused you pain. You know, I wrote a letter to explain everything. I gave it to the porter to deliver. When it arrives, promise me you'll burn it."

They reached the Van Bergen house and Lex lifted Ginny down to the sidewalk.

"But tonight. I really do think it would be better if I pretend to have a cold," Ginny said. "That way, there's no chance I mess up the dinner with the minister."

Lex kissed the end of her nose. "Ginny, no more pretending. You are equal to anyone. The Canadian minister will be charmed by you."

He took her hand as they went up the steps.

FIFTY-SIX

Ginny asked her maid to make her appear sophisticated but drew a line at the laces of her corset being pulled so tight. Ginny tied the ribbons of the crinolette and then the skirt of her new dress. The maid helped her into the bodice and fastened the tiny buttons. Looking in the full-length mirror, Ginny chewed her lip. She loved the shimmering silk, but the scarlet and black seemed to be making a statement.

Phoebe knocked and entered. "Oh my!"

"It's too much, isn't it?"

"Too much? It's beautiful. And your complexion is glowing. The day in bed seems to have done the trick."

Ginny was relieved Lex had not told Phoebe she'd actually spent most of her day at the railroad station. She felt embarrassed about her desperate behavior. She had come so close to throwing everything away. She had to trust Lex's faith in their future.

"Stand still," said Phoebe, "I need to adjust this."

She lowered the fabric to reveal Ginny's shoulders and adjusted the bodice.

"Phoebe, are you sure? I feel a little... exposed."

"This is how Boston ladies are wearing evening dress this season."

"But most Boston ladies have snow-white arms and décolletage. That can't be said of me."

"But you have the perfect figure for this dress. I've seen many women in this style and it looks all wrong." Phoebe leaned in to whisper: "Florence, for one."

The maid swept up Ginny's hair in a coiffured arrangement with curls tumbling down her neck and touching her shoulder blades.

Phoebe studied the effect. "You need some jewelry to finish it off."

Ginny held up the black velvet choker, but Phoebe shook her head.

"Everyone is wearing those, but you need something more." She rushed from the room, returning a minute later with a black box. "Let's try these."

Ginny opened the box to find a diamond pendant necklace and a pair of matching earrings. Her mouth fell open.

"They were Grandmother's."

Ginny snapped the box shut. "I couldn't wear them. Not if they're family heirlooms."

Phoebe took the box and lifted out the necklace. "Why not? You're gonna be Mrs. Van Bergen very soon. They're as much yours as anyone's." She fastened the clasp at the back of Ginny's neck and helped thread the earrings.

Ginny stood and Phoebe looked her up and down.

"Perfect."

Lex waited in the hall, fidgeting with his cufflinks. He had made small talk with the early arrivals, but his mind was elsewhere.

Phoebe swept down the staircase in a gold-and-cream gown. She made eye contact with Lex, a knowing look on her face.

Then Ginny stood at the top of the stairs. Lex was breathless as she put her hand on the banister and carefully made her way down. The warm glow from the gaslights made her dress shimmer and the jewels at her neck scattered beams. Her shining eyes locked on to his. The hubbub of chatter paused as people turned to watch her.

Lex put out his arm as she reached the bottom step and kissed her on the cheek. His chest expanded and he knew he was enjoying everyone else's admiration as much as his own.

"Thank you for not saying anything about today to Phoebe," Ginny whispered.

Lex squeezed her closer. He led her down the corridor to the garden room, looking for somewhere private.

"There's something I haven't done yet." Lex unpeeled the white glove from Ginny's hand. "I'm afraid you won't be able to wear gloves tonight." He slid a ring onto Ginny's finger—a ruby surrounded by diamonds. "I hope this fits."

Ginny's mouth opened, her lips full and pink, and made a soft "oh" sound. She looked up at him, blinking with astonishment.

"D'you like it?" Had he got this wrong?

Ginny extended her hand, fingers pointing upwards. "I love it. It's beautiful."

"I can't wait to introduce you to everyone as my fiancée. Call me shallow, but I have to admit, it's gratifying to have envious looks from the other gentlemen."

Ginny blushed and he was tempted to stay in the garden room a little longer. But the sound of more people arriving reminded him of his duties and he led her back to the hall. There he saw Thaddeus shifting his weight from foot to foot. His brother scanned Ginny, her hair, the jewels around her neck, her striking dress, but his face did not reveal his thoughts.

"You go up to support Mother in the reception room," he

said in a low voice to Lex. "I'll wait here to greet the minister and bring him up."

"Anything to be of assistance, brother," Lex replied.

Ginny walked into the reception room, which was full of women in vivid dresses with swags and ruffles, contrasted by men in plain suits. Mrs. Van Bergen held court near the unlit fireplace, dressed in her customary black silk, her iron-gray hair pulled back from her face. Spotting Ginny, her face tightened as if she had a toothache.

"I'm glad you are feeling better, Miss Snow. Although you missed an exciting day at the regatta."

Ginny curtsied but thought it better to remain silent. Mrs. Van Bergen's attention moved on.

There was a flutter of excitement as Thaddeus brought the minister and his wife into the reception room.

"May I present my dear mother, Mrs. Van Bergen. This is the Canadian Minister for Public Works."

The minister bowed. Ginny had expected him to be taller. The generous mustaches across his cheeks did not match the thinning hair on top of his head.

"Delighted to meet you, Mr. McIntyre," said Mrs. Van Bergen.

"This is my wife, Clotilde." The blonde, doll-like woman on the minister's arm was at least ten years younger than her husband.

"We are honored." Mrs. Van Bergen smiled, but the minister's wife did not reply. Her eyes remained on the carpet as she shook Mrs. Van Bergen's hand. Mrs. Van Bergen began the introductions. "Minister, you have met Mrs. Florence Van Bergen before, I believe. Thaddeus's wife."

"Of course. Charmed, once again." There was a distinct Scottish burr to Mr. McIntyre's accent.

"My daughter, Phoebe. I don't think you have met my other son, Alexander."

The minister greeted each of them and turned to Ginny, clearly anxious for an introduction. "And you are?"

"My fiancée, Miss Geneviève Snow," said Lex.

"Exquisite," he said, touching his lips to the back of Ginny's hand.

Thaddeus stepped forward. "A drink before we go down for dinner?"

The minister agreed and a servant brought a tray of champagne flutes.

"May I introduce you to other guests?" The cream of Boston politicians and industrialists were assembled and would not be pleased if they were prevented from establishing a rapport with the guest of honor. The men moved away, Lex glancing back at Ginny to check she was comfortable. She gave a quick smile of reassurance.

"Shall we sit? At my age, I cannot stand for long." Mrs. Van Bergen tried to raise a smile from Mrs. Clotilde McIntyre.

With no reaction, she sat anyway, and the rest of the women followed. Ginny found herself on an uncomfortable sofa next to Clotilde and thought she could sense a tremble, like a foal who has just found its feet.

"And what do you think of Boston?" Mrs. Van Bergen asked.

"Pardon?" Mrs. McIntyre replied.

"Boston. You like it?"

"*Mais oui*. Yes. *Grande*... big."

Mrs. Van Bergen's smile did not reach her eyes. She spoke louder and slower. "How... long... have... you... been... here?"

"Pardon?"

Mrs. Van Bergen repeated herself but with hand signals.

"Long... *trois*, three days." Clotilde held up three fingers.

Mrs. Van Bergen nodded enthusiastically. "Three days! Ah.

How interesting." She turned to Florence. "She's been here three days."

Florence then tried. "And what do you like best about our city. About Boston?"

Clotilde shrugged to indicate she had understood nothing.

Ginny felt for her, knowing what it was like to be under the Van Bergen ladies' scrutiny. She stepped in. "*Qu'est-ce que vous aimez le plus à Boston?*"

Clotilde's eyes opened wide at Ginny. "*Rien. Je n'aime rien du tout.*"

Ginny hesitated. A kindred spirit? But she couldn't really tell these Bostonians that there was nothing to recommend their city.

"It's so hard to choose," Ginny said.

Clotilde eagerly turned to Ginny. "*Où l'avez-vous appris, le français?*"

Ginny looked at the other women. "She is asking where I learned French."

"*Ma mère,*" Ginny returned to Clotilde.

"*Elle était française?*"

"*Non. Ma grand-mère.*"

Having found someone who shared her native language, Clotilde began to fire questions, not giving Ginny a chance to translate for the other ladies. Clotilde seemed to forget there were other people in the group.

The marble clock above the fireplace rang out the hour. Mrs. Van Bergen rose. "Shall we go down to dinner?"

The Minister for Public Works returned, delighted his wife had found someone to talk to. "Americans often forget that Canada has two languages," he said as he accompanied Thaddeus out of the room. "There are as many Canadians who speak French as English. Or, in my case, Scots."

Thaddeus laughed heartily. "But I thought all Canadians would speak *some* English."

"Depends where they're from."

"It's good to learn something new about your fascinating country," Thaddeus continued with a stiff smile that showed his teeth.

The table ran the full length of the dining room in order to accommodate so many guests. Roses tumbled from the centerpiece vase. Although gas lamps lit the walls, candelabras spaced along the table gave the room a honeyed glow.

Mrs. Van Bergen had printed names on small cards at each place. Ginny was at the lower end of the table. *Where I can do no damage*, she thought.

Phoebe noticed the look of dismay flash across Mrs. McIntyre's face as Ginny took her place, well out of earshot. This dinner needed to go well for the Van Bergen family and a happy minister's wife might make all the difference.

"Mother, as my French is lamentable, and Mrs. McIntyre is getting on so well with Miss Snow, wouldn't it be nicer if we swapped? And Geneviève sat next to her?"

Mrs. Van Bergen raised her eyebrows. "The seating has been planned most carefully."

"What a kind thought, Miss Van Bergen," said Mr. McIntyre. "My dear wee wife has to sit through so many dinners as part of her duties. It would be nice if she were able to converse at this one."

Ginny stole a look at Thaddeus, who frowned at this development. But, by now, Phoebe was beside her and Ginny had no option but to walk back to the top of the table. As she took her place beside the minister's wife, Clotilde looked at her, eyes round with gratitude. Ginny took her seat, afraid that a few ill-advised words from her could lead to the Van Bergens failing to win the lucrative contract.

FIFTY-SEVEN

From that moment on, Ginny kept all her attention on Mrs. McIntyre. They conversed in French throughout, their voices low.

"Call me, Clotilde, please, Miss Snow."

"Thank you. And though I am Geneviève, my friends call me Ginny. I hope you will do so too."

She found that the McIntyres had only been married a year and the minister had been married once before. Clotilde feared she did not live up to the previous wife, who, people never tired of telling her, had been a society hostess who had made the minister's residence a cultural salon.

"I don't know much about marriage, Clotilde, but from the way your husband looks at you, I think he cares about you very deeply."

"You think so?" Those big eyes fixed on Ginny again.

"I do. And I'm finding that the love of one man is enough to take us through the hardest things." She glanced down the table at Lex, and, just at that moment, was rewarded with a look and a grin. Her stomach seemed to flip over.

"How long have you known your fiancé?"

"Around eighteen months."

Clotilde asked how they had met and was greatly amused by the tale of Lex arriving at the homestead, disheveled and injured. Ginny told how their love had grown, how he had saved the farm without her knowing.

"That is the most romantic thing I have ever heard!" Clotilde declared.

"But I nearly lost everything." Ginny told her about meeting him at the ball, how she was sure Lex was a confidence trickster and how she had threatened to expose him. Clotilde laughed out loud. Florence frowned from across the table.

"I would have made such a fool of myself. And caused a scandal at the state ball. They would never invite me to play again!"

"To play?"

"The piano." Ginny told her about her mother's gift of teaching her to play the piano, how she had persevered no matter how busy the farm. They discussed their favorite music and Ginny told of the score that Lex had sent as a gift.

Clotilde sighed and looked across at Lex, who was in conversation with a politician's wife. "And he is *so* handsome. I wish you every happiness."

"Remember, at the time I had no idea who he was. I suppose I should have been more curious about a cowboy who knew of Chopin."

Clotilde gave a giggling sideways look at Ginny, who smiled and shrugged at her own stupidity.

The meal ended and Mrs. Van Bergen led the ladies back to the reception room, leaving the gentlemen to spirits and cigars.

Florence squeezed Ginny's arm as they passed on the curving stairs. "You mustn't monopolize her like this," she hissed.

Ginny raised her eyebrows. "What do you mean?"

"The minister's wife. There are plenty of other ladies who want to make her acquaintance."

"Yes, of course. But I thought I was helping. Mrs. McIntyre has so little English."

"I've discovered Mrs. Murgatroyd learned French. Perhaps if you hadn't pushed yourself forward, we would have found out earlier. Particularly as Mr. Murgatroyd is running for office next year."

Ginny inclined her head. "Whatever you think best, Florence."

Florence narrowed her eyes and stepped ahead to enter the reception room with a flourish.

Mrs. Murgatroyd's French was more elementary than Florence had hoped, but enough to encourage Mrs. McIntyre into a game of cards.

"The perfect pastime," Florence said. "Numbers are the same in any language."

Mrs. McIntyre looked doubtful but settled at the card table with Florence, Mrs. Murgatroyd and a lady from an old Boston family.

Ginny looked across and felt for her new friend's predicament. She sat with Phoebe, who introduced her to a pair of fashionable ladies who were eager to hear about the wedding preparations.

At the end of a round of cards, Clotilde made it clear she did not want to continue and looked over at Ginny. Florence put her hand on Clotilde's arm to keep her close.

"Perhaps you would enjoy some music?" Florence asked, ignoring the dark look from her mother-in-law. "Musique?" she said with a French tone, and was delighted when this was enough to be understood. "Phoebe, might you start?"

Phoebe snorted. "Florence, you know my playing isn't good enough for company. It would be as painful for everyone else as it is for me."

"I'll lead the way, then." Florence scampered to the grand piano, where music for appropriate pieces and songs had been laid out in advance. She settled herself ostentatiously until the room gave her its attention.

Florence played well but with a heavy rhythm. Each piece sounded like a march. Florence then performed a song, struggling to play and sing at the same time. Again, her voice was passable and she hit the right notes, but the tone was forced; she worked too hard to fill the room.

At the end of the song, Florence stood and smiled at her audience, taking in the applause. "Mrs. McIntyre, do you play?" Her hand signals made it apparent what was being asked.

"*Mais non.*" Clotilde's hand fluttered to her mouth and she shook her head. Then she looked at Ginny. "*Mais, Geneviève, pourquoi pas jouer la pièce que Monsieur Van Bergen vous a donnée*?"

Ginny looked startled for a moment.

Florence picked up on something that had lain secret. "What did she say?"

Mrs. Murgatroyd translated. "She is asking Miss Snow to play something Mr. Van Bergen wrote."

"Alexander has taken up writing music?" asked Phoebe.

Ginny smiled at the thought. "No, something he *gave* me."

"Chopin," Clotilde continued, looking from woman to woman, trying to help. She nodded at Ginny.

After Florence's modest efforts, Ginny knew she would appear to be displaying her superior talents. She tried to put them off. "I'm afraid it's quite a difficult piece for me to play. I cannot manage it without the score."

Florence raised an eyebrow. "Complicated?"

"Is that the score in your room?" asked Phoebe.

Ginny pursed her lips.

Phoebe gave an apologetic shrug. "Sorry. I noticed it when you unpacked and wondered about it."

Florence's smirk suggested she was on the scent of something that might expose Ginny to ridicule. "Miss Snow, you seem to have presented yourself as quite the pianist to our honored guest."

Mrs. Van Bergen slapped her fan shut and used it to point to Ginny. "Come on now, Miss Snow. If the minister's wife would like to hear this piece and you have the score upstairs, go fetch it without delay."

Ginny left the room, Phoebe following her into the lobby.

"I'm so sorry, Ginny. I spoke before I thought. As always. Do you really not want to play the piano? I can think up some excuse."

Ginny took a deep breath. "No, I'll play. It's just that... well, the piece is suitable for a larger room. And it's quite long."

"Half an hour?"

"Goodness, no! More like ten minutes."

"Sounds perfect."

Ginny ran upstairs and fetched the precious score. When she and Phoebe returned to the reception room, conversation was bubbling again, but the fashionable ladies turned as one, like a flock of wading birds, as Ginny took her seat and unfolded the score.

"Miss Snow tells me the piece lasts around ten minutes," said Phoebe.

Mrs. Van Bergen set her black fan fluttering as if to tell Ginny to get on with it. Florence sat bolt upright next to her, eyes narrowed and one side of her mouth curled in a smile.

She remembered Lex's words from earlier that evening: no more pretending. She was equal to any of them. If her playing outshone Florence's, so be it. She would honor her mother's memory by playing as well as she could.

Ginny began the familiar notes, starting quietly, almost tentatively. Then the piece grew louder before the romantic theme broke forth. The emotion of the music burst through and filled the room. Clotilde smiled with recognition of a piece she had heard before. Florence's half-smile fixed into a grimace.

In the dining room below, the gentlemen were finishing their brandies and discussions of ambitions for the Canadian Pacific Railway.

"Mr. Van Bergen, you have arranged a concert for us?" the minister asked Thaddeus as music seeped through the floorboards.

"I... er... yes. Well... I'm not sure."

Lex listened more closely. "That will be Miss Snow. My fiancée."

Thaddeus looked at him and grunted.

"Truly. That's Geneviève." Lex clapped a hand on Thaddeus's shoulder. "Brother, have I not mentioned she adores the piano? Perhaps you were not listening at the time."

"Let's go and enjoy it," said Mr. McIntyre. "I am a great lover of music myself."

Thaddeus led the way upstairs. Opening the double doors to the reception room, the sound flowed out. Ginny was so absorbed in the music, she did not notice the men quietly taking their places around the room.

Lex stood at the door, his arms folded and leaning against the jamb as he felt the emotion of the music. He watched the woman he loved, completely engulfed in the melodies she was conjuring. His mother's stern face softened slightly, whilst Florence's features sharpened, her eyes fixed on Ginny's back. Thaddeus stood behind his mother's sofa, lines of confusion on his forehead and stealing glances at the minister to check he was not bored.

Mr. McIntyre reached down and took his wife's hand. Clotilde was enthralled by Ginny's playing. She held his hand close to her cheek and glanced up at him with a smile.

Lex slipped into the room. He made his way round to the back of the piano so he could watch Ginny's face. Momentarily, she glanced up and caught his eye, a smile flashing across her face as she gave herself to the lyricism of the music. She built to a crescendo and then to the final quiet chords, before sitting back, the piece complete.

There was a moment of silence as everyone sat transfixed, knowing something very special had taken place. Then the applause filled the room, the minister crying bravo.

At the end of the evening, Mr. McIntyre pulled on his coat in the hall.

"Thank you, Thaddeus, thank you, Alexander, for an exceptional evening." He lowered his voice. "My dear first wife made our home a place of culture. We would entertain writers and bards. It was good to be reminded of those times."

McIntyre took Alexander's hand. "And please convey my deepest gratitude to your delightful fiancée. Wee Clotilde has not taken naturally to dining in company, particularly here in the United States. Miss Snow made her *so* welcome. It was by far the most enjoyable evening we've had in a long time."

He put on his hat and shook Thaddeus' hand. Without letting go, he leaned in.

"I'll be at your office tomorrow, young man. I'm sure there's some paperwork we can get underway." He tapped the side of his nose with his finger and gave a wink.

"*Viens, ma chérie,*" he called to his wife, who was saying farewell to the ladies.

Clotilde whispered in Ginny's ear in French. "Come and have tea with me tomorrow. Make my time here more bearable. And we can laugh about all those pompous Boston women who try but fail to make us feel small."

EPILOGUE

The light scattered between the branches of the trees overhanging her open landau as it juddered down the street next to Boston Common. Although sunny, there was a nip in the September air. Cousin Madeleine took her hand and gave it a squeeze; Ginny smiled briefly, despite her wedding-day nerves. Mary Lou sat opposite, swiveling from one side to the other, looking up at the buildings. Ginny loved how excited Mary Lou was by the city, how she had taken this new experience in her stride.

The landau pulled up in front of the Old South Meeting House. Its elegant steeple soared above and bells rang out. Maddie and Mary Lou got out first, each in new dresses, and helped Ginny down. They were met by Phoebe, smiling widely, and Monsieur Demarque, ready to perfect his creation.

Ginny tried to keep her tense fidgeting under control and stand still while Monsieur shook out the lace-edged levels of the skirt of her dress to ensure it fell properly. He smoothed the satin bodice and adjusted the garland of flowers threaded from one shoulder and across her neat waist to the opposite hip. He attached the delicate veil with pins hidden among the wreath of orange blossom. The translucent silk gauze fell to the floor and extended behind her.

Maddie gave one of her dimpled smiles and slipped into the church with Phoebe, leaving just the sisters.

"This is all down to you, Mary Lou," said Ginny softly.

"How so?"

"If you hadn't dragged that half-dead, raggedy stranger through our front door, none of this would have happened. This is all because of the kindness of your heart."

Mary Lou arched an eyebrow and gave Ginny her bouquet of cream roses and white dahlias with sprigs of myrtle. "And who taught me the importance of being kind to other people?"

Organ music started and the wooden doors opened in front of them. The congregation stood and turned to watch the bride. Men in starched collars standing as straight as if on parade. Women in an array of colors, hats flopping with feathers and fabric flowers. Ginny's ivory dress looked restrained beside the high-fashion outfits.

The Meeting House was wide, rather than long, and full of light from the arched windows on each side. Ginny walked down the aisle, Mary Lou a few steps behind. She nodded to Aunt Josephine and Uncle Thomas, who beamed in return. The smiles of Mrs. Van Bergen and Florence seemed less spontaneous.

Because the congregation was standing, she could not see Lex and her heart beat faster as she approached. He had been waiting with Thaddeus. He stepped forward, caught sight of her and the familiar smile spread across his face. He was dressed in a black frock coat, a cravat and high collar framing his jaw. As their eyes met, Ginny felt the familiar rush of love.

She drew next to him as the organ music ended. Mary Lou lifted the front of the veil back over her head until it formed a cloud around her shoulders, and then took the bouquet.

Lex held both her hands and leaned his head toward hers.

"This is where I'm meant to be," he whispered. "And this is where I'll always be. Right beside you, holding your hands."

A LETTER FROM THE AUTHOR

Dear Reader,

Thank you so much for reading *Under a Gilded Sky* and I hope you enjoyed Ginny and Lex's story. If you would like to join other readers in keeping in touch, here are two options. Hear about my new releases and bonus content by clicking this link:

www.stormpublishing.co/imogen-martin

Or you can pop over to my website and sign up to my monthly newsletter. You'll get giveaways, sneak peeks and historical snippets:

www.imogenmartinauthor.com

Or do both! I look forward to meeting you.

If you enjoyed this book and could spare a few moments to leave a review, that would be hugely appreciated. Even a short review can make all the difference in helping other readers discover my book for the first time and every single review helps. Thank you so much.

The origins of this book go back a long way. When I was a teenager, I took a Greyhound bus from San Francisco to New York. Over those three days of staring out of the window at the majestic mountains and endless flat plains, stories wound themselves into my head: tales of brooding, charismatic men captivated by independent women. My second novel, *To the Wild Horizon*, returns to this theme—you'll find out more if you sign up to the newsletter.

Please read my acknowledgements if you want to know the very personal way that *Under a Gilded Sky* came to be written. I have, of course, done years of research and this book draws on some events that really happened. But it's fiction: an imagined story. If you want to make contact to find out more, the best place is my Facebook page.

I can also be found on Twitter for more time than I care to admit. Come and say hello.

Thank you again for being part of this amazing journey with me, and I hope you'll stay in touch—I have so many more stories and ideas with which to entertain you.

Imogen

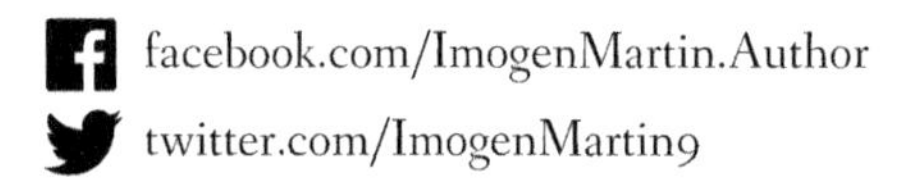

ACKNOWLEDGMENTS

Writing a book might be a solitary occupation but getting it to publication isn't. I have many people to thank, and the first is you, dear reader, for choosing this book. I hope you have enjoyed it.

People remember where they were for life-changing moments and one of mine was at Cardiff Airport. I opened an email from Storm Publishing editor Vicky Blunden, saying she was enjoying reading my book and asking what my writing plans were. Little did I know that Vicky would become the wisest of editors, guiding me through the development of this book and bolstering my confidence when it was flagging. I don't know what I did to deserve her!

Storm Publishing is a new venture from the visionary Oliver Rhodes and is full of talented people. I am grateful to Jade Craddock and Maddy Newquist for their sharp eyes as copyeditor and proofreader; to Elke Desanghere for marketing; and Anna McKerrow for publicity.

I wouldn't have got this book anywhere near publication were it not for the Romantic Novelists' Association. Many thanks to my anonymous Readers and the RNA's unique New Writers' Scheme.

It's been a privilege to be part of the RNA Cariad chapter, learning from published authors every month at meetings in Cardiff. Whilst I am in peril of missing people out from a list, thank you, Jan, Sue, Pat, Evonne, Laura, Sandra, Amanda,

Jessie... Thank you, Jane Cable, for the pep talk about protecting writing time. And to Luisa A Jones; if she hadn't said "why don't you just...", this book wouldn't be here.

In 2020, I was delighted to be selected for the Kate Nash Literary Agency BookCamp to accelerate promising writers. I hugely value the enduring friendships and excitement as we have each moved towards publication. Thank you, Laura, Samantha, Georgia, Kate, Annabel, Ina, Kathryn, Katie, Joanne, Adam and Jon. Thank you to Robbie Guillory for giving me faith in my writing and that this book would one day find the right editor and an audience.

The Writing Angels were busy on Platform 7 at Crewe station in 2019, engineering a meet cute with fabulous author Kiley Dunbar. Thank you for all the love and support, and let's keep setting our goals!

Thank you, Faye Chamberlain, for making the experience of taking author photos fun rather than cringe-making.

My deepest love to my daughter Naomi, the kindest soul in the world. I admire you more than words can say.

I could not have written this book without the unfailing love and support of my husband, Peter. He is my first reader and greatest cheerleader.

And finally, thank you to my elder daughter, Becky, to whom this book is dedicated. From her teens onwards, she lived with a chronic illness requiring regular medical treatment. Perhaps she sensed she wasn't going to be with us for long, because she got busy making the world a better place. She did an MSc in Humanitarian Studies, worked for a health charity, was active in international peacemaking, and so much more. She was fierce and gentle in equal measure. Despite the heroic efforts of our NHS and her own determined spirit, Becky died in 2018 aged twenty-seven. A month later I began to write what became *Under a Gilded Sky*. It took me a year, pencil on paper, and became the place where I could escape while I healed. Her memory reminds me to take every opportunity and live, as she did, to the full.